WINGS OF ENCHANTMENT

They have cast their spell over our imaginations for countless centuries—those most deadly beasts of prey, the fading race which once ruled the skies, hoarders of treasure both magical and golden, or benevolent keepers of universes beyond human ken. These are some of their stories:

"Fluff the Tragic Dragon"—The modern world can be lonely for a dragon on his own. After all, doesn't everyone need a friend?

"Take Me Out to the Ball Game"—When a dragon attends a baseball game, "winning" is likely to take on a whole new meaning. . . .

"Shing Li-ung"—Was the dragon pin a fanciful parting gift from her grandmother or a magical talisman that could change her life?

DRAGON FANTASTIC

Other FANTASTIC anthologies
from DAW Books:

HORSE FANTASTIC *Edited by Rosalind M. Greenberg and Martin H. Greenberg. With an introduction by Jennifer Roberson.* Here are magical tales for anyone who has ever wished to gallop off into the sunset. From a racer death couldn't keep from the finish line to a horse with the devil in him, these are original stories by such top writers as Jennifer Roberson, Mercedes Lackey, Mickey Zucker Reichert, Judith Tarr, and Mike Resnick.

CATFANTASTIC *Edited by Andre Norton and Martin H. Greenberg.* For cat lovers everywhere, a unique collection of fantastical cat tales, some set in the distant future on as yet unknown worlds, some set in our own world but not quite our own dimension, some recounting what happens when creatures out of myth collide with modern-day felines.

CATFANTASTIC II *Edited by Andre Norton and Martin H. Greenberg.* An all-new collection of fantasy's most original cat tales! Join such memorable cats as: Bomber, the ship's cat out for revenge on the German warship, *The Bismarck*; Graywhiskers, who ruled his kingdom with a weapon of his own creation; and Hermione, who protected her astronomer not from falling stars but from unexpected dangers lurking in his own home.

THE NIGHT FANTASTIC *Edited by Poul and Karen Anderson.* Let Poul Anderson, Ursula K. LeGuin, Isaac Asimov, Alan Dean Foster, Robert Silverberg, Fritz Leiber, and a host of other fantasy masters carry you away to magical realms where night becomes day as the waking world sleeps and sleeping worlds wake.

Dragon Fantastic

EDITED BY
ROSALIND M. GREENBERG
& MARTIN H. GREENBERG

DAW BOOKS, INC.
DONALD A. WOLLHEIM, FOUNDER
375 Hudson Street, New York, NY 10014

ELIZABETH R. WOLLHEIM
SHEILA E. GILBERT
PUBLISHERS

DAW Book Collectors No. 879

First Printing, May 1992

1 2 3 4 5 6 7 8 9

CONTENTS

INTRODUCTION

by Tad Williams

Where do you find a dragon?

Any explorer or hunter can tell you that before you can even start looking you have to know what it is you're looking for. So what is a dragon?

My dictionary says: "A fabulous monster represented as a gigantic reptile. . . ." Well, there is a certain truth to that, I suppose—a dragon is indeed a fabulous monster. But dictionaries are cold, factual things, and dragons tend to be huge, powerful, only incidentally factual, and generally (although not always) rather hot. So a dictionary may not be the best place to look for dragons.

A better place to look for fabulous beasts is, of course, inside ourselves. The most common habitat of the dragon—at least these days—is in the human mind. Or, perhaps it might be more true, if less factual (but remember, we're talking about dragons here, and facts just aren't very important) to say that the best place to look is in our *hearts*.

So when you say "dragon," what do you see in your heart?

If you're anything like me, you don't see just one thing, but instead many different things that mean "dragon"—claws, teeth, wings, eyes, fire. But there are other important characteristics that cannot be described in simple words. I can't simply give you a list of attributes that describe a dragon the way I could with a giraffe or a tuna or an armadillo . . . or even a unicorn. A dragon is far more than just an animal, even a mythical one.

A dragon is a force of nature, swift as a thunderclap, powerful as an earth tremor; it may strike with the sudden unpredictability of a lightning storm or spout fire like a volcano. If dragons *are* only mythical (as some of the less imaginative zoologists claim) our ancestors may have invented them to represent the fierce unpredictability of the natural world. For people who owed their existence to hunting and simple farming, the swift changes of earth and weather were to be respected, even feared. For those who lived and worked beneath open sky, nature was often something dangerous and unpredictable that needed to be placated. In fairness to the diversity of dragons, we must also note that these fabulous beasts sometimes represented the benevolent side of nature as well. The ancient Chinese used the dragon as a symbol of, among other things, the rains that fed the crops and thus fed the world.

But just as a dragon is more than simply an imaginary animal, it is also more than just a nature symbol, far more than a representation of wind and water. There is also a strong tradition in myth and literature of the dragon as a keeper of wisdom, or as a keeper of treasure . . . or both. The classical dragon is a beast of great age and frightening wisdom. Some, like Fafnir of the old Norse legends or J.R.R. Tolkien's Smaug, use that wisdom mainly to protect their hoards—the great piles of gold and jewels and other treasures upon which it is their wont to lie, and in defense of which it is their habit to munch treasure-seekers of various sorts. However, they seldom eat these interlopers without first regaling the knights or bandits or burglars with a little dragonish double-talk. If the legends are to be believed, it is not a good idea to listen too carefully to what a dragon has to say: you are either being bamboozled—and soon after the bamboozlement you will be dragon-dinner—or you are being told things that No Mortal Should Hear.

Dragons can be confusing creatures. Take as an example the great riddle of dragon-hoarding: what are they going to do with all that gold and all that wisdom? The gold is the more puzzling of the two—anything that lives as long as a dragon cannot help but acquire a great deal of knowledge, but what does a huge and possibly mythical beast want with gold? In the case of

Fafnir, this behavior could perhaps be excused by the fact that before he became a dragon he was a covetous dwarf, and thus might have carried prior bad habits over into dragonhood. But what of Smaug? What of all the other dragons who lie, stern and smoldering, atop their ill-gotten gains? Why would a dragon want a pile of bent plates and old crowns and over-decorated goblets? Perhaps that is one of those questions that has no answer. The immense and bad-tempered fireworm in John Gardner's *Grendel*, after a long disquisition on the nature of time and reality, describes all of life as a brief pulsation in the black hole of eternity, then sums up: "My advice is to seek out gold and to sit on it."

If the dragon himself doesn't really know, who are we to ask?

The more we try to define dragons, the more confounding it becomes. Of all the so-called mythical beasts, there are none quite so various in nature and appearance as are dragons. In fact, none of the others are even close. Take unicorns (which are lovely animals, but frankly not in the same league). How many unicorns are clumsy? How many are fat?? How many have more than one horn, or dislike virgins, or are really and truly evil? The answer, of course, is "none." A similar exercise can be performed with basilisks, yetis, cameleopards, gryphons, harpies, even manticores. Similar results will be obtained. These other imaginary creatures are timid, conformist types, each imitating his or her fellow with scarcely a maverick in the bunch. But not so dragons.

There are flying dragons and sea-swimming dragons, fire-drakes and cold-drakes, dragons wingless and wide-pinioned. There are friendly dragons and decidedly evil dragons and more than a few morally ambivalent dragons as well. There are trustworthy worm-folk upon whom you can stake your life (and often have to), and others upon whom you turn your back at risk of finding yourself abruptly toasted like a marsh-mallow. Dragons can be as old as time—and usu-ally are—but there are a few youngsters on record as well. Even dragons have to start somewhere.

Big and small and everything in between: you name it and there's a dragon to fit the bill. Green and scaly, golden and smooth, red, orange, pur-ple, black as burnt iron, white as milk—dragons are also available in a range of designer colors. (Never try to find one to match the furniture, though: that is taking dragons far too lightly, and will likely cause offense.)

But we started out to try to find a dragon. In-stead, we have fallen into the all-too-human trap of trying to discover something by defining it. A dragon is a great deal more than the sum of its extremely variable parts, and the worst mistake of all to make in searching for dragons is to un-derestimate them. A dragon cannot be easily de-fined any more than it can be successfully kept as a pet. They are far more than any listing of their hues and volume-displacement and other personal statistics, far more than any brief personality sketch.

That is why a dictionary definition is such a useless tool for the pursuit of dragons. The same dictionary I used earlier describes *sunset* as ". . . the daily disappearance of the sun below the western horizon." Would you run out of your house to see that? Would you call someone up about a mere daily disappearance and say "You missed it! It was sublime! Gorgeous!" Words are a poor cage for transcendent things. Calling a dragon a "fabulous animal" is a start, but remember, the dictionary folk use "fabulous" only to mean "fabled"—that is, imaginary.

Now, are dragons, all the dragons that you see with your heart, only imaginary animals? What about the incredible wingspan, the shadow that sweeps across the fields making grown men and women dive for cover, hearts pounding? Don't you *feel* the terrifying weight of that shadow? What about the roaring voice, as loud as any windstorm, more fearsome than a thousand lions? Can't you hear that, and feel it shuddering your bones? Or the dragon-fires that burn deep within their belly-forges, the flames hotter than any ordinary blaze, flames that can burn castle walls to dust and roast a knight in his armor in an instant. We have nightmares about how hot those fires are.

What about the deep, rumbling breath down in the heart of a dark cavern? What about the transfixing eye, a hole into the ultimate secrets of Creation? What about the tail ... the long, lashing tail that might merely swipe down buildings, or, in the case of the legendary Ouroboros-worm, reach all the way around the universe until the beast can bite it with its own teeth, making the great Circle of Time? (The worst thing about finding yourself next to a dragon's tail is the realization that, awesome as it is, the rest of the dragon is going to be even more frightening.) And teeth. Dragon teeth make an entire subject themselves. Jason and his Argonauts discovered that. Now, is this all only imagination? Or is there something more to it than that?

"Fabulous" and "imaginary," we are finding, are both pretty useless words when we are searching for dragons. Dictionary definitions, while extremely handy for some tasks, are no real help here. In fact, the only halfway useful definition I can offer is this: dragons are Very Powerful Things.

That's the reason we have revered them and whispered of them and feared them since a time long before there was such a thing as the written word. Their power, whether it frightens us or fills us with joyful wonder, is what makes them so important. Dragons are more diverse and powerful than anything ... except dreams. Maybe that's why we see them best with our hearts.

So, as we knew we would, we at last find the dragon we were seeking, and it's inside of us— but it's also greater than we are, more than we are. A dragon is everything we fear and wonder about and worship—everything we don't quite understand—given powerful, fiery flesh.

Because a dragon is a dream. And this book is full of dreams.

LETHAL PERSPECTIVE

by Alan Dean Foster

They assembled in the Special Place. Though a considerable amount of time had passed, none forgot the date and none lost their way. It took more than several days for all to arrive, but they were very long lived and none took umbrage at another's delay.

It was the very end of the season and a small team of climbers from France was exploring a new route up the south col of K5 when one happened to look up instead of down. He shouted as loud as he could, but the wind was blowing and it took a moment before he could get the attention of the woman directly ahead of him. By the time she tilted her head back to scan the sky, the apparition had vanished. She studied her climbing companion warily and then smiled. So did the others, when they were informed.

They put it down to momentary snow blindness, and the climber who'd looked up didn't press the point. He was a realist and knew he had no chance of convincing the least skeptical of his friends. But to his dying day he would know in his heart that what he'd seen that frigid morning just east of Everest was not an accident of snow blindness, or a patrolling eagle, or a figment of his imagination.

The Special Place was filling up. Legendary nemesis of the subcontinent, Videprasa had the least distance to travel and arrived first. Old Kurenskaya the Terrible appeared next, making good time despite his age and the need to avoid the limited air defense radar based in southern Kazahkistan.

O'mou'iroturotu showed up still damp from hours of flying through the biggest typhoon the South China Sea had experienced in a decade, and Booloongatta the Night soon after. They were followed by Cracuti from central Europe, Al-Methzan ras-Shindar from out of the Empty Quarter, and Nhauantehotec from the green depths of Central America.

It grew crowded in the Special Place as more of the Kind arrived. They jostled for space, grumbling and rumbling until the vast ancient cavern resounded like the Infinite Drum. Though solitary by nature, all gathered eagerly at this singular predetermined time.

Despite the incredible altitude and the winter storm which had begun to rage outside, conditions within the Special Place remained comfortable. Creatures that are capable of spontaneous internal combustion do not suffer the cold.

As the Elder Dominant, Old Kurenskaya performed the invocation. This was concluded with a binding, concerted blast of flame the largest napalm ordinance in the American armory could not have matched, resulting in a massive avalanche outside the Special Place as a great sheet of ice and snow was loosened from beneath. The French climbing team far to the west heard but did not witness it.

"It is the time," Kurenskaya announced. He was very old and most of his back scales had shaded from red to silver. But he could still ravage and destroy with the best of them. Only these days, like the others, he had to be more circumspect in his doings.

He glanced around the crowded cavern, vertical yellow pupils narrowing. "I do not see As'ah'mi among us." There was a moment of confusion until Nhauantehotec spoke up. "He will not be joining us."

Kurenskaya bared snaggle teeth. "Why not? What has happened?"

Nhauantehotec sighed and black smoke crept from his nostrils. "He was not careful. As we must all be careful these days. I think he forgot to soar in the stealthy manner and was picked up on U.S. Border Patrol radar. Not surprisingly, they mistook him for a drug runner's plane and shot him down. I heard him curse his forgetfulness as he fell and altered my path to see if I could help, but by the time I arrived he was but combusting brimstone and sulfur on the ground."

A smoky murmur filled the cavern. Old Kurenskaya raised both clawed forefeet for silence. "Such is the fate of those who let time master their minds. We sorrow for one of our own who forgot. But the rest are come, healthy and well." He gestured to the one next to him with a clawed foot the size of a steam-shovel bucket. "As first to arrive it falls to you, Videprasa, to regale us with tales of your accomplishments."

She nodded deferentially to the Elder Dominant and instinctively flexed vast, membranous wings. "I have since the last gathering kept myself properly hidden, emerging only to wreak appropriate havoc through the stealth we have had to adopt since humans developed advanced technologies." Raising a forefoot and looking thoughtful, she began ticking off disasters on her thick, clawed fingers.

"Eleven years ago there was the train wreck north of New Dehli. The devastating avalanche in Bhutan I instigated twenty years ago. There was the plastics plant explosion in Uttar Pradesh and the sinking of the small freighter during the typhoon that struck Bangladesh only a few years past." She smiled, showing cutlery that would have been the envy of a dozen crocodiles.

"I am particularly proud of the chemical plant damage in Bhopal that killed so many."

Al-Methzan ras-Shindar snorted fire. "That

was very subtly done. You are to be commended." He straightened proudly, thrusting out his scaly chest and glaring around the cavern. "You all know what I have been up to lately." Quong the Magnificent flicked back the tendrils that lined his head and jaws. "You were fortunate to find yourself in so efficacious a situation."

Snakelike, Al-Methzan's head whipped around. "I do not deny it, but it required skill to take advantage." Eyes capable of striking terror into the bravest man glittered with the memory. "It was purest pleasure. I struck and ripped and tore and was not noticed. The humans were too busy amongst themselves. And around me, around me every day, were those wonderful burning wells to dance about and dart through and tickle my belly against." Al-Methzan ras-Shindar stretched luxuriously, the tips of his great wings scraping the ceiling.

"I haven't felt this clean in centuries."

There was a concerted murmur of envious delight from the others, and Old Kurenskaya nodded approvingly. "You did well. How else have you fulfilled the mandate?"

Al-Methzan ras-Shindar resumed the recitation of his personal tales of mayhem and destruction. He was followed by Booloongatta the Night and then the rest. The hours and the days passed in pleasant companionship, reminiscence, and safety, as the storm howled outside the gathering place. They were safe here. The Roof of the

World saw few humans in the best of times, and in the winter was invariably little visited.

There was more to the gathering than mere camaraderie, however. More to the boasting of accomplishments than a desire simply to impress others of one's kind. For the gathering and the telling constituted also a competition. For approval, surely, and for admiration, truly. But there was more at stake than that.

There was the Chalice.

It hung 'round Old Kurenskaya's neck, suspended from a woven rope of pure asbestos fiber, thick as a man's arm. It was large for a human drinking utensil, tiny by the standards of the Kind. The great Berserker Jaggskrolm had taken the prize from the human Gunnar Rakeiennen in 1029, in a battle atop Mt. Svodmaggen that had lasted for four days and rent the air with fire and fury. When all had done and the killer Rakeiennen lay dead, his fortress razed, his golden horde taken, his women ravished (the great Jaggskrolm having been ritually mindful of the traditions), practically nothing remained unburned save the jewel-studded, golden chalice with which the most beauteous of Rakeiennen's women had bought her freedom (not to mention saving herself from a rough evening).

Ever since it had been a symbol of dominance, of the most effective and best applied skills of the Kind. Old Kurenskaya had won it during the last Tatar invasion of his homeland and had kept it ever since, having last been awarded it by acclamation (the only way it could be awarded) for his work among the humans during the purges and famines of the 1920s and 30s. Admittedly, he'd had human help, but his fellows did not feel cheated. Such assistance was to be welcomed, and cleverly used. As Al-Methzan ras-Shindar had utilized events so recently.

It seemed truly that because of his most recent accomplishments ras-Shindar had the inside track on securing the Chalice. Nhauantehotec had been working particularly hard, and the devastating achievements of skillful Mad Sunabaya of the Deep impressed all the assembled with their breadth and thoroughness. Despite his years, Old Kurenskaya wasn't about to give up the Chalice without a fight, and it had to be admitted that his brief but critical presence at Chernobyl would go down as a hallmark accomplishment of modern times.

When at last all had concluded their recitative, and waited content and with satisfaction for the vote of acclamation, Old Kurenskaya was pleased. It had been a gathering free of discord, unlike some in the past, and had demonstrated conclusively that the Kind could not only survive but prosper in their efforts despite the technical exploits of their old enemy, humankind. He was elated, and ready. All, in fact, were anxious for the choosing, so they could be on their way. Though all had enjoyed the gathering, they preferred to keep to themselves, and by now were growing irritable.

"If, then, each has stipulated and declaimed their deeds, and retold their tales, I will name names, and call for the choosing." He raised a clawed forefoot to begin.

Only to be interrupted.

"Wait, please! I have not spoken."

Dire reptilian heads swiveled in the direction of the voice. It was so slight as to be barely intelligible, and those of the Kind with smaller hearing organs than their more floridly earred brethren had to strain to make out individual words. But it was one of them, no doubt of that, for it spoke in the secret and ancient language known only to the Kind.

Something like a small, scaly hummingbird appeared in the air before Old Kurenskaya and hovered there noiselessly.

"What is this?" Videprasa emitted a smoky burst of flame and laughter. "A bird has slipped in among us, to be out of the storm, no doubt!"

"No," roared Cracuti, the sharp spines of her back flexing with amusement, "this is not a bird, but a bug!"

The miniscule speaker whirled angrily. "I am Nomote, of the Kind." Laughter and smoke filled the gathering place. "I demand to be heard!"

Old Kurenskaya raised both clawed forefeet and the ferocious, terrific laughter gradually died down. He scowled at the tiny visitor. "There are three recent-born among us. I did not know of a fourth."

"Who would admit to birthing *this*?" snorted

Videprasa, and another round of awesome laughter shook rock from the walls of the cavern.

Old Kurenskaya looked around reprovingly. "This Nomote is of the Kind—if . . . somewhat lesser than most of us. Give to him the deference he deserves, as befits the traditions." An abashed silence settled over the gathering.

The Elder Dominant nodded to the hovering mite. "Speak to us then of your exploits." One of the assembled sniggered but went quiet when Old Kurenskaya glared threateningly in his direction. "Tell of what you have done to fulfill the traditions of the Kind." He sat back on his hindquarters, his leathery, age-battered wings rumpled elegantly about him.

"I am young and have not the experience or strength of others who have accomplished so much." A few murmurs of grudging approval sounded among the assembled. "I have had to study our ancient adversaries and to learn. I have struggled to master the stealthy ways needed to carry out the work without being noticed by the humans and their clever new machines." It hesitated, wee wings beating furiously to keep it in place.

"Alas, I have had not the skill, nor the strength, nor the prowess to do as so many of you have done. I have done but one thing, and it, like myself, is small."

Nomote's humbleness and modesty had by now won for him some sympathy among the assembled, for who among them could not save for the intervention of fortuitous fate imagine himself in such a poignant condition.

"Tell us of what you have done and what you do," said Old Kurenskaya encouragingly. He glared warningly one more time, but by now the gathering was subdued. "None of the Kind will laugh, I promise it. Any offender will have to deal with *me*." At that moment Old Kurenskaya did not look so old.

Nomote blinked bright, tiny eyes. A small puff of dark smoke emerged from the tip of his snout. "I go invisibly among those humans who are ready and those who are reluctant, I breathe the addiction into their nostrils and their mouths, and then when they weaken and are susceptible, I light their cigarettes."

They gave him the Chalice, which was too large for him to carry, much less wear around his neck. But Nhauantehotec moved it to a convenient lair for him, and though he could not fly with it shining broadly against his chest as had his glorious predecessors, it made a most excellent bath in which to relax upon returning from a good day's work among the execrable humans.

THE CHAMPION OF DRAGONS

by Mickey Zucker Reichert

The rising sun haloed a red-tiered fortress on the mountain's highest peak. Far below, in a glade partially covered by mats of woven grass, Miura Usashibo and Otake Nakamura knelt in silence, chests rising and falling from the strain of mock combat. Nearby, their sensei watched, stroking his wispy beard.

Usashibo closed his eyes, and a familiar quiet darkness overcame his world. His heart pounded from a mixture of exertion and excitement. Sweat rolled down his face. The reed mats cut their regular pattern into his knees, and the euphoric afterglow of combat consumed him. Victory no longer granted him the unbridled sense of triumph it had scarcely a year ago. Winning had become mundane. But the physical and emotional peak attained in combat never dulled. It seemed as if no reality existed beyond the feelings of inner peace and power he could reach only through all-consuming violence.

Usashibo turned his thoughts to the dragon that Sensei had chosen and trained him to fight. Sensei either would not or could not describe the creature and its method of combat. His initial explanation detailed all he would reveal of Usashibo's enemy. "Every ten years the Master and I select a champion to seek out and slay the dragon. We train him to reach beyond his limitations and drive him until he surpasses even the Master. We have chosen you, Miura Usashibo, as the fourteenth champion of dragons. The others never returned." Yet, despite this grim appraisal, the possibility of failure never occurred to Usashibo. *In the quiet of my soul, I am invincible. I will return.*

A sharp handclap snapped Usashibo's attention back to his surroundings. Sensei bowed, signaling an end to Usashibo's last practice session before setting out to destroy the dragon. As the old man turned, his linen jacket and pants hissed gently. Pausing, he bowed to the shrine of the mountain's spirit and climbed the long flight of stone steps which led to the Master's fortress.

Otake Nakamura remained kneeling where Usashibo had landed what Sensei had judged a killing blow. The interlocking squares of his abdominal muscles rose and fell, and blood beaded from the vertical red line where the champion of dragons' wooden sword had cut his stomach. Silently, he stared at the mats before him. Usashibo searched Nakamura's face for signs of the friendship they had shared a little over a year ago, but none survived. Usashibo studied his old companion, hungry for recognition that he was still a human being if no longer a friend.

Nakamura touched his forehead to the ground, then rose. "May you return from tomorrow's battle victorious and the gods of the winds and the mountains watch over you." Etiquette demanded Nakamura remain until Usashibo responded to his overly formal gesture.

Usashibo shifted uncomfortably, recalling the many times he had tried to force Nakamura to acknowledge how close they had been in friendship. But the mountains they had climbed together, the girls they had known, and the fights they had started became distant memories. Early in his training, Usashibo vented his frustration and loneliness on Nakamura during their practice sessions, battering him until he could barely walk. As he withdrew further, Usashibo's anger lessened. But the feeling of betrayal remained. The soul mate who would have urged Usashibo to rip the dragon's ugly head off was gone, and Usashibo missed him.

Usashibo rose and pressed wrinkles from his pants with the palms of his hands. He replied with exaggerated formality. "Thank you, Otake." Usashibo dismissed his sparring partner, anxious for the solace of being alone.

Nakamura turned and followed Sensei up the stone staircase, apparently unable to understand the inspired madness that goaded Usashibo to consecrate his life to a goal no one had ever achieved and the fleeting glance at immortality it offered. As boys, Nakamura and Usashibo had shared visions of greatness, but it seemed Nakamura dreamed with his mouth instead of his heart.

Over the years of training, Usashibo had paid a high price for his dream. He denied himself many of the indulgences of youth, gradually surrendering pieces of himself to his art until only the warrior survived. Only one aspect of life remained inviolate: his love for his wife, Rumiko. He knew she fought to maintain the spark of desire within him. He wished her task was easier. Usashibo turned toward the narrow path which led to the village of Miyamoto and resolved to grant Rumiko the only gift which remained his to give: the last night he knew he would be alive.

At the edge of the rice mats, Usashibo slipped his feet into his sandals and slid his swords through his belt. Despite his melancholia, his mind entered his familiar regimen of imaginary combat. As he walked, he consciously controlled each step and shift of balance. His left hand rested on his scabbarded sword, draped over the handguard. He recalled Sensei's words at times when he had doubted his purpose: *Once a raindrop begins to fall, it must continue to fall or it is no longer even a drop of rain. A man must finish his journey once the first step is taken.* Usashibo laughed to himself and wished Sensei spoke more directly.

As Usashibo entered Miyamoto, he tried to close his mind against the ordeal mingling with its citizenry presented. The townspeople regarded him as the epitome of virtue or the target of envy, not as human. Soon, peasants and the rough wooden huts of the village surrounded him. Although people jammed the streets, the throng parted before him. Young girls leered invitations, and men he had known since childhood pretended not to notice him with exaggerated indifference. A child asked him if he could really slay the dragon, only to be snatched away by an embarrassed mother before Usashibo could answer. He felt the tension of hastily averted stares.

Stories of Usashibo's feats, provided and embellished by Nakamura, endeared the teller but not the subject. Many attributed Usashibo's prowess to magic or unwholesome herbs. Others sought tricks to make his accomplishments fall within their narrow view of possibility. Even those people who dismissed Nakamura's tales as lies managed to attribute the blame for the deception to Usashibo.

Quickly, Usashibo crossed the town and traversed the white gravel path through his garden to his cottage. He paused before the faded linen door and removed his sandals. Closing his eyes to help escape the cruel reality of Miyamoto, he stepped through the curtain. The starchy smell of boiling rice mingled with the pine scent of charcoal and the musky aroma of freshly cut reeds. Rice paper walls shielded him from the attentions of people who believed him either more or less than human. Gradually, Sensei's demands and the unattainable goals the peasants projected onto him were borne away on the breeze as wisps of smoke. His own aspirations still burned obsessively in his mind like an endless fire in a swordsmith's forge. He basked in the feeling of power it inspired. He accepted the flame he knew he could never entirely escape or extinguish. Without the desire it inspired, he would not be Miura Usashibo. He opened his eyes.

A ceramic pot rested on a squat, black hibachi. Steam and smoke rose, darkening the tan walls and ceiling. Rumiko knelt on the polished wood floor, and the brush in her hand darted over a sheet of paper. The soft beauty in her round face and dark eyes belied a wit that could cut as quickly and deeply as his sword and a strength which, in many ways, surpassed his own. The rice pot's lid rattled. White froth poured over the sides and hissed as it struck the charcoal. Rumiko rose, turned toward the hibachi, removed the lid, and stared into the boiling rice. Quietly, Usashibo waited for her to meet his gaze.

The steam freed several strands from Rumiko's tightly coiffed hair. Her face reddened. Droplets of sweat beaded on her upper lip, but she did not look up.

Tension filled the room. It seemed almost tangible, as it does when a delicate glass bottle has fallen but not yet shattered on the floor. He could deal with Rumiko momentarily, but Usashibo knew his swords demanded their proper respect. In four strides, he crossed the room and knelt before a black, lacquered stand. He withdrew the longer sword from his cloth belt, applied a thin coating of clove oil, blotted it nearly dry with powder, and delicately placed it in the stand. He slid the companion sword free, repeated the process, and hung it above its mate. Respectfully, he bowed, then rose.

Rumiko stood, stiff-backed, stirring the rice. Her wooden spoon moved in precise circles.

As Usashibo walked, the green reed mats crackled beneath his feet. He stopped behind Rumiko, swearing he would allow nothing to spoil this night for her. With a finger, he traced a stray lock of hair along her neck and trailed off across her shoulder. His hand discovered taut muscles beneath her thin robe. Confusion and concern mingled within Usashibo. "Rumiko?"

The faint, hissing explosions of Rumiko's tears striking the charcoal punctuated the silence. Usashibo's grip on her arms hardened, as if to lend her his own strength.

Rumiko shifted uneasily in his grasp. "Always the swords first. If you loved me as much as you love them, you'd stay. Let someone else try to kill the dragon."

Usashibo snapped Rumiko toward him and wrapped his arms around her. She braced her elbows against his chest. Carefully, Usashibo pulled her to him, despite her resistance, and buried his face in her hair. "Ah, Rumiko. I will return. You must believe."

Rumiko ceased struggling. Usashibo relaxed his arms and dropped them to her waist. She leaned away from him and stared through red-laced eyes. "Do you really believe the thirteen others thought they would lose? Why risk your life here with me to fight a dragon that never hurts anyone who doesn't attack it? Stay. Please."

Usashibo had never questioned his reason to slay the dragon. The thought of surrendering his dream seemed so alien it did not merit consideration, but her words raised doubt. *Perhaps the dragon could kill me as it did all the others.* After so many consecutive victories, the thought of defeat appalled Usashibo. He knew he must fight the dragon, if only to prove himself invincible. If he quit now, all his striving and sacrifice meant nothing. One moment of weakness would make him and everything he believed in a deadly joke. *Ideals are worth dying for. I have trained my entire life for this one fight. If I cannot win, I deserve to die. Once a raindrop begins to fall, it must continue to fall, or it is no longer even a drop of rain. I've lied to myself; Rumiko never understood my dream. She is the same as all the others.*

Usashibo recalled a clear winter day half a year and a lifetime ago. His first sensei, the consummate warrior in action and spirit, had died in his sleep. He had much left to teach, and Usashibo had much he still wanted to learn. It seemed unfair for Sensei to die as quietly as a peasant. Shortly after learning of his teacher's death, Usashibo fought with Rumiko over how the rice was prepared and left her.

Then, distraught, Usashibo had walked to the falls north of Miyamoto and sat on the crest, watching water crash to the rocks below. Mist swirled around him as he folded a small square of paper into a swan. He tossed the bird over the precipice as a gift to the god of the cascade. It spiraled gently downward until it struck the water. Then it plummeted and disappeared beneath the foam. He had seen his future as a warrior perish with old Sensei, and he had lost Rumiko, too. At that time, he realized he wanted to follow his swan over the falls.

A hand had touched Usashibo's arm. He spun, drew his sword instinctively, stood, and faced Rumiko. Resheathing his sword, he had turned back to the waterfall. She stood beside him, and forced him to face her. He felt tears run down his face, and Rumiko smiled sadly. Her presence spoke more deeply than words. He thought he sensed an understanding and similarity of purpose that transcended love.

But the love Usashibo had believed in was a lie. Now, the muscles at the corners of his jaw tightened as well as his grip. Rumiko winced and twisted, pushing desperately at his hands. He released her, and she retreated, kneading bruised arms. "Go now. I refuse to spend the night with a man who would rather die alone than live with me."

Rage and self-pity warred within Usashibo. His stomach clenched, and thoughts raced through his mind. He was truly alone. Sweat formed on his forehead, and he walked mechanically from Rumiko. He stooped, lifted the swords from their stand, and returned each to his belt. The familiarity of his weapons became an anchor for his troubled thoughts. In the past year they had cost him much, but they had returned far more in a way no one seemed to understand. While the world changed, they remained reassuringly constant. Though they tested him unmercifully, they never doubted or judged. *Rumiko cannot force me to give up the direction that shaped my life. I refuse to become her servant.* He dropped his left hand to his long sword and sprinted for the door.

The linen curtain enwrapped Usashibo like a net. His momentum carried him blindly through, tearing cloth from the doorway. Anger and frustration exploded within him. He shredded the faded linen. When the cloth fell away, he snatched up his sandals and resumed running.

Stones crunched beneath Usashibo's tread. Their sharp edges bit into his feet, and he sought the physical pain to replace the hurt Rumiko's betrayal had caused. He burst from his garden and into the street. He crashed into a young man and both sprawled in the dust. The man rose, swearing viciously. But when he recognized Usashibo, he broke off and apologized for his own clumsiness. *The bastards won't even curse me.* Unconsciously, Usashibo placed his right hand on his hilt. *The dragon won't single me out as different.*

Usashibo leapt to his feet and raced down the street, knocking peasants aside when they did not dodge quickly enough. Soon, they cleared a lane before him, and he ran between walls of people to meet the dragon.

The damp warmth of the pine forest surrounded Usashibo. He scrambled across a small waterfall. Thick boughs shielded him from the sun and freed the ground from undergrowth. The terrain remained level, and Usashibo quickly neared the isolated clearing where legend claimed the dragon lived. In the three days since he had left Rumiko, he existed only to slay the dragon. The rigor of solitary sword practice and travel occupied every waking moment, though Rumiko haunted his dreams.

Stray beams of sunlight pierced the forest's canopy. In the distance, a head-high wall of brambles signaled an end to the trees, the edge of the dragon's clearing. Usashibo squatted near the base of a tree. The muscles at the nape of his neck tightened. A wave of warmth passed through him. His chest prickled with the first drops of sweat.

The scene was a sharp contrast to Usashibo's

imaginings. The hollow whistle of a songbird echoed from the edge of the clearing. A brown and black beetle peered cautiously from beneath a loose curl of bark above his shoulder. No evil presence exerted its control over the woodlands. But perhaps the clearing would be different.

Usashibo's left hand rested on the mouth of his scabbard, and his thumb overlapped the sword's guard. He crept from tree to tree, paused, and peeked through the wall of briars. In the center of the clearing stood a cottage surrounded by a garden similar to his own. Usashibo stared, unable to believe that anyone would dare to live this close to the dragon.

Usashibo circled the clearing, searching for a gap in the wall of thorns. At the far edge, he found a path that led through the garden to the cottage. He pushed through the briars and emerged into the sun. As he blinked, eyes adjusting to the light, a man stepped through the cottage's door. Although Usashibo had never seen this man before, much about him seemed familiar. The powerful shoulders and mocking eyes marked him as a warrior, even without the two swords resting in his belt. Usashibo's left hand resumed its position at the mouth of his scabbard. The two men stared at each other in silence, mirror images separated by clusters of red and gold blossoms.

Wind ruffled the strange man's wide black pants. Slowly, he moved toward Usashibo, feet skimming the ground but never losing contact.

Just beyond sword range, he stopped and met Usashibo's stare. He grinned, and the creases that formed at the corners of his eyes made him look immeasurably older. "A champion of dragons. Ten years so soon."

Usashibo forced himself to relax; tension would slow his reactions. From the combination of ease and precision that permeated the man's movements, Usashibo knew he followed the way of the sword with a dedication most men cannot imagine. He knew this man shared his obsession to master his sword and himself and the isolation it brought. Curiosity broke through the strange feelings of companionship welling in Usashibo's mind. "How did you know I am a champion of dragons?"

A smile again crossed the man's face. "The way you walk, the way you hold your shoulders, and the unconquerable look in your eye. The last man I fought recognized me as I now recognize you. I was the last champion of dragons."

Usashibo's eyes narrowed accusingly. He feigned wiping sweat from his palm on the left side of his jacket to bring his hand nearer the hilt of his sword. "The last champion died fighting the dragon. He never returned."

The man's hand also casually drifted to his sword. "And you saw the body? Why should I return to people who inspired me, drove me to achieve beyond their dreams, then condemned me as different. They made me become the dragon, as shall you if you survive me." The man unsheathed his sword slowly and raised the blade, hilt gripped two-handed near his shoulder. "You cannot escape them. I've lived many places. All people are the same. It's easier being alone."

Usashibo drew both his swords and retreated two steps. His short blade hovered at waist height, the long one poised above it. The thought of killing the only person who truly understood the hell he survived appalled him. "I don't want to fight you."

The man lowered the tip of his sword until it nearly touched the ground. "You don't need to know who'd win? If you're afraid, you're a disgrace to the swords you carry."

The possibility of losing this combat had never occurred to Usashibo. Surrender would render the years of training and self-denial meaningless. The minutes of immortality during this fight had cost too much to be given up now. After sacrificing Rumiko's love, one man's life would not keep Usashibo from his goal. Despite the bond he shared with this man, or because of it, Usashibo knew he must kill the dragon he faced. *In the quiet of my soul, I am invincible.*

Usashibo thrust with both swords. The man dodged and retreated. The two men circled. They probed each others' defenses without fully attacking. The man struck for Usashibo's forward leg. Usashibo leapt above the attack. The man lunged again. Usashibo batted the blade aside with his short sword. He countercut at the man's wrists. The man jerked his sword back and caught Usashibo's blow near his hilt. Spinning away, he cut beneath Usashibo's guard. Pain seared Usashibo's thigh. Reflexively, he lowered both swords to block the blow which had already landed. The man's sword arched toward Usashibo's undefended head.

Usashibo dropped his short sword and pivoted away. As the blow descended, Usashibo blended with the man's movement. His free hand caught his opponent's hilt and continued the forward motion. Pulled off-balance, the man stumbled. Usashibo drove his long sword into his opponent's chest. He continued the cut as his blade slid free. The man dropped to the ground.

Red froth bubbled from the man's mouth as he clutched the wound. "Brother, you did not disappoint me." A final smile crossed his face before death glazed his features.

A horse's whicker snapped Usashibo's attention from the man he had killed. Snatching up his short sword, he whirled, poised for combat.

Rumiko sat astride a dun stallion at the edge of the clearing, bow in hand, arrow nocked. She answered Usashibo's question before he asked it. "If he'd won, I'd have killed him."

Usashibo lowered his swords and stared at his wife, puzzled. The entire situation confounded him, and the burning cut on his thigh clouded thought further. One question pressed foremost in his thoughts. "Why didn't you shoot him before the fight?"

A shy smile lit Rumiko's face. "When I heard him talk, I knew he was right. You had to fight." She shrugged. "That's the way Miura Usashibo is."

Suddenly, Usashibo realized the force that had driven and shaped his life had disappeared. The dragon was dead. The joy he should have felt at Rumiko's revelation lost itself in the void the dragon had filled. For the first time in Usashibo's life, he experienced panic. Tears welled in his eyes.

Rumiko's grin broadened as her horse danced sideways. "I understand Mimasaka has been plagued by a demon for three hundred years."

An inner warmth and new sense of purpose suffused Usashibo. *There are many dragons and only one Rumiko.* "Let's go home."

PHOBIAC

by Lawrence Schimel

There is a glut of small shops on the upper east side of Manhattan, filled with antiques and fine art pieces. They are clustered around Museum Mile, catering to the affluent masses who emerge from their small doses of culture inspired to buy an *object d'art*.

Of these stores, one of the most popular and most enjoyable is Fennwick's, located down 84th street closer to 5th than Madison. The proprietor is a small old man who has never been seen without his thick horn-rimmed glasses. It's a local joke of sorts, like trying to guess how old he is, because we're pretty sure that they're just plain glass. He's got sharper eyesight than a microscope, and the glasses can't help that much. It's assumed he wears them as part of his costume. He's balding on top and dresses conservatively in somber grays and charcoal, the darker browns. Exactly the type who *should* own an antique shop.

One of the things that makes Fennwick's so enjoyable is that he has a story to tell about each piece he sells, told in a faint British accent that must also be part of his affectations. Something about where he found it along his travels, or an amusing anecdote about the person he had bought it from.

His pride and joy was a tenth century suit of armor which he refused to sell. They came in hordes to buy it from him, but he remained adamant in his refusal to sell. It was the only piece in the shop that didn't have a story, or if it did, he kept it to himself.

Fennwick's became one of the regular stops along Museum Mile, sightseers coming in to look at the armor, having heard whispers of it in the nearby museums. While they were there they often decided to purchase something, maybe a miniature portrait, or a small sculpture. When forced to give a reason why he wouldn't sell the suit, the proprietor would reply, "It's too good for business."

The proprietor held a bronze figurine in each hand, trying to decide which to put in the display case to replace the one he had sold that morning. He saw the man looking in through the window and knew that he would ask to buy the suit of armor. The proprietor chose the satyr and placed it in the case, carrying the nymph into the back room with him. The door chimes rang while he was still in back.

The man, dressed in a dark navy business suit, a lawyer perhaps, stood before the suit of armor. "How much?" he asked when the proprietor stepped out from the back room.

"Not for sale." The proprietor sat on a stool located behind the counter.

"That's a shame. It's very nice."

The proprietor merely nodded as a response that he had heard. The man looked around the shop, stopping to study a Fraggonard sketch, running his hand over the smooth marble of a fountain sculpture, and peering closely into a display of Russian *plique-à-jour* cases. Finally he picked up the bronze satyr and brought it to the counter without looking at the price.

"Will that be cash or charge?" the proprietor asked.

"Charge. Do you take American Express?"

The proprietor nodded and accepted the card the man produced from his wallet. He pushed his glasses farther up his nose and glanced at the name on the card, George Ba—

A gurgle tried to escape his lips but was choked off by the burst of flame rising spontaneously from his snout. "Damned reflexes," the dragon muttered, once the dizziness from the transformation had subsided. He sneezed twice, then cast the spell to transform himself back into an old man. Again the dizziness and he leaned back to sit on his stool before realizing it had been destroyed during the first transformation. Sighing, he fumbled along the floor for his glasses and put them back on. The left lens was cracked. The green plastic had mingled with the bronze slag from the satyr, giving the molten puddle a patina as it sank into the dark oak counter.

The proprietor leaned over the counter to see the pile of ash where the man, George, had stood. He looked up at the suit of armor which still glowed red as if the metal was being tempered. The Fraggonard was catching on fire as the flames from the wooden frame moved inward. A chunk of burning wood dropped onto the pile of Persian rugs, one of which he had seen fly in an era long gone.

The proprietor sighed again, took one last look to make sure that enough objects near the man would catch fire, then ran out into the street screaming, "Arson! Help me, someone! Arson!"

HOME SECURITY

by Karen Haber

I didn't intend to rent a dragon to guard my castle, but in the end it actually seemed like a sensible thing to do. The day I took the first step toward making that fateful decision seemed, at first, like any other late summer day in San Francisco.

A white tendril of fog curled its way under the Golden Gate Bridge but the sun was still high in the sky as I left work and only a slight coolness to the air foretold the famous bay city summer chill to come. I stopped at Embarcadero Bakery #5 for some sourdough bread and picked up MacHeath at the vet's. The bread under one arm, cat in his micromesh carrier under the other, I turned the corner onto Bill Graham Memorial Alley, opened the gate at Forty-three and a half, scurried up the steps of the green concrete duplex, and stopped. The front door gaped open like my former father-in-law's mouth.

"Not again," I said.

"Quarch," said MacHeath tartly. I put him down on the stoop and considered my options.

I could call the police, as I had the last time and the time before that. I could call the nearest gun dealer. Or I could just go in. Chances were that the intruder was long gone. And if not, well, I could always club him or her with my bread loaf.

The apartment had an empty feel and my shoes echoed on the hardwood floor.

I called out, "Hello? Anybody here?" Right, I thought. If I were a burglar, I would certainly just yoo-hoo back to that cheery greeting.

Moving deeper inside, I saw that the panic button I kept by my reading chair to call the fire department and/or medics just-in-case was still there. I grabbed it up and felt slightly less vulnerable. Pallas Athena and her panic button. Right.

Nobody in the bathroom. The kitchen was empty. Ditto the guest room. That left my bedroom. Brace up, I told myself. This was no time to wimp out.

I kicked open the door to my bedroom and wished I hadn't. The place looked like a small tornado had been unleashed inside. The drawers had been pulled from the bureaus and the contents liberally dispersed around the room. A quick look into the bathroom revealed that my best lipstick had been used to scrawl obscenities over the mirror and shower stall. Someone had even left me a present in the toilet. I told myself to be grateful that he or she had used the toilet and not the red kilim rug.

"Goddammit," I said to the toilet. "I'm getting tired of this shit!"

"Warooo," MacHeath called. I had almost forgotten him and he knew it. I hurried to the front door, brought him inside and set the pressure lock to release him. He appeared in all his orange tabby glory with his tail three times its normal size, gave me a reproachful look, and began sniffing the rug near the door. "Fssst," he said.

"You can say that again, Mac. We've been robbed. For the third time."

The vidset was gone, as was my new food processor/waver, and the mega amp for the apartment stereo. Inconvenient, yes. But I could replace them easily on my salary—thank God I had decided to become a lawyer instead of a dancer. I was almost getting accustomed to coming home after a long day of battling to protect other people's possessions and finding my own things missing. In fact, I half-anticipated the stomach-hollowing sense of violation that came with every break-in. I had wanted a nice apartment, right? Finally, I had gotten one. Unfortunately it lived in a bad neighborhood.

At this point I didn't exactly begrudge the burglars my electronic equipment: I even fantasized working out a 50/50 split. But when they got close to my grandmother's jewelry, well, that was different.

I had made a special trip back to 1962 to beg

some pieces for a big date. Grandma was a good sport and finally told me just to keep it all— she never used it. I was happy to comply. We're talking quality goods here, handed down from her mother: gold Victorian earbobs with dangling pearls, diamond-studded stickpins, and, the best piece of all, my great-grandmother's engagement ring. It was anachronistic, sure. No iridescent silver or multi-hued gems. No, it wasn't flashy and hardly anyone noticed it. That's why I liked it. The intricate settings seemed almost architectural to me: a tiny, secret metal fantasy which I alone appreciated.

For a while I flattered myself that I was pretty good at hiding the loot. But the burglars were getting smarter and smarter all the time. My heart was pounding as I checked the hoard where I had stashed it in the hollow compartment of my dining table. I saw deep scratches in the polished oak surface that hadn't been there that morning. The son-of-a-bitch had located my stash, probably by using an ultrasound probe. He had found my treasures, but the lock had foiled him. This time. Soon somebody would just trash the table to get at the jewels and Grandma's goodies would be gone forever. I was getting desperate.

As I stood in my raped and plundered abode, the lights flared, dimmed, went out, then came flickering back on. Every digital clock in the apartment let out a series of chirps, beeps, and buzzes to announce that yet another power surge had occurred. I spent the next hour resetting my clocks and gadgets, muttering darkly. By the time I was finished, I was really ready for some tea and sympathy.

My boyfriend Wiley brought both, along with dinner from my favorite Chinese restaurant. He commiserates, does Wiley. It's one of his best qualities.

"Poor baby," he said. "Give us a kiss."

"Get your own kiss," I snarled. Nevertheless, he backed me into a corner and convinced me to give up the goods. Then we sprawled across my blue sofa and dug into stuffed tofu and chili pepper peapods.

I had met Wiley in court, and although I have a certain built-in antipathy for public defenders, his goofy sense of humor won me over. Not to mention his dark hair, his blue eyes, and his height, which at a respectable 6'4" dwarfs even my stature. What's more, he passed muster with MacHeath, who sniffed him twice and immediately claimed his lap for a nap. We had been dating steadily for six months, which meant that Wiley thought he was part-owner, with MacHeath, of my life. I was beginning to feel like a co-op.

Between mouthfuls, Wiley said, "Why don't you move?"

"Where? I told you what a problem I had getting this place."

"You could move in with me. I don't know

why you don't. I've got a much bigger place. And tall, gray-eyed women deserve more space."

"Uh-uh," I said. "Forget it."

"Why?"

"Your music, for starters. That recidivist rock and roll gives me a headache. And then there's cooking: doing it for one is trouble enough. Two is unthinkable."

He persevered: after all, he is a lawyer. Not a bad one, either. "I can cook. And you could buy noise dampers, you know. Or bring your own stereo along and we'll duel."

"How about I just stay here in my own apartment?"

"Chris, be reasonable."

"I like to think I already am."

"In other words, no, right?"

He was sweet, but I wasn't interested in sharing my personal space with anyone larger than MacHeath. I had fought too long and too hard to get it. But in the interest of keeping other people out of it I was losing sleep. And weight. Which meant that Wiley kept trying to cram food into my mouth every time I opened it.

"Listen," he said as he dangled a succulent piece of twice-cooked pork before me. "I know this guy."

"I don't do pro bono work," I said. "I've told you that before." I snagged the morsel from his chopstick and chewed thoughtfully.

"No, it's not like that. He's a specialist in virtual reality rigs."

I looked up from the take-out carton and glared at him. Wiley knew I hated those techno-heads and their electronic hidey holes. As far as I was concerned they were all a bunch of vid masturbators romping around in their imaginary worlds. "Must be nice," I said. "If life gets too tough, just switch to another reality channel."

"Don't be so hostile, Chris. He might have a solution to your problem."

"Like what? A virtual police officer?"

"Something like that."

"Look, Wiley, what I need is a living, breathing berserker with a fully-equipped arsenal, not somebody's electronic daydreams."

"You've got to do something about your technophobic tendencies," Wiley said, raising his voice to be heard above the din. "They really get in the way."

"Oh, yeah?" Crossly, I pulled back into my corner of the couch. "How?"

The lights dimmed, blazed, dimmed again, almost went out, came back on, to the accompaniment of chirps, beeps, and buzzes from my clocks and appliances. It sounded like mating season at the electronic zoo.

Wiley raised his voice to be heard above the din. "At least you could get the wiring in this place fixed."

"When I have time."

"I worry about you, Chrissie."

Wiley's always bugging me about something. For instance, he has been bugging me forever to take a vacation with him someplace quiet, say California before the Gold Rush. But he knows how I feel about time travel. I don't think I'm technophobic. I just don't like time travel. Or virtual reality. Or being called Chrissie.

"You're sweet," I said. "Save it for your men's group, okay?"

Most guys, faced with that kind of hostility, glare and leave. At least that's what they've always done to me in the past. But Wiley just smiled patiently as if he thought I was cute. It was maddening. What's more, I was starting to worry that I might do something dumb and impulsive like marry him. I've made that mistake before. I decided I had to do something to wipe that smile off his face, so I kissed him, which led to all sorts of interesting complications and ended any further conversation for the night.

Wiley's suggestion wasn't really off-base. He just wanted equal time with my new best friends, locksmiths. Whenever he couldn't reach me, he knew I was out making time with them. They were always so happy to see me and sell me the latest state-of-the-art security system. And when each one in turn failed, they had another they wanted to show me. Sound-sensitive, air-sensitive, light-sensitive. Nothing worked.

I thought about staying home and waiting, with a gun, by the door. But my boss might not understand. I thought about getting a dog. But MacHeath might not understand. I thought about moving. No, I couldn't do it, even if it was the intelligent choice. I loved the hardwood floors, the built-in bookcases, and, most of all, the fifteen minute walk to work.

One locksmith had offered what I actually thought was the solution. "You'll like this system," he told me. "It's the best, absolutely the best. I have one at home, myself."

What could be more convincing? Of course, they all said that. But I was a sucker for an earnest locksmith.

The perfect security system would not only call the police but alert me at work via a buzzer. Great. I could greet the cops at the door and together we could catch the robbers. And would I press charges? Boy, would I ever.

Unfortunately, MacHeath developed a fondness for setting the damned thing off. After the third false alarm, the cops stopped coming. After the fifth, I decided that MacHeath was using the system the same way the Edwardians had once used a bell to summon the butler—press a button and Chris appears to break up the long, foodless desert of MacHeath's day. Well, I love his furry face a great deal, but he was already running far too much of my life. Faster than you can say "Pavlov's cats" I had the perfect alarm removed. Then I called Wiley.

"Okay," I said. "Introduce me to Mr. Wizard."

The next day, Wiley produced his friend Marsh. Marsh was about what I had expected:

short, pale, balding, and slightly overweight. He looked like an ambulatory pudding with bright red eyebrows and a trim goatee. His home was apparently his office as well: the small apartment in the Mission was festooned with printouts, stray bits of computer parts, coffee cups in which something had died, and crumbs of numerous wave 'n go pizzas.

He fanned out a group of tri-d pictures across his desk as though he were a riverboat gambler. "What'll it be?" he said. "Battle cruisers? A platoon of elite palace guards? Or maybe you'd prefer a ninja assassin?"

"Wait a minute. Do you mean these guys would be creeping around my house? Would I see them? Have to talk to them?"

"Yes, but only if the system got triggered."

"I don't know," I said. "If I were at home and suddenly I saw one of these soldiers creeping around, I might try to brain him with my portascreen. Meanwhile, who—or—whatever triggered the system would get away."

Marsh nodded gravely. "Hmmm. Good point. Maybe you would like something less realistic?"

"But scary," I said. "Especially to burglars. I want them to be violently allergic whatever we choose."

He turned to his screen and flipped quickly through a series of images.

A flash of scales, of slavering green jaws, and great, wide-spanned wings caught me. "Wait!" I said. "What's that?"

"Oh, no, that's not what you want," Marsh said quickly. "That's for a gaming program—it's a hobby, really. Not set up for what you need at all."

I gave him my best dimpled smile. "Oh, come on, Marsh. You said I can have whatever I think will work best, right?"

"Yes. I guess so." He didn't sound very convinced.

"Well, what I want is a dragon," I said. "A big, green, scaly, snaggle-toothed, terrifying watch-dragon."

Wiley moved closer and whispered in my ear. "Chris, I think we're losing a bit of our objectivity here—"

I brushed him away. "It's my apartment."

"He's my friend."

"What's wrong with a dragon?"

"No, it's okay," Marsh said. "I think I can do it. It'll be interesting. Fun."

Right, I thought. Only a technohead would say that.

It took Marsh two weeks to set up his spare rig in my apartment, festooning my living room ceiling with translucent sensor bands. Wiley helped, demonstrating certain practical skills like wiring and programming which almost made me propose to him on the spot. Almost.

"There." Marsh was crouching on his hands and knees over a triple keyboard, playing it the way I imagined Mozart might have if he had ever gotten a fair shot at high tech. "I think we're ready for a run-through."

When we switched the system on, the soles of my feet began to itch and tingle.

"Preliminary vibrations," Marsh said. "They should fade with time. Okay, now let's say a burglar has broken into the apartment." He pressed a quick series of command buttons.

A sound like a shuttle taking off split the room. The combined scent of sulfur and burning rubber made my eyes water.

"The olfactory effect is one of my proudest achievements," Marsh said. He beamed like a new father.

I blew my nose with a loud honk. "Couldn't you get it to pump out something a little less hellish?"

He ignored me. "Now for the dragon." He punched in another command.

A dazzling flash of light, all colors and no color. When it faded, a dragon sat in the center of the room and stared at me with green, baleful eyes. The top of his head was pressed against the ceiling. His leathery wings swept the width of the room, pushing against the tables and chairs. Spiked green claws curved down from his feet, claws that looked even sharper and more evil than did MacHeath's.

"Tell him to watch the rug," I whispered.

He had scales that glistened with iridescent fire at their edges. His nostrils emitted twin tendrils of gray smoke. He was the size of an extremely large elephant. He was perfect.

I nodded approvingly. "I'll take him."

"Does he cook?" Wiley joked.

MacHeath wandered into the room to see who was getting all the attention he deserved. At the sight of the dragon, he fuzzed up to twice his size so that he resembled a furry basketball, and began hissing.

The dragon hissed back.

MacHeath scuttled under the sofa.

"Uh, Marsh, better make sure the system recognizes MacHeath," I said. "Just to be safe."

"Good idea." Marsh said. He positively glowed with pleasure: his pale face looked like a big lightbulb with a beard. Hands flying over the keyboard, he made some minor adjustments, showed me how to set and disarm the rig, and wished me luck. With a merry salute, he left to catch a shuttle for a gaming tournament in Sri Lanka.

Wiley stayed over that night so I didn't bother with the dragon field. The next night he had to work late on a case. I followed Marsh's instructions and got into bed feeling snug and safe as a fairy princess.

I dreamed of a room whose windows and doors opened out onto a broad green meadow. In the distance white horses cantered along a fenced path, their whinnies faintly audible on the wind. I carried a large wicker basket through the door and out into the green meadow. The broad base of an oak tree seemed like the perfect picnic spot and I spread a soft red blanket on the grass and set out an array of succulent tidbits.

A white rabbit hurried by, checking a pocket watch and muttering to himself. I waved gaily and opened a bottle of chardonnay. The wine was young, and a bit sharp. Soon the bottle was empty. I lay back on the blanket and stared through the green glass at the huge cumulus clouds floating above. There, that one with its pointed hat and nose was a witch. And that one over there with a jaunty prow slicing the air was an ocean cruiser scudding through the white caps of the lesser clouds around it. The next one was harder: a huge snowy mass that cast a moving shadow upon the ground and seemed to change shape as I watched. It was an elephant. No, a dinosaur. Finally, I decided it looked most like a dragon. As if to confirm this, the cloud drifted lower and lower, becoming more distinct the nearer it got. I could make out wings, talons, even a head of sorts. The cloud-dragon hovered in the air above me for a moment and I put down the bottle I had been peering through.

Almost as though it were moving by will, the mist descended, drenching me with fine drops of water until my cotton shirt was matted to my chest. I couldn't move. An enormous weight held me immobile as the cloud dragon floated mere inches above me, staring right at me.

I thrashed my legs, trying to lever myself away from the thing.

Suddenly the sun went out and I was lying in the dark, staring into a pair of baleful green eyes.

The dragon was on top of me. I couldn't breathe. I would be crushed.

"Prrrrr," said the dragon as it prickled me with its sharp claws. "Prrrrrr," and he began to wash his plumy red tail with great delicacy.

"For God's sake, MacHeath!" I sat straight up in bed. Gracefully, the cat rolled off me without missing a beat in his toilette.

"You jerk," I said. "Don't tell me you've got a case of dragon envy? Stop goofing around and let me sleep."

He gave me a pained glance and began to work on his right front paw.

As my pulse beat slowed to normal, I slid back under the covers and closed my eyes. If I dreamed about anything else, thankfully I don't remember.

The next day was busy, and the day after that even worse. I was subbing for an office mate as a favor, covering the progress of an arraignment for him while trying to keep track of my own caseload. Things really began to heat up in the latter portion of the week, and I got home later and later each night until I was forced to set up the mechfeeder for MacHeath or risk a visit from the SPCA on charges of cat malnutrition. This went on for two weeks, until even Wiley started to complain.

So I decided to take my life into my own hands, be reckless, and leave work early, before five. Maybe even before four. I would go home, fill the tub three-quarters full, and take a leisurely bath that would use up most of my water allotment for the month. But so what? I could always buy more on the black market. I walked home in a happy daze, thinking about sybaritic pleasures, about dinner with Wiley and—

The front door to my place was wide open.

"Not again," I muttered. "Not today. Please."

As I neared the apartment I heard the faint sound of roaring. A wisp of something foul-smelling leaked out the door; it smelled like burning tires crossed with rotten eggs.

"Help!" cried a high, vaguely male voice. "Oh, God, somebody help me!"

Goody, I thought. No doubt the dragon had cornered the intruder. This was going to be fun

I found them in the bedroom. MacHeath stood by the door hissing. The dragon was in the middle of the bed, roaring. The burglar was crouched down by the bathroom door, crying. He had long blond hair, muddy brown eyes, and looked disturbingly familiar.

"Hey," I said. "Don't you live downstairs?"

"Please, lady, save me. Don't let this thing eat me."

"Have you robbed my house before?"

He looked at me like I was crazy. That doesn't happen very often but when it does I really don't like it. Especially coming from some punk who has just broken into my sanctum sanctorum. I have a fine grasp of reality, thank you, and wish I could say the same of most other people. Actually, it's just as well that three-quarters of the general populace *is* deranged—otherwise I might be out of a job.

I glared down at the intruder. He was a short man. Good.

"What the hell is that thing, a giant lizard?" His teeth chattered with fright. "If you let that alligator get me, I'm going to sue your ass!"

"Save it. I'm a lawyer."

He scowled at me. "Shit. So that's why you got all that good stuff around here."

The dragon roared at him again and moved closer.

"Hey, Ms. Lawyer, do something," he said. "Anything. Call the police."

"Fine idea." I turned on the hallscreen and dialed 911. "Burglary in progress," I reported. The answermech took my name, my address, and promised to get back to me soon. Damned budget cutbacks.

"They're on their way," I lied.

"Thank God," the burglar said. "Did you tell them to hurry?"

The lights dimmed, almost went out, flared, went out completely, flared back on. And things got weird.

The rear wall of the bedroom rippled and disappeared. In its place I saw a stone wall upon which an assortment of wicked looking pikes and lances were hanging. The wall shined faintly with moisture—it was distinctly dungeonlike.

My sleek leather pants and vest had disappeared. Instead, I was wearing some kind of long, flowing gown made of a pale blue, silky material. It was the sort of thing my mother would have worn to her school dance. My head felt heavy and I realized that my hair had grown in an instant until it hung beneath my shoulders. On my head was perched a conical hat. A filmy veil hung down from its tip, tantalizing MacHeath who began to bat at it.

I heard a screen ringing, but MacHeath distracted me by snagging my hat. When I finally disentangled myself, I turned to answer the screen and saw that wall had disappeared as well. I was peering out into a courtyard of a castle where horses were being shod and fitted with armor for battle.

Behind me, the dragon roared.

Men with leather hats and tight-fitting tunics came racing toward me. "It's Gaolbreath," they yelled. "He's come back. Get Sir Rodney. Hurry!"

"Hey, guys," I said.

They ignored me.

"Just a minute, please."

I could hear the screen ringing again, somewhere. But the apartment was gone. Even MacHeath was wearing some sort of strange little heraldic blanket which bore a coat of three blue lions rampant upon a golden field. He didn't seem to mind it, in fact, he sat right down in the middle of the courtyard and washed his face.

"Sir Rodney's coming," yelled a guard. "He'll slay the dragon."

I looked for Sir Rodney, but I couldn't see him. The burglar from downstairs had fainted from fright and/or confusion, or maybe he had hit his head on a cobblestone. Whatever the reason, he was lying, unconscious, in a corner of the dungeon. Suddenly I heard the drumbeat of hoofs against stone.

A noble gray charger in full battle armor came galloping into sight. In his saddle sat a knight who looked eleven feet tall. He was covered from head to toe in gleaming silver armor and he held a lethally sharp-looking sword in his gauntleted hand.

"Stand aside, maiden," a deep, musical voice intoned. "I would not have thee harmed."

At least he was polite. I swept up MacHeath and got out of his way.

The dragon turned, snarling, and fixed upon the knight. They squared off. I was certain that Sir Rodney would carve him into dragon cutlets in short order. Idly I wondered if dragons bled green blood.

Sir Rodney feinted.

The dragon pulled back.

The knight moved in closer and struck the dragon a mighty blow with the lance.

Seemingly undaunted, the dragon, with a great scream and a gout of black smoke, spread its huge leathery wings and took to the air.

Sir Rodney stood straight up in his saddle, slashing at the dragon's belly as it passed over his head.

That proved his undoing.

The dragon plucked him from the horse's back and tossed him against the far wall of the castle. Sir Rodney hit with a sickening crash of metal on rock. He slid, gratingly, to the cobblestoned courtyard, where he lay, unmoving.

"You have lost three hundred points," the dragon announced cheerfully.

Sir Rodney's horse bolted from the arena and raced down an alleyway, out of sight.

"Sir Rodney has fallen," a guard yelled. "Run for your life."

I took a step and felt my skirt catch on something. Then the something tugged at me again. I whirled around. A dwarf in full court jester's dress—bells hanging from his two-pronged hat, the works—held the hem of my skirt and gazed up at me. At least he did with one eye. The other was turned in permanently, staring at the side of his long, hooked nose.

In a piping Cockney tenor, he cried, "Run, maiden. Run to the wizard. He'll know what to do."

"Wizard?" I said. "You have got to be joking. I don't remember ordering up any wizard." Of course, I hadn't asked Marsh for Sir Rodney, either, had I? This virtual reality seemed to have a mind of its own.

"Flee, ere you be slain!"

"Beat it, shorty." I didn't trust this program any farther than I could throw it. If I went to see the wizard, where would I end up? In Emerald City?

The dragon alighted upon the fallen knight, grabbed hold of his helmet, ripped his head off, and began to feed. It seemed like a good time to leave. MacHeath was squirming in my arms and I shook him in annoyance. "Stop it," I hissed.

The dragon's massive jaws paused in midchew. He turned and looked at me. His eyes glittered as he sighted fresh prey.

I began to back away.

He stood up and stalked toward me on big dragon feet.

I backed away faster. But there was nowhere to go. A solid wall stretched behind me, blocking my way. His savage green eyes sparkling with hunger, the beast drew nearer.

"This is a dream," I muttered. "An electronic dream."

The stones of the wall pressed into my back.

The dragon licked his chops.

"Maiden!" A guardsman appeared on my left. "Here!" He tossed me a sword and vanished.

I hefted the heavy blade with some difficulty. "This is ridiculous," I said.

The dragon took a swipe at me with his front claws, knocking MacHeath from my arms.

"Son of a bitch!"

MacHeath landed on all fours and shook himself. The dragon grabbed for me.

Taking the sword hilt in both hands I slashed awkwardly, desperately, upward. The blade connected with something meaty, and I put all my weight behind the blow. There was a sudden wrenching and the sickening, wet sound of heavy flesh hitting stone.

The dragon reared back, roaring. I had severed one of his front claws. "You have gained fifty points," he said.

I swung again and lopped off the other claw.

"You have gained another fifty points."

The front of my gown was ruined: the beast bled a foul ichor that was of an oily greenish-brown hue.

The dragon lashed at me with his tail, caught the sword, and yanked it out of my hands. I looked around desperately, but no guardsman, not even a dwarf, appeared with a replacement weapon.

As the dragon moved in for the kill, I wondered what would happen. Would I die and awaken in a virtual heaven or hell? I didn't really want to try and imagine a hell designed by technoheads. The dragon's slavering, sharp-toothed maw was directly above my head. I shut my eyes.

"Mmmrowwll!

I opened my eyes. MacHeath was at my feet, yowling. I kicked at him, trying to chase him away.

"Get out of here, stupid. Do you want to be hors d'oeuvres for this guy?"

"Fsssst! Fsssst!" MacHeath batted at the scaly dinosaur. I had to give him credit for spunk. But I expected to see him squashed into cat mousse beneath the dragon's feet any second.

The dragon stopped, peered down, and seemed to focus on MacHeath for the first time.

"Systems check," the dragon said. "Lifeform identified as cat, twelve pound mixed breed. Positive identification. MacHeath. System owner. No threat. Shut down."

And with that the dragon froze, flattened to two dimensions, fragmented, went sideways, and, with a loud pop, disappeared, taking the illusion of the medieval town with him.

Stucco walls and hardwood floor again. I was standing in my own living room. There was no castle, no cobblestones, no dead knight. Just one burglar lying by the door to my bedroom, out cold.

I sighed with relief. So much for knights riding to my rescue. I'd sooner count on MacHeath any time. I felt something in my hand and looked down, expecting to see a sword. But I wasn't holding a sword. Instead, I was grasping a serrated breadknife that usually lived in the kitchen. When had I gotten that? No matter. I put it down as the doorbell rang. Just for good measure, I shut off the security field. Then I went to let in the cops.

Wiley came running, with food, when I called. "You don't mean," he said, "that Marsh forgot to provide the system with permanent identification for you? What a jerk."

"No." I shook my head in between bites of dim sum. "He gave it my I.D., all right. But that power surge must have wiped part of the memory, causing the program to revert to its gaming configurations. The only thing that saved me was MacHeath. The system recognized him. In fact, it called HIM the system owner."

"I knew that cat was good for something. Is he smug?"

"Insufferable. He's taken to sitting above my jewelry stash with a possessive air, smiling a positively lizardlike smile."

"He thinks he's a dragon?"

"I hope not."

"So I guess this means you're going back to standard security measures."

"I don't know how badly I'll need them now that my erstwhile neighbor is in the pokey."

"Marsh thought he had gotten all the gaming glitches out of the program. He's really sorry, you know."

"He's lucky I don't take him to court," I said. "That system should have been surge-protected. He should know better than that."

Wiley looked dismayed. "Chrissie, you won't—"

"Relax. Marsh distracted me by offering to split any profits he makes from commercial applications of the program."

"Sounds good. But what about protecting your apartment right now?"

"Oh, I don't know," I said. "I might not need it."

"What do you mean?"

"Talk to me again about moving into your

place," I said. "And start with the noise dampers."

He beamed like an imbecile. "Chris, do you mean it?"

"No. Well, maybe. How safe is your electrical system?" And I gave him a crocodile smile.

THE STOLEN DRAGON

by Kimberly Gunderson

"May the Great God Shiran freeze his guts, may his bed be one of a thousand sand fleas, and may camel spit be his only drink." Jud cursed into his beard as he shuffled out of the desert toward the city gates. The morning sun rising over the sandstone walls reflected in his eyes and highlighted the numerous sand scores on the breastplate of his uniform. The thought of the hours that would be spent to get it into condition for an inspection sent Jud into another round of cursing.

He snarled at the smirking gate guards who passed him through, but the object of his darkest thoughts was Captain Zalman, Captain of the Guard, expert horseman, adequate archer, and lousy card player. The Captain had assured Jud the fact that he had lost two gold to him, had nothing to do with Jud's being assigned to sentry outpost duty for two shifts. Jud believed him about as much as he believed the desert sand would turn to mulled wine and the Great God Shiran would personally escort him through the gates of paradise. Although that fantasy sounded very good, right now all Jud wanted was something cool to drink. Something sweet to remove the desert sand from his mouth.

Jud found it at the first winemaker's stall. This stall was a rough wooden cart covered by a white canopy offering some measure of shade against the morning rays. Although the stall looked like a hundred others scattered throughout the city of Garn, to Jud it looked better than the famed water pools of the royal harem. Jud bought a whole skin of sweet plum wine, still cool from the evening air, and headed deeper into the market on his way to the barracks.

The crowds were growing as quickly as the day's heat. Jud had to stop several times to avoid running into a push cart or being spit on by a camel. Dirty children played with colored stones between bright striped tents while veiled women held up a variety of edible delights. Hawkers bellowed the distinctive cry of their guild to advertise their wares. Their cries mixed with donkey brays and the sweet strains of strolling lute players. The dew gave the dirty canvas awnings a damp earthy smell that was overpowered by warm bread, sweaty bodies, and the perfumed fragrance of honeysuckle. To the wandering tribes who came to Garn to trade horses and wool, the diversity and confusion of the market was wondrous. And now, with Garn swollen by caravans hoping to make a few more deals before heading west ahead of the fire storms, it was overwhelming. But to Jud, city-born and city-bred, everyone, everything, and every sound was just an annoyance created by the gods for his personal torture. All he wanted was a meal to fill his belly, a bath to remove the sand, and a bed free of spiders or scorpions. That was all Jud's mind could focus on when he tripped over a dirty street urchin and lost his wineskin under the feet of a camel.

"You dirty, no good—"

"Please officer, don't hit me!" the boy cringed.

"I'm not an officer, and I'm not going to hit you."

"Good," yelled the boy as he kicked Jud in the shins and bolted into the crowds.

Jud roared out a curse and ran to follow. He was tired, but not that tired, and he caught the boy before he had taken a dozen steps. He grabbed him by the back of the shirt collar, slapped his free hand under the boy's neck, and lifted him off his feet.

"All right street scum, you just cost me my drink and in return earned yourself a mountain of trouble."

"Please, officer, I've done nothing," the boy pleaded.

"Lying, probably, thieving little tramp, why were you running? What'd you steal?"

"Nothing."

"Give it to me, or I'll shake it out of you." Jud stormed.

"But I didn't . . ." By this time the boy was beginning to turn purple.

"Last chance, what'd you steal?"

"Nothing," the boy gasped.

Jud dropped the boy on the ground in frustration and began to roughly search his pockets. His hand closed on two coins and then he felt something about the size of his fist. His eyes caught the glint of gold. Jud removed it and held it up for inspection. It was a small statue of a dragon and it appeared to be made of pure gold.

"So this is what you think is nothing," he said holding the statue in front of the boy's nose.

The boy paled under the layers of dirt and sun browned skin. "That's mine, I didn't steal it."

"Of course, dirty street urchins always buy gold statues."

"I didn't buy it. It belongs to—"

"To whoever you stole it from. Now, where did you get it?"

"The lady in the blue and yellow stall, end of the last row."

"Finally, street scum, you told me what I wanted to hear. This is how the game is played. I'm too damn tired to take you into the courts now, so I'm going to let you go with a warning this time. I'll take this," he said, lifting the boy to his feet by the front of his shirt and taking the two coppers he had found in the boy's pocket during his previous search, "for the wine you cost me. Now, get lost," and he threw the boy into the watching crowd. Much to Jud's surprise, the boy turned around and staggered back. "But you can't keep that dragon."

"That's not your problem." Jud stepped forward, his face dark as a desert storm. When the boy didn't move, Jud grabbed him by the wrist and forced his hand down on the counter of a neighboring fruit stall.

"Do you know what happens if I turn you over to the courts?" he asked his captive.

The boy shook his head.

"They find you guilty of thieving and they cut off your hand, or, if it is your first offense, maybe only a finger or two. Now, if you continue to bother me, I won't bother to take you down to the courts, I'll take off your fingers right here!" Jud roared as he drew his sword.

The boy screamed and struggled furiously to break free. He finally twisted away from the guardsman and disappeared into the crowd. Jud laughed as he sheathed his sword and went in search of more wine.

Once he was back in his barracks, Jud put the statue under his pillow while he went for a bath and some food. When he returned, he checked; it was still there. As he lay in his bunk, he couldn't help admiring it. It was beautifully and delicately crafted, a long slim dragon, covered with scales. The dragon had a ridge of sharp horns on his back and a slim tail that circled the statue's base. It had one front foot raised as if to warn off intruders and its open mouth seemed ready to burst into golden flame. It was the work of a fine craftsman. Artistry the likes of which Jud would never own. Unless he decided to keep it.

Keep it? The idea just seemed to pop in his head of its own accord and Jud looked around to see if someone might have said it out loud. No one else was in the barracks. But why shouldn't he keep it? He worked too hard for the small pay the Governor allowed and he was due for some small reward. And the owner obviously didn't miss it or she would have been in the area searching for the thief. No one knew how he came by it, so he could just tell them he received it as a favor from a friend. Yes, a lady friend, a lady of quality and wealth. The idea grew and grew until Jud drifted off to sleep.

A pain in Jud's hand woke him a few hours later. He had been lying on that side and had apparently numbed it from sleeping on it. He rolled over and fell back to sleep. Again he awoke with a pain in his hand. But this time it had spread to his elbow and felt as if he were holding it over flames. In his mind he could see the fire surrounding it. He sat up and looked at his arm. It looked the same as it had when he had gone to sleep, the same as his other arm. Jud shook it a few times to try to get the feeling out and decided to get up and eat. He dressed quickly, only stopping to admire his new treasure for a few moments before securing it in a pouch he carried beneath his tunic. Then he headed for the kitchen.

By the time Jud finished eating, the pain had spread to his shoulder and felt as if the skin were being burned off slowly. He could almost see the spreading redness as he heard the sizzle of fried flesh. The acrid smell of scorched muscle and skin was almost more than he could bear. Jud let out a scream as he rose, knocking his chair backward. He stared at his arm. The arm still looked the same as it always had, but the pain felt as if it were never going to stop. Jud decided to admit his problem and go see the company healer, Mirald, a minor mage assigned to patch up the members of the company after street fights, barroom brawls, and an occasionally unsuccessful amorous evening. Jud wondered how Mirald would handle things if there ever was any real fighting.

The mage occupied a private room on one side of the barracks compound. It was made of desert mud like the rest of the buildings but was covered with marks and runes that Mirald said aided his power and kept out evil spirits. The healer was home when Jud arrived, resting to escape the day's heat. Jud quickly explained his growing pain and Mirald examined the affected appendage. He questioned the private about his last few days.

"Did you eat anything new to you?"

"No, just the usual camp grub."

"Were you bitten by anything. Any insects?"

"Mirald, you can't do outpost watch without being bitten a dozen times. In the desert, there are flies out for blood, spiders out for flesh, and scorpions out just to be mean. But I didn't get bit any more than normal."

"Have you acquired anything new?"

Jud thought of the gold dragon statue. "Nothing new."

A sharp shooting pain stabbed across his shoulder and down his chest. The pain in his hand was becoming a constant throb that was almost too much to bear. In his little finger the pain suddenly stopped. Jud breathed a sigh of relief until he looked at the numbed finger; it was hanging on the end of his hand, white and at an unnatural angle. Mirald reached over to touch it, and without warning it fell off and shattered into thousands of crystal pieces. Jud couldn't catch his breath and his shocked expression was mirrored by Mirald.

"Whatever it is, Jud, for your own health, hand it over."

Jud reached in his pocket, took out the statue, and set it on the table in front of the healer. Immediately the pain in his chest stopped and his hand went back to just a dull ache.

"That does explain a lot," Mirald began. He noticed Jud's questioning look and continued. "Magic, I can feel it. Either the statue itself is magic, or it is cursed to prevent thieves. Some vendors use such curses to protect their wares. When the items are legitimately purchased, the curse is removed by the shopkeeper. But if the item is stolen, it causes the thief some form of discomfort. The most common is for the thief's hand to turn blue, that was always my favorite. I've never heard of one so strong. This statue must either be very powerful or very valuable to carry such a powerful curse."

"So how do I get rid of the curse?"

"Simple. Get rid of the statue. Return it to its owner."

Jud flexed his hand and nodded, resigning himself to the loss of his prize. He hesitated before picking up the statue but realized he had no choice. He tentatively picked it up with two fingers and gingerly put it back in his pouch. It caused him no additional pain.

Mirald chuckled at his performance. "When you are done with that, I expect to hear how you acquired it."

"I didn't steal it if that's what you mean."

"I never said you did."

Jud left the room, slamming the door behind him as hard as he could. He headed for the market.

The market was as congested as it had been yesterday but for a different reason. Tents were being removed as out-of-towners began to form the long caravans that would head across the desert before the fire season began. Twice Jud was almost caught under collapsing canvas as tents fell before being removed. He had to detour three times to avoid camel chains being loaded with dry goods purchased for the western lands. But finally, he got to the last row. The blue and yellow stall was gone. There was nothing he could do now, he thought. The searing pain in his chest caused Jud to gasp, but his ring finger went numb cold. Jud stifled a scream of horror as he watched the scene from Mirald's repeat. The finger just hung there unnaturally. Then, without further warning it fell off, shattering into thousands of crystal pieces. Jud gasped and staggered over to the young woman in the neighboring stall.

He grabbed the young woman by the shoulders and shook her violently. "Where'd she go? Where'd the old woman with the blue and yellow stall go?"

"She left," the girl gasped, scattering the flowers she held.

"I know she left. Where?" Jud yelled.

"Master Rukan's caravan. She left a message for anyone who came looking for her that she would be there."

Jud released the girl and bolted away from the stall. He had seen Master Rukan's banner at the northwest gate, so he knew where the caravan would be forming. If it had already left, he would just have to borrow a horse and follow it. The pain in his chest stopped.

Jud ran as fast as he could through the crowded rows toward the gate. He got there as the last members were forming up for the trip across the desert. He stopped one of the mercenaries hired to protect the caravan on its journey and asked about an old woman who had a blue and yellow market stall. The guard pointed to a wagon at the back of the line. Jud approached the old woman who was checking the reins of the wagon's horse.

He hid his injured hand behind his back as he stood as if at attention.

"Excuse me, I'm Private Jud of the Governor's Guard, and I believe I found something that belongs to you."

"I was wondering how long it would take to get my toy back. I worried it would cause problems if it fell into dishonest hands. How did you find it?"

"I caught a young street urchin yesterday and took this from him." Jud removed the little dragon and handed it to the old woman.

The old woman held the dragon close for a moment. Then her eyes widened briefly in surprise, which quickly faded. The old woman looked intently at Jud. "Well, that naughty boy. What happened to him?"

"I let him go," Jud answered softly.

The old woman smiled sadly. "He's lucky you took the dragon and let him go. What is the punishment for thieving in Garn? Loss of a hand or just a finger or two?"

Jud nodded, unable to answer.

The old woman packed the dragon safely in the wagon and returned her intent gaze to Jud. "Thank you for all your help, Private, I do appreciate it. It's nice to know that our Governor's guard still contains honest men."

Jud bowed and turned to leave. But as he walked away, he caught a glimpse of a face behind the wagon. He turned to see his street urchin climb onto the wagon seat and take the reins from the old woman. She climbed up beside him and the caravan began to move away. But as the wagon passed, Jud could swear the little boy sneered at him.

"Just a finger or two," Jud whispered with realization. "Just a finger or two."

COLD STONE BARROW

by Elizabeth Forrest

Morning, as if it were as battered as they felt, crept up the slate colored hills slowly like the fog rolling off knife-sharp rivers cutting into the foot of the cliffs. Alben stopped, panting, the shafts of the cart jabbing splinters into the palms of his hands. Much taller than their dead horse, he strode hunch-backed to pull it and he straightened with a crackling stiffness. The two-wheeled carrier bucked his heels as it jarred to a halt. Every bone in his body ached.

His passenger cried from the cart bed. He turned about quickly to see Rain awake, holding weakly to the edge, her hands pale white and her nails blue with cold.

"Fool," she got out. "Why did you come this way? You'll kill us both."

"I thought to give you company," he said dryly. "I came because I saw the smoke from hearth fires this morning, before the fog came in. There's got to be somebody living up here. A village, I think." The dog came trotting up, *kefer* fur about his mouth from hunting.

Rain gave him a spiteful look, spat out, "Coward," and the dog slunk back into the moist grayness. Alben watched him go before looking back at Rain. If she thought Redstar a coward, what would she think of him? He coughed once, spitting the dragon's black smoke into his palm that he had inhaled during the brief fight and looked back to Rain. She had shrunk into her shroud, but he could see the fever spasms trembling her. "You need help I can't give you."

"Fool," she husked again. "No one travels back in these hills. It's forbidden."

"Why?"

"How should I know? Headhunters, maybe."

"Really?"

"Yes," she hissed with a hint of her old irritability. "And if they take ours, they'll find nothing but thick bone stuffed with air!" She fell back into the cart on the last word.

Alben paused, weight shifted forward, to go to her side quickly, but he didn't dare do it as long as she was scrapping with him. The slender fingers of her hand surfaced, pointing upward.

"Water," she beseeched.

Alben unslung the skins from about his neck and went to the cart then. He steadied the bag in her hands. Their touch thrilled through him like ice on a winter-etched pond. "Not too much," he said.

"I *know*," Rain answered. Her dark eyes

flashed. Nonetheless she gulped at the bag a second time before surrendering it and wiping her mouth. "It's never enough."

"Blackthorn fever," Alben stated. He knew much of the symptoms, nothing of the cure. Like the plague, it rendered him helpless. A blade would not cut the fever from her body. Not that he fared much better with a blade, he thought bitterly.

She lay back, staring upward at him and the sky. "Even the Tirendan don't come here," she said.

"Why?"

She closed her eyes in a blink so long he thought she had succombed to fever sleep again, but finally she opened her lids. "Headhunters," she said weakly, with the corner of her mouth quirked. "How the devil should I know? My father used to call it the Forgotten Lands. Mountains, too high and jagged. The land, too barren."

Alben said stubbornly, "I saw smoke curls."

Rain turned her face from the sky. "If you think so. If you're searching for the dragon, this is a good place to find him."

"It didn't fly this way. Besides, you defeated him before. Why should I worry?"

Rain subsided with a deep, rattling cough of scorn. Alben's sympathy with her extended only so far. If she had not drunk blackthorn elixir to augment her powers, he would not be hauling her carcass up these forsaken hills. She shook again, violently, curling her hands into her cloaked body so vehemently he thought the cloth would part under her nails. His concern for her came flooding back.

Redstar barked once from the fog banks. Alben relented. He had to get help for her or she would never last the day. He went back to the shafts and bent his back to balancing the weight. The cart jolted into movement as he leaned forward. The dog picked out the road for him, unerringly, running back and forth, coursing. Alben caught only bare glimpses of his sorrel flanks and big, square head, the jowls and tongue lolling and then the dog was off again. His trust in the dog was gone, as well. After Redstar had fled the dragon, Alben knew he could not depend on the creature's help pulling down any enemy they might meet.

The fog thickened, though the youth knew the sun had had to have risen somewhere over Faran. He could hear birdsong and the kefer rustling through stone and grass at the trail's side. He thought ruefully of their slain horse and tightened his slick palms upon the wood shafts. He would have to bind his hands against bloodblisters if they went much further. It was better than carrying Rain, but only just.

The sun's heat, if not light, reached him through the fog and his shirt was soaked with sweat and his knees going weak when the cart went into a stubborn spot on the patchy trail and balked, setting Alben back on his heels. He sworn as a long daggerlike splinter cut across his palm, his voice booming in the quiet. He paused, fingers pinched to pull the splinter, realizing he heard nothing but silence, and did not like the possibilities.

The dog, who'd gone ahead some time ago, began to bark, loudly, his voice belling to Alben that he found something, found, found, found it. The edge in Redstar's call woke Rain who sat up in the cart. She held onto the slab side with both arms, the hollows in her face sunk with deep shadows of hurt under her eyes. "Alben," she said, and worry shook her voice.

He unslung the water bottles from about his neck, freeing the long sword's sheath. He tossed her the bottles. Rain clutched them in one claw-like hand. He drew the sword overhand and stood, on guard, waiting for the thinning fog to break entirely.

It didn't and the dog kept barking and Alben knew he couldn't let Redstar face whatever it was alone.

He started forward.

"Don't leave me here!" Rain cried out.

"Kalkus," he swore. His shoulders ached, his hands were riddled with splinters already bringing pus up in blisters. He stomped back, hoisted the shaft under his left arm and began to pull again, carrying his sword in his free hand. Rain said nothing and he thought ironically that he had finally managed to please her—even if it so handicapped him they would both be mowed down.

They entered a narrow cut which even the fog could not obscure, slate and blue sides of the mountain leaning in upon them until Alben thought he could not drag the cart through. With a jolt and a lurch, they were through and the sudden brilliance of the noonday sun dazed him as he staggered into the open.

He was on a rutted road, more or less, with a broken stonewall pasture fence beside him, and Redstar bounding on stiff legs facing a wild-haired old farmer holding him off with a hoe he used like a quarterstaff. The hoe had a metal head to it which gleamed wickedly in the sun, but the silver-haired wielder seemed to have no intention of hurting Redstar, only holding him off. The haft, the dog's massive head and the lanky man's guts were all on a level. Star had gone for him at least once, Alben could see scars from the dog's teeth gleaming in the wood. The attack and prey surprised him.

"Star! Drop!" he shouted.

The dog went down, but stayed alert, his hind-quarters bunched under him, eyes never leaving the hoe-wielder. He could spring from that position, Alben thought. He let go of the cart and felt it settle.

A lush mountain vale opened beyond the road, terraced and dotted with fences and cottages and livestock. Its bowl of farmland and pastureland concentrated into what must be the main streets of a village and then spiraled outward again into woodlands so dense they were blue-green against the foot of implacable mountains that stretched purple vistas as far as he could see. Man had eked out only a tiny purchase against the wilderness.

"He yore dog?" the farmer asked, his words accented with a guttural inflection that made it difficult for Alben to understand him at first.

"Yes," he answered hesitantly, trying to keep sword in hand nonchalantly.

The farmer's seamed visage turned toward him. Redstar crawled along the ground to keep between them and stay in front of the peasant. "He's a good one. Mite young though. Still green. Or else ye've not trained him well enough."

"Haven't trained him at all," Alben said defensively, not wanting Redstar's faults blamed on him. He had enough trouble with his own flaws.

"No?" The farmer lowered the hoe head to the ground and leaned upon the staff.

Rain had sat up in the cart again. "The Packmaster's dead," she said, her voice reduced to a husked whisper.

The peasant looked past Alben to her. He appeared not to have heard her catastrophic news or it meant nothing to him. "The Eye of God sent me up here to meet you. But she said nothin' about plague." He seemed neither fazed nor impressed that they traveled with a dragon-dog among them.

"It's not plague," Alben countered quickly. He tightened his grip on the sword. "It's blackthorn

fever." He wondered what in the frozen hells an
Eye of God was.

"Blackthorn, eh?" The man squeezed his eyes
into a keener gaze aimed at Rain. "Only three
reasons I know of for your woman to be usin'
blackthorn. Riddin' yourself of an unwanted
babe. Riddin' a possessor." He paused and Alben
was minded of the sharp eye of a hawk as the
man looked closer at Rain. "Or honin' the edge
of powers that ought to be left alone."

Alben could see Rain's cheek flush darkly,
stark against the pallor of her skin. Her mouth
puffed and then she got out, "I'm not his
woman."

It seemed to take the last of her strength as
she sagged back.

"What does it matter as long as it's not
plague?"

The farmer looked at him, then at the dog still
showing his teeth between them, and back to
Alben. "It matters," he said. "And ye know it
does. Best come with me now. Without a horse,
it'll take us a while to get down."

Alben knew the village folk watched them
come in, watched without seeming to, just as he
used to when he lived among steads like this.
Peering about corners and through shutters,
eying through the tines of pitchfork, through the
cloud of a bellows and forge. He wondered what
they saw in him, tall, big shouldered young man
with a massive dog at his heels, pulling a rickety

cart by himself, its passenger moaning on the shuddering bed. They would fear plague and not come out. They would spit between the forked fingers of their hands to avert the evil he might bring with him. One or two would envy him for the long sword on his back and maybe a handful might think of stealing the dog. They wouldn't if they knew of the base nature of this dog, he added wryly to himself.

From every pitched eave swung a wind chime, and the midday breeze that began picking up sluggishly from the river that was this village's heartline rattled at the chimes. A few who ventured out to stare openly reached out and deliberately set the chimes to swinging. Alben watched back, thinking they must use the noise to drive away demons. Redstar gave an anxiously pitched whine. He dropped his hand down to the dog's head and kneaded him gently behind one soft flapped ear. He could not forgive or forget the dog's failure, but his own was just as heinous, and he'd grown fond of the pup.

They crossed a floating bridge that bobbed slightly under their weight and the cart's weight. Redstar stopped and hung his head over, looking at the river.

"Flood often?" Alben asked.

"Not much. Ever' ten years or so. Never too high."

The far side of the bridge was a grove and a few, scattered huts, the pungent smell of the tanners' row and stockyards. Also the ramshackle building the old farmer headed him toward. From the hex signs painted on every surface, and the abundance of wind chimes hanging about, Alben knew this must be the residence of "the Eye of God" and also precisely who she might be, as a figure nudged outside and waited for them. This was the witchy woman, it could be none other.

Wrapped in a blanket woven in all the colors of the rainbow and leaning against the dull hut, she had once been heartstoppingly beautiful. Neither old nor young, she was still remarkably handsome. Did Tirendan blood run in her that she could look so? When they were alone, he would risk using the little Tirendall he knew. Alone; so that she need not worry about revealing herself and he did not need to fear scorn because of his terrible pronunciation. He began to slow his walk.

"Not *her*," the old man said in scorn, dodging away from her. "That's the town slut." Back ramrod stiff, he marched away from the woman.

Alben thought he heard a muffled sound from deep in the cart bed which might have been Rain coughing or stifling her amusement. His face heated. The woman smiled widely and called after him throatily, "Visit me on the way back."

The elder farmer gave a loud harrump and she called after softly, "Good day, father."

Alben did not look back though he could feel the woman's gaze burning a hole between his shoulder blades which his long sword gave him no protection from.

They strode deep into the grove, and the trees began to grow with majesty, their auburn bark deepening and their girth and height expanding so that it seemed they could canopy the stars. Ferns and small thickets bushed their massive roots, and the air felt damp and clean.

The farmer had to give him no sign when they found a massive tree whose trunk had been blackened and hollowed by fire, yet the tree still thrived. A hide curtain for proof against the wind was pegged to one side, and he saw a modest bed and table and brazier in the hollow.

The girl who stepped out of the ferns did surprise him. Over her homespun shift, she wore the crowning rack of a forest stag, its hide her cloak, and her dark, long hair was unbound down her back. Her eyes, dark and deep as a mountain tarn on a moonless night, watched them. As her gaze met his and searched his face for what he didn't know, he could see the fine, tiny lines about her eyes and mouth. Not as young as he thought, then ... perhaps ageless, like these trees.

She spoke and her voice carried no trace of the guttural accent of the elder, clear as rainwater in a meadow freshet. "Thank you, Bertie, for bringing them here."

"You didn't tell me 'bout the plague," said the old man somewhat sulkily.

"There's no plague here. It's blackthorn fever, as he told you, and you'll be fine."

Bert cleared his throat and slung his hoe over his shoulder. She stopped him in his tracks. "Stay. You'll be needed to guide them later."

He twitched at that. "Nawt," he said.

She turned her head to look the old man fully in the eye, a graceful, even movement, done slowly to keep the massive rack balanced. "Bert," she said.

The farmer looked at the ground. "Al' right," he growled in submission. Redstar whined at the tone in his voice.

The girl then turned her dark, clear eyes on Alben. "Bring her in," she ordered and stepped within the fire-grooved hollow. She unfastened her crown and rack. He saw it was the stag's skull, bone and horn and all, as she put it carefully on the table. She kept the hide tied about her shoulders, cloaking her slender body.

Rain felt light as thistledown as he carried her. As he lay her down, she kept her hands fastened about his neck a moment, unwilling to let go and when she lay back and shut her eyes quickly, she didn't keep him from seeing the fear in them. Alben straightened, puzzled. Why should Rain fear this slip of a girl? Wouldn't they have an understanding of power between them?

He stepped back as the Eye of God came to the cot and kneeled on the mossy flooring. Her sable hair rippled down her back with the movement. Alben found himself staring and drew his gaze away and caught old Bertie watching him with a knowing look.

Alben's neck flushed. Redstar brushed up against his legs, searching for comfort, and he knuckled the dog to quiet him.

The forest girl held a gourd to Rain's parched lips and let her drink long and deep. The water set off another spasm as if it warred with her fevered flesh.

"This is the price you pay," the girl said to Rain, "for forcing that which might or might never have come to you on its own terms."

Rain clenched her teeth to stop their chatter. She gritted out, "I had to."

"There is always a choice." The forest girl's voice never rose, but Rain winced at the condemnation in it.

Alben said, in defense, "She did it to protect us—"

The forest girl twisted on her knee, turning her uncompromising gaze at him. "We saw the beast darken the sky. We know what you have driven our way. We know far better than you what you have done."

Rain's hand came out and caught the other's wrist. "Alben nearly slew it—"

"They heal quickly. If crippled, it will be more maddened than ever. It will have to be dealt with." The forest girl twisted her wrist. Rain's hand fell away and she gasped with the pain, and lay shuddering, pale as morning dew. Alben felt her pain with her.

"I have some medicinals, but not enough to cure her. I can slake the fever and put her back on her feet, but she needs to drink the tea for a least a moon's cycle if she wishes to be free of blackthorn fever." The forest girl spread her hands.

Alben had his double-headed coin tucked inside his boot shaft. "I can pay."

"Indeed you will. But coins have no tender here, and her payment requires more. I have no moss for tea. It is up to you to gather what you need for yourself and to replenish my stock."

Old Bertie startled at this, and rolled a wild eye at the girl, but she paid him no attention. "The moss grows inside the gateway barrow. You'll have to scrape it from the rocks. You'll need as much as you can gather." She bent to Rain's side and pulled the girl into a sitting position. From under the cot, she pulled a woven reed bag and set it into Rain's trembling hands. "Fill the bag to bursting."

"You can't send her," Alben protested. "It'll be the death of her. I'll go."

Without looking at him again, the forest girl said, "Yes, you'll go, to guard. But the price to be paid comes from her." She leaned over Rain, who swayed back and came up short against the tree's charred flank. "You must be soul-strong as well as quick and clever. You were quick to reach for this . . . now let's see if you have the strength to hang on." The forest girl straightened abruptly. "It might be there waiting for you, or it might have returned to its own lands. You'll need your sword and the dog."

Alben's jaw dropped, but he did not utter the question that started to brim out of him. With a sudden clarity that pierced his fatigue and aching muscles, he knew what the forest girl referred to.

The dragon was in the barrow. To heal Rain, they must finish what they had so raggedly, unsuccessfully begun. No wonder old Bert quaked in his sandals.

The forest girl scooped up another gourd of rockmoss tea and forced it down Rain. When the last drop had been drunk, she stepped back, put on her skull crown and left, walking into the shadows and thickets and disappearing as quietly as a stag.

Rain patted her mouth dry. She looked miserably at Alben. "We make a fine threesome," she said. "A coward, an invalid and a ... a brave fool." She had stopped shivering, but her skin looked as translucent as an egg held before candlelight. At any moment, he thought he might see her skeleton shifting within.

Alben decided. "To hell with rustic mystics," he said. "Give me the bag."

"No." Rain curled her arm about it. "No. She promised me...." Rain's voice dropped away suddenly.

"She promised nothing." Alben fought to keep

his anger reined in. "She promised you nothing!"

Rain looked beseechingly at him as he tried to wrestle the bag from her. She whispered, "She promised me everything . . . if I live."

He saw the desperation in her, the hollowness, the life in her that had caved in, sucked away with the loss of her power and the first flush of blackthorn fever. It was something he could not give her. As the Eye of God had said, he could only guard her back when she went to seek it. He let go of the reed bag abruptly.

Redstar had approached the cot and stood by it, head lowered. Alben toed him away. "When do we leave?"

"Nowt," old Bertie said loudly. "As soon as yore woman can walk." He dug the end of his hoe into the lengthening shadow of the tree in emphasis.

The old farmer found a whetstone in his baggy pouch and handed it to Alben who silently made use of it as they walked, though no amount of attention could mend the nicks where the dragon's heavy scales had nocked the edge.

"Ye look like ye knowt how t' use that thing," Bertie said with grudging admiration.

"Not really. I'm better with an ax."

"A war axe?"

"No. I cut timber."

"Ah," said the elder. "Not wit'out the permission of the Tirendan, I hope."

"Never." Alben looked at him curiously. "You're one of the few I've heard mention the proud nation lately, without fear."

"Up here," Bertie said, "we've only one enemy t' fear. Unless a traveler brings th' plague to us. But the Eye of God keeps us safe, mostly. Not to say that life passes us by . . . we get th' same hard knocks as most folk. But it's wickedly hard for a friend to find us, let alone an enemy." And his eye twinkled at Alben.

"The fog. I knew it wasn't natural."

"Maybe it is and maybe it tisn't. But it works, all the same." Bertie reached out to point out a spot needing attention on the blade and got a wee slice along his finger for his effort. He sucked on it to take the sting out. "Sharp, thet is."

"Yes." Alben turned about quickly as he heard Rain stumble.

She caught herself and put her chin up, one hand knotted in the loose skin about Redstar's withers. "I'm all right," she said.

She wasn't. He could see it, but knew she would not take his hand if he offered it. Bertie looked past him to the girl.

"The Packmaster's dead, ye were saying," the farmer said agreeably, as if that had just been mentioned.

"Murdered," she husked. "By the false king's guard."

Bertie tched. "We'll be needin' a new one, then," he said, and strode away again. Rain threw Alben a look of utter despair, wiped her hand across her face as if she could erase it and lurched back into motion.

The sun was lowering into the third quadrant of the sky, and the purple vistas of the harsh mountains the only view ahead, when Bertie came to a sudden halt. Among the purple, shifting shadows, he pointed his hoe to a darker maw.

"Th' barrow," he said, and turned away.

"Wait." Alben caught his elbow. "What can I expect?"

The farmer's jaw worked as if he chewed cud. "Expect?" he finally echoed.

"I've no torch. Is it dark in there, a cave, or just a cut? And will the . . . beast be in there, waiting?"

"I don't knowt," answered Bertie. "And my guesses will do ye no good. I'll be nappin' under thet tree," and the hoe swung back around. "I'll wait for ye." He marched away. Redstar bounded off with him, paused, and then came back, as if knowing his destiny lay in a different direction. In the long shadows, the dark star on his chest looked more than ever like a crimson flower of blood staining his chestnut hide even darker.

Alben wondered if that mark was a portent.

Rain swung the reed basket from under her arm. "With any luck," she said, "the old lizard's flown back to wherever he came from to lick his wounds." She glared down at the dog. "Stay out from under my feet!"

The dog leaned against Alben's leg as the girl walked off unsteadily. The two looked at one another. Alben stroked Redstar's head. "You don't know what it's like to be a coward," he murmured. "To fail. It's always a new day with you, ready to do better. But I can't trust you, and I can't protect you. Go with the old man. Stay out of our way. Go on!" and he nudged Redstar back toward the forest. The dog went off a little way and sat, head cocked. Alben picked up a stone and threw it.

Redstar yelped and skittered away, disappearing into the forest fringe. The farmer lying on the ground never twitched. Asleep already, Alben thought. He pocketed the whetstone and dried the palms of his hands, first one and then the other, before hefting the sword securely.

The barrow was not an enclosed tunnel for its ceiling was cracked, fractured, and though dark, a lightning bolt of illumination ran as far as Alben could see. He strode in, narrowing his gaze, waiting for his eyes to adjust to the dimness, Rain ahead of him scraping rock with her eating spoon.

The barrow could encompass two or three dragons, if it needed, although the way would be close. It was not, however, big enough to allow the wings unfurled. Alben took a small comfort in that observation. The stone cried and moss pooled amply along the flooring. He put a finger out to touch the weeping rock. The water was both gritty and ice cold, as if being squeezed through changed its properties into an element containing both stone and ice.

He said to Rain, "Why'd he call this a gateway barrow?"

She grunted as she bent, frantically harvesting the moss. "Legend says the dragons are held back until their time. They press the limits of that magic constantly." Rain turned to look at him, her face a pale moon. "This must be one of the fractures in that boundary. That's why these mountains are forbidden. . . ."

"And the village?" He swung his blade along a rockface, shearing off a panel of moss as large as a sheephide. Rain knew the histories from the Packmaster. He knew only old timber tales about the Tirendan.

Rain gathered it up and compressed it into a third of its size, stuffing it into the reed bag. "There're supposed to be guardians. I don't know."

Guardians with hoes. Alben smiled crookedly in spite of his splinters and weariness. He strode deeper into the barrow and stumbled.

Redstar pushed past him with eely eagerness, chuffed his kneecap, and disappeared down the barrow. Alben righted himself. The jagged crack above let enough light in so that he could see what he had stumbled over.

A score so deep into the rock and dirt floor

that it had rutted furrows. He frowned, looking downward. A dragon raked here, he thought, marking his ground. But he did not smell the rank, evil, musty scent of the canny old beast he'd wounded. He strode across the marking in search of Redstar whose faint belling sounded down the barrow. He followed its curve.

"Here," the girl said, moving forward from the shadows. "I'm here."

The Eye of God came to him, her sable hair shining in the twilight, her dark eyes filled with his image. She put her slender hands out, pushing away the sword barrier and slipped close to his chest, her legs entangling with his. Taller than Rain, she had only to left her chin slightly to meet his kiss.

But he did not have one for her. Alben staggered back a step, startled. "What—"

"I know what you want. I know what I want. As for her—" and the rack-crowned head turned. "Leave her to her own."

The hairs prickled on the back of his neck. The palm of his left hand itched unbearably and Alben knew something was not quite right. "I'm here to guard her," he said. "You said it was her task alone, but you're wrong. She did what she did to save me . . . me and Redstar. We blundered into the old lizard. We started a fight we couldn't finish. He ran. I would have died if she hadn't taken blackthorn."

The girl's lips pouted. "Forget her. Forget the

dog." And she put her hand out to his brow. "She betrayed you."

"No. I failed her."

"Never. You have the strength."

"But she has ... the soul," Alben answered weakly.

A misty curtain started to fall. He felt the unmistakable stirring of his body for what she offered ... the girl was like the forest beast she mimicked, her body in rut, and wanting only satisfaction. He could smell the herbs in her sable waterfall of hair. He wanted her as well. Despite her name, Rain was a drought of sexual comfort. He moved toward the offered embrace.

Redstar howled. Once, sharp and clear, in warning.

Alben's head shot toward the direction of the noise, a veil falling away from his senses. He stepped back and into guard out of habit, and the Eye of God hissed with displeasure.

He looked into a dragon muzzle, widespread eyes a-gleam with refracted light, scaled and bedazzling skin a deep cobalt blue. The wings lightened to a gentle sky blue, drawn over its back, spines crowning its head and down its back. Far more beautiful than the human illusion it had projected, this vision was enough to hold Alben in his tracks. It coiled, snakelike, to strike.

It shook its mane of spines, the scales rattling against one another, a multitude of wind chimes sounding with its movement. There was none of the stink of corruption about this beast, or the aroma of evil, the venomous stink of deep and dire thoughts. The dragon, save for its size, could have been new struck from the dragon forge, its scales freshly minted, its eyes just mined from the jeweled depths of the underworld.

"You are too wonderful to kill," Alben said. "Run from me!"

The dragon peeled its lips back. Alben tensed, readying himself. When it spit, he was already in motion, dancing away from the corrosive miasma. It burst into blue-licking flames on the dirt and smoldered out where he'd been standing. The dragon lunged forward on its six legs, wings straining to come up, roofed in by the barrow.

Alben's throat had gone dry. He parried the snapping jaw. Metal rang against tusk. The sword blade skittered uselessly off. His arms ringing with the shock of the contact, he gathered himself once again. He could hear Rain shout, faintly.

The dragon skittered forward once more, forcing him back. Its eyes glowed like irridescent rainbow wings. He did not wish to see them dim.

Could it be that dragons were born innocent and became corrupted, tainted, by their exile? Just as he had once been a killer of nothing but trees?

The beast swiped a paw at him, ebony talons gleaming. He moved quickly. Rock sliced through. With the flat of the blade he slapped the paw before it could recoil. The dragon wailed thinly in pain.

"Run," Alben pleaded. "I'll not let you pass."

The dragon spat again. Alben shrugged out of its way, but the cave wall lit up with the fervor of its spittle, and the moss, damp as it was, blazed. He could feel the heat against his face, plucking at his brows and eyes. He put a hand up to shield himself.

It was then the beast pounced, bowling Alben over, the sword wedged awkwardly between them, its hilt keeping the jaws from savaging Alben. He'd let out a gasp of surprise, its noise echoing off the stone.

Redstar answered with a savage bark and growl. From out of the gloom and nowhere, the dog leapt up the dragon's flank. Bounding upward, teeth gleaming, he went mercilessly for the sky blue wings of thinnest skin foil and began to shred.

The dragon slid backward, lashing its tail about, unable to dislodge the dog. Alben crawled to his knees and then levered himself to his feet.

"Star! Down!"

The dog did not heed him. He mauled the wing rack until the leathern membrance hung in tatters, dashing this way and that to avoid the lashing tail as it curled up to smack him, and the gnashing jaws as the dragon vainly tried to snap him off. Redstar made a move too rash and the tail thudded into his haunches, tossing him from the beast's back. He grunted into the dirt.

Alben saw the gleam of hatred and lust light in the dragon's eyes. He turned to run, to get the dragon off the dog, and to chase Rain from the barrow.

He shouted his throat raw as his boots pelted the stony floor.

"Rain! Get out of here! Go, go, go!"

The dragon charged at his heels. Incredibly swift, keening with pain, it snapped at his wake. He could feel its hot breath with every jolting step. Star belled behind them, his dog voice raggedly determined. *A dragondog, nothing fiercer or more loyal or more determined.* He would run the dragon down to its or his death this time.

Alben had no choice but to fight the beast.

Rain looked up, her hands full of the bulging reed bag, as he rounded a wide bend. He scooped up her down light body, hauling her with him. From the thundering commotion behind them, she knew. She had to have known.

"Alben—"

He threw her aside as they burst into the open, pivoted off the maw, braced himself and waited for Redstar to drive the crippled beast into his untender mercies.

It exploded into the sunlight, its damaged wing braces curled about its spined back, jaws a-gape with saliva and hatred. Redstar slid under its belly with a daring that made Alben gasp, for the dragon burst sunward, barreling straight at Rain. Alben cocked the sword and charged himself.

The dog leapt, catching the blow of snapping jaws instead. With a truncated yelp, Redstar went limp, his body crashing to earth at Rain's feet.

He had no time to look. He cut at the exposed flank, and then the wattle under the neck as the dragon swung about with a cry to meet him head on. Alben gathered himself, pivoted about and hamstrung the dragon where plates did not meet together smoothly, to allow for the bending of the leg. The dragon went down clumsily on that side, keening.

Alben drove in, slicing the saliva pouch open so that it could not spit again. The spittle spewed forth, setting the grass on fire, the dragon's head thrashing about in the smoke and flames.

But it still lived.

It would heal, he thought, if he let it go. And he wanted to let it go. It knew nothing of the battle between Alben and the other beast. Perhaps it had only been defending the gateway.

And, bleeding and mauled, it was still wondrously beautiful as it lay heaving in the sunlight.

Alben paused. Over the bellows panting of the beast, he could hear the rip of cloth. Rain knelt by the dog, quickly wrapping him. She cried soundlessly, water glistening on her face. He saw the crimson flower on the dog's breast.

"What are you waiting for?" she shouted, as she got to her feet. "Kill it!"

"I ... don't want to." He paused, sword gripped tightly in both hands. The weight of the blade made the cords stand out on his forearms. His wrists trembled slightly.

The beast twisted its muzzle about, putting one eye on him. It fluttered its ripped wings.

Rain said, "Those will never heal."

And what was a dragon without wings? His gaze met the creature's and with a jolt, he knew the thought was both his and not his. It let out a call, a trumpeting as fresh and pure as the ice across the purple mountains behind them. It set the flesh to creeping and brought his eyes to brimming. Alben sucked his breath in and drove the blade across the back of the outstretched neck.

The dragon twitched once, and then lay still. Its eyes closed, so Alben did not have to watch the dimming of its fantastic lights.

Something shambled in the opening of the barrow. Alben looked, and smelled the ancient stink, and saw a flash of old scale. He drew his sword up, blade dripping with ichor, but the old dragon was gone before he could reach it. Alben stood in the mouth of the cold stone barrow and listened to the echo of its retreat.

It had driven the young one out ahead of it. Testing the waters? Challenging the strength of the magic and the guardians at the gate? Whatever its reasons, the old beast had fled.

Alben swallowed a bitter taste in his mouth.

He gathered up Redstar in his arms. "I think," he said slowly, "we've paid the price."

She hugged the swollen reed bag and only nodded. Her fingers caressed the ear flap of the moaning dog. "He was no coward this time."

"No. Perhaps a bit too brash and brave."

They crossed the meadows slowly, ponderously, the stink of dragon blood heavy on the air, Rain still weak. She nibbled a bit of moss as she walked, and the color came slowly back into her cheeks. When they reached the forest fringe, Bertie stood waiting with their rickety cart behind him.

Alben put the dog onto the straw bedding. Redstar rolled a mild brown eye at him and cleaned the back of his hand before he pulled it away. Rain filled her packs with fresh moss and handed the rest to the wild-haired farmer. "Take this back to the Eye of God. I've what I need."

Bertie narrowed his gaze at Alben, splashed with dragon blood. "Ye've wet your blade."

"We paid the price, but I'll tell you now, I killed the wrong beast. There was nothing evil about that creature."

"No, ye dinna kill the wrong one. The old one's gone, pulled back into the mountains, and he'll stay there for a time. He sent the young one after ye. That's what they do."

"A sacrifice?" said Rain, and her voice rasped higher with every sound.

"Mayhap. Who knows the mind of a drake? The world of man has all but forgotted about them ... and they're biding their time until they come down in earnest. They'll be bringing war with them, take me sincere, dragonwars, and the earth will wash with our blood and theirn. I doubt," and Bertie stretched his neck, scratching at his scrawny, patchy skin, nails scraping across his beard stubble. "I doubt we'll stand against them then," he said in a faraway voice.

"There was no evil about him," the youth said, to no one, his face stricken. "But I had no choice. He attacked."

"A-course he did. That's what the old one sent him for. Make no mistake, boy, you killed the better beast. The young ones have more fire in th' blood, more poison in their venom. The elder knew what he was about, sending the young one after you. It's the way o' the world, itn't it or—" and Bertie looked closely at the two of them. "Or th' two of you wouldn't be here, would ye?"

He opened his mouth to retort differently, but Rain stopped him, her hand across his forearm. He clapped his lips shut.

Bertie straightened up, taking his weight off his hoe. "So will ye stay the night, tell your tale to the others? The inn will be full listenin' to you."

He thought of the clarion call let out by the dragon, the high pure voice of the wind keening across mountain peaks, challenge and innocence. He shook his head. "No. No, I don't think I want to talk about it."

Bertie's eyes widened in disbelief. "We'll

stand a night of drinks for you, take me sincere,"
he said. "For you and your woman."

"I'm not his woman," Rain corrected softly.
She touched him again, drawing him away.
"Let's go." She picked up the shaft of the cart,
leaving the other one for him. Red Star whined
slightly as the cart bed shifted, but he lay quietly, bound as Rain had bandaged him.

Bertie watched as he picked up the other
shaft. The old man nodded then.

"I unnerstand," he said. "Forgive us for
showin' you a truth o' the world too soon. But
remember us. When the dragonwars come, remember we stood the best we could, and no sacrifice was too great."

Alben didn't answer. He thought only that he
had come close to leaving his heart and his soul
in that cold stone barrow—and did not know if
he thought Bertie and the townspeople heroic
for stemming the tide at the dragonsgate . . . or
monsters worse than the one he'd agreed to slay.
He put his sore back into pulling the brunt of
the cart weight, but Rain was at his side, and
she gave him a look from her cool eyes that told
him she would not let him pull alone.

There was some small victory gained, after all.

FLUFF THE TRAGIC DRAGON

by Laura Resnick

"Esther, dear, there's a dragon in the basement," said Mrs. Pearl.

I climbed up the rain-splattered steps outside the apartment building on West 93rd Street as I perused the casting announcements in *Backstage*. "Hmmm?"

"I said there's a dragon in the basement," Mrs. Pearl repeated.

"That's nice." *Backstage* proved to be just as depressing as I had feared. Since I couldn't type and I had already failed miserably at telephone sales, I would probably have to go back to waiting tables again.

"I went down to the basement with a load of laundry," Mrs. Pearl said excitedly, "and when I was putting my quarters into the machine, one of them rolled away. Well, dear, you know that I always say if you watch out for the pennies, the dollars will take care of themselves."

I looked up to see her standing in the doorway.

Her little tote-cart was full of groceries and took up whatever part of the entrance that her not inconsiderable bulk didn't.

"Yes, you *do* always say that, Mrs. Pearl," I said mildly. "Can I get by?"

"So when my quarter rolled away, naturally I went after it."

"Oh, good, Mrs. Pearl. I'm glad you got it back. Now, could I just get through here? My feet are killing me, and—"

"But I *didn't* get it, Ester. That's the point."

"I'm sure you'll find it tomorrow, then."

"No." She positioned herself in the doorway as if she planned to take root there. "I'm afraid I may never get it back."

"Well, that's too bad, but you know what all the tenants say about the greedy basement troll," I said lightly, trying unsuccessfully to get by. Things were always disappearing from our basement—coins, coffee cups, articles of clothing. The washing machine had apparently eaten my favorite T-shirt two months earlier.

"It's not a troll that's living down there," she cried, moving with a pro basketball player's agility to block my way again. "It's a dragon!"

"Mrs. Pearl," I said, trying to maintain an even tone, "I've been pounding the pavement since first thing this morning. I've spent the day waiting in humid, stuffy, un-airconditioned rehearsal halls, auditioning before casting directors with faces so stony they could grace Mount Rushmore, and wondering how I'll pay not only this month's rent, but last month's rent, too. Now I'm drenched from this charming summer shower we've just had, and the one thing I want out of life is to go upstairs to my apartment, take off my shoes, and die in peace on my own couch. And if you will either go in or come out so that I can accomplish that feat, I will *give* you a quarter to replace the one you lost. What could be fairer than that?"

Mrs. Pearl's doughy face looked disapproving beneath her blue hair. "No wonder you're always having financial trouble. You'll never hang onto your money by giving it away."

"I'm not *always* having financial trouble," I snapped. The hell with maintaining an even tone. "Just lately." After a six month regional tour and lots of heady anticipation about our New York opening, the show I was in—a musical based on *Clan of the Cave Bear*—had folded after only four weeks on Broadway.

I, like everyone else in the cast, had anticipated that it would be a big success and that I could count on a pleasant interlude of regular income. Unfortunately, *Clan* had instead proved to be the greatest Broadway debacle since *Shogun*. Considering that the New York theater community gave last year's Tony Award to a show with singing cows, I had thought they would welcome singing Neanderthals with open arms, but such was not the case.

So there I was, still out of work more than three months later and completely broke. Having expected to be steadily employed for a while, I had finally invested in some furniture for my one-bedroom apartment, some clothes for myself, and even a motorcycle for my Significant Other after his had died. He used the new one to pick up another woman. The next time I spend my last fifteen hundred dollars on a man, someone should throw me up against a wall and beat me with a lead pipe.

"I'm sorry, Mrs. Pearl," I apologized wanly, trying to forestall a lecture on how to run my life. "I didn't mean to snap at you. It's just that things haven't been going so well lately. Summer is a lousy time to be in the city anyhow, but it's a *horrendous* time to be looking for acting work. And when I got cast in *Clan*, I really thought that my table-waiting days were behind me at last."

"Yes, and I'm sure that losing Lloyd to a younger woman hasn't helped," said Mrs. Pearl, whose sympathy is something of a double-edged sword.

I sighed. "Thank you for those comforting words, Mrs. Pearl. Now can I go upstairs?"

"But aren't you concerned about the dragon in the basement?"

"The dragon in the basement?" I repeated. "Do you mean a member of one of those gangs, like the Pell Street Dragons or something?"

"No, no, not a gangster. A large, fire-breathing lizard with wings. You know." She made a bizarre attempt to demonstrate by imitation. "A *dragon*."

"In the basement," I said.

"Living down there, on a level below the laundry room, in caverns of primordial darkness and gloom."

"A dragon? Living below the laundry room? What makes you think that?" I asked as if there could be a good reason.

"He spoke to me."

"Indeed?"

"Yes. My quarter rolled under the stairs. When I followed it, I found an old, rusty, dusty door built into the wall. I thought my quarter must have rolled into the crack under the door, so naturally I pried it open."

"Naturally." Prying has always come naturally to Mrs. Pearl.

"There's a series of steep iron stairs behind the door." She lowered her voice, and it took on a dramatic intensity I might have admired in other circumstances. "I started down the steps, and then . . ."

Hey, I'm an actress, I know a cue when I hear one. "What happened then?"

"I heard a voice coming from far below me, from the bowels of the very earth it seemed."

"Uh-huh." Subway tunnel, no doubt.

"I said, 'Who's there?'"

"And lo, there came a voice."

"Yes!"

116

"Really?" A homeless person, perhaps? "What did it say?"

"I'm not sure. It was sort of muffled."

"I see."

"So I descended another step."

"Wait a minute! Are you nuts, Mrs. Pearl? You don't want to mess around in old tunnels in this city. You could have been hurt."

"And as I continued downward, step by step, becoming enveloped in darkness—"

"Good God."

"Suddenly, there was a great heaving sound, and then a burst of fire shot across the ceiling of this cavern—"

"I'm calling the police," I said firmly, trying to push past her. "We could all be murdered while sorting our colors."

She got a good stranglehold on me and kept talking. "And I saw his shape outlined in the darkness, highlighted by the fire pouring from his nostrils."

"What?"

"He had a great lizardlike head, with square nostrils and tiny, pointed ears, a long, serpentine body, an enormous tail, vestigial wings, claws...." She shuddered and released me. After a moment of profound silence, she added wistfully, "He did have a certain strange, horrific beauty about him though...."

Poor Mrs. Pearl. She was clearly the victim of too many episodes of *Beauty and the Beast*. Taking one of her trembling, clammy hands into my own, I asked, "What did you do then?"

"I went to the grocery store."

"You what?" It seemed rather anticlimactic.

"Well, we were out of a few things," she explained matter-of-factly.

"But . . . what about this fire breathing dragon you had just seen?"

She placed a hand on her bosom, which heaved alarmingly. I suddenly wished I knew CPR. "Oh, Esther, what are we going to *do*?"

"I think you'd better tell this whole story to Mr. Pearl. I'm sure he'll know what to do." If he had any sense, he'd have her evaluated immediately.

I stepped past her at last and, finally free to go my own way, I climbed four flights of stairs to my apartment, took off my shoes, and lay down to die. A knock on my door interrupted my nap a couple of hours later. "Who is it?" I called groggily.

It was my neighbor Arnaud. His real name is Arnold, but when he opened his own hair salon, he felt that *Arnaud!* in red neon had a certain quality that *Arnold!* somehow lacked. Arnaud works out every day and is a damn good-looking guy. His lover Scott, who's a model who's always off on location somewhere, is even better looking.

I let Arnaud into my apartment and said, "Are you a weekday widow again?" When Scott is away, Arnaud practically lives with me. He apparently has some kind of phobia about being alone in closed spaces. A therapist is currently linking the problem to a past life experience.

Arnaud nodded with noticeable agitation before adding rapidly, "Did you know there's a dragon in the basement?"

"You've been talking to Mrs. Pearl, haven't you?"

"No, I haven't told a soul!"

I stared at him. "You mean you've seen it, too?"

He stared back. "You mean you knew it was there and didn't tell me? Esther, I might have been killed!"

"Wait a minute, wait a minute. Are you trying to tell me there really *is* a dragon in the basement?" I'd heard there were some pretty weird things wandering around subterranean Manhattan, but *really*. "Did you lose a quarter, too?"

"Quarter?" He pushed me roughly into a chair. "What are you babbling about?"

"Me, babbling? Arnaud, who came up here shrieking about a dragon in the basement?"

"There *is* one, I tell you!" He started pacing. "I took a basket of laundry down, and I noticed some peculiar sounds coming from under the stairs. Naturally, I went to investigate—"

"Naturally?" I snapped. "In a building with no doorman and a front door lock that wouldn't keep out a determined three-year-old? In a dank basement where no one could hear you if you screamed for help? What's wrong with you people who keep investigating strange noises? You *deserve* to be eaten by a dragon!"

"My God, you're vindictive," he said critically. "How long have you known it's there?"

"I *didn't* . . ." I stopped myself. "Tell me what you saw that makes you think there's dragon down there."

I'll spare you the histrionics. He peeked under the stairs and saw the rusty iron door that Mrs. Pearl had carelessly left open after her little tête-à-tête with St. George's old foe. Unfortunately, his description of the dragon living behind that door matched hers perfectly.

"Of course, everyone knows what dragons look like," I said rationally, "so your mind naturally filled in the details it thought you should perceive."

"Come down and have a look," he challenged.

"Oh . . . my feet hurt."

"Ah-hh! You're afraid!"

Me, afraid? What was there to be afraid of?

"We could be murdered by some lunatic with a warped sense of humor. We could be eaten by an alligator—I've heard they're spawning in the sewers. We could be run down by some kind of city-operated subterranean vehicle. We could stumble upon a secret crack laboratory." I was still enumerating all the things I was afraid of when we reached the door to the basement.

Mrs. Pearl and all the other tenants were standing there, peering fearfully down the stairwell.

"Hey, man," said Ricardo, the bongo player who lived on the top floor. "Do you know there's, like, a stinking, fat, hairy, dragon in the basement?"

"I thought he was scaly," I said repressively.

"You've seen him before?" Mr. Rivman demanded. "How long have you known he was in the basement, young lady?"

"*Santa Maria*," cried Mrs. Castrucci, crossing herself fervently. "The beast, he could have eaten us at any time. And you say nothing about it?"

"I *didn't* know. . . . Why am I trying to deny there's a dragon in the basement?" I said in defeat. "This is crazy."

"Hey, man," said Ricardo. "This is New York. *Anything* could be down there."

"So let's call the police," said Fumiko, the sociology student who lived in the studio apartment at street level. She shivered. "It gives me the creeps to think of that thing being down there."

"We should call exterminators," said Mrs. Pearl.

"We should call the stinking, fat, hairy landlord," said Ricardo.

"If we ask him to deal with it, we'll be waiting till the Second Coming," Arnaud said acidly.

"I say we call the police!" said Mr. Rivman.

"We must call a priest!" cried Mrs. Castrucci.

"Hey, man, this ain't no exorcism."

"I say we call the papers," said Arnaud, with

an expression that suggested he had thought of a way to turn this into a human interest story for *Arnaud!*

"I say we take a little dose of reality," I snapped. "We can't call the cops, the rodent man, or the *Times* and say we have a *dragon* in the basement, for God's sake."

"No, but the *Inquirer* would go for it," said Arnaud.

"Maybe even the stinking *Post*," added Ricardo.

"All right, Miss Reality," said Mrs. Pearl a trifle snidely. "You go down and see what's living in the basement, and then you tell us what to do about it, you're so smart."

Everyone fixed their gazes unwaveringly upon me. Stalling for time, I suggested, "Why don't we wait and bring this up at the next tenants' meeting?"

"Darling, nobody *ever* goes to tenants' meetings. That's so Midwestern of you," Arnaud chided.

"Look, Arnaud, the landlord may be slow, but this really is his responsibility," I said, sounding mature and wise.

"That's so naive of you," he replied dismissively.

"Besides," said Mrs. Castrucci, fingering her rosary with one hand as she gestured against the Evil Eye with the other, "whadda make you think he gonna believe more than you believe, without you see with you own eyes?" Her English, usually rather good, deteriorates sadly under emotional stress.

"Fine," I said, losing patience with the whole scene. "Fine! I'll go and look at your dragon, and then I will make a rational suggestion. After that, you can do as you please. I'm supposed to be lying on my couch right now, dying in peace and comfort."

Akemi bowed, and Ricardo made some sort of voodoo gesture. He added, in the kindest tone I'd ever heard him use, "Hey, man, they gonna remember you in this building for years to come. You gonna be like a saint on West 93rd Street."

"Okay, okay," I said, descending the stairs.

"Those who are about to die salute you!" Arnaud cried.

"See if you can find my quarter while you're down there!" Mrs. Pearl called.

"I'm going to move when my lease comes up," I muttered.

I reached the bottom of the stairs and turned the corner to the laundry room. It was utter chaos down there. The hastily dropped laundry baskets of half a dozen tenants cluttered up the place. It was while I was wondering who was stupid enough to wash a silk blazer in an industrial machine that I heard the noises.

I froze when I heard the first heavy, echoing sigh. When it was followed by a deep, primordial growl and the scent of smoke, I did everything a good Gothic heroine does—I gasped, I pressed a trembling hand to my heaving breast, the hair on the back of my neck stood up, and a deathly chill raced down my spine. Believe me, it's not a routine a girl wants to go through every day.

"Who's there?" I demanded, my voice squeaking in a manner that would have appalled my singing coach but probably pleased my method acting teacher.

A low, forlorn, hollow moan answered me. It came, of course, from the ancient, heretofore unnoticed doorway beneath the stairs. I approached it with stiff legs and dragging feet, terrified, yet too fascinated to turn away, for surely the moan was followed by a faint glow and another wisp of smoke.

I reached the doorway at last and peered into the stygian darkness beyond. As my eyes grew accustomed to the dark, I thought I perceived an enormous, bulky shape about thirty feet away.

"Who's there?" I repeated, leaning forward as I tried to make out more of that elusive shape.

"Fluff!" came the answer a moment before all hell broke loose. Flames shot forward, smoke clouded my vision, and the bulky figure moved and took on the form of my childhood nightmares, a horrible, ferocious, firebreathing, winged lizard at least fifteen feet high. Never having been the most coordinated Neanderthal in *Clan*, I tripped clumsily in my terror and pitched headlong into the subterranean cavern.

I nearly lost consciousness for a moment, and I was so winded that even with the adrenaline pumping through me, I lay on the cold, damp floor for a full minute, too stunned to move. I was sure I was going to die.

"Say, are you okay?"

That did it. I hopped to my feet. "Who said that?"

"Me. Fluff." When it spoke, its nostrils glowed.

"You can *talk*?"

"Of course. I'm a dragon."

It spoke with a faint Chinese accent and sounded vaguely hurt. "Yes, I see that." I swallowed. "But I . . . I didn't think you'd *talk*."

"All dragons can talk." It sighed suddenly, and a soft blue fire poured from its nostrils. "If they have someone to talk to, that is."

"This is incredible." I sat back down rather suddenly and gracelessly.

"Careful. The floor is very damp. I've had rheumatism for thirty years."

"Is that how long you've been down here?" I asked in amazement.

"More or less. Sometimes I go to Chinatown to hang out and have a few meals. They have the best produce, and it reminds me a little of the old days. But . . . it's just not like it used to be." He sighed again, looking directly at me this time.

"Hey, watch it!" I ducked before I could be singed.

He raised a dreadful claw. "Sorry, I forgot. It's been so long."

"Since you barbecued anyone?" I asked carefully.

"No!" He sounded hurt again. "Since I had someone to chat with."

"Chat?" I clenched my jaw to stop my teeth rattling.

"I never see anyone," he said despondently. "I just live down here by myself, in the dark, with no one to talk to. I was friendly with the land-lord when I first got here. He used to read me the paper, play chess with me, look at my trea-sures, ask me to grant him wishes." Fluff's fear-some features looked sort of nostalgic. "But then he died, and no one else ever came to visit me again."

"So you've been alone down here all that time?" I started to feel a little sorry for him. When he nodded, I asked, "What do you do with your time?"

He shrugged, making his wings quiver. "Some-times I crawl through tunnels and see if any-thing interesting is happening." He sighed again. "But there's seldom anything new to see, and even if there is, who would I tell about it? So, these days, I mostly just keep collecting treasure, since it's sort of a biological imperative, and I sit around here and think about the old days."

Now for the sixty-four thousand dollar question. "What do you eat?"

"Bok choy, onions, apples, snowpeas—"

"Not people?" I asked hopefully.

"No, of course not!" His glowing, yellow eyes widened in shock. "Oh, that Saint George!" he growled suddenly. "He's got a lot to answer for.

He decides to pick on some poor innocent dragon who's minding his own business. And then, just to make himself look like a hero, he goes around telling everyone that we're evil, voracious beasts who devour children and burn down whole villages. And centuries later, we're still suffering because of that bully! It's so *unfair*."

I actually thought he might start to cry. "Hey, I'm sorry. I didn't mean to hurt your feelings."

He hid his eyes with a claw. "You just don't know what it's like to be such an outcast. Sometimes I wish I'd never left China. Everyone there knew a dragon's real worth."

"That's where you're from? China?"

He looked up again. "Well, of course. All dragons come from China. Everyone knows that."

"I'm sorry I'm so ignorant." I frowned. "What was that dragon doing in England, then?"

"He was a tourist. Naturally, when we found out what had happened, no dragon ever went *there* again."

"No, I suppose not. Tell me, why did you leave China? It sounds like you miss it."

He scratched one pointy little ear and shifted his great bulk into a more comfortable position. "It just wasn't the same anymore after 1949. The Cultural Revolution left no room for dragons, not real ones anyhow. So, I decided to come to America. But San Francisco had so many dragons that all the good tunnels were taken. Anyhow, earthquakes make me hysterical. So I just got right back in the water and swam all the way to New York. That Panama Canal of yours is very handy, by the way."

"Aren't there any other dragons in New York for you to talk to?" Other dragons? Oh, Esther, Esther, I thought, it's time to go back to Iowa.

"There's one in Queens and another in Brooklyn. To tell the truth, though, dragons are very people-oriented. We don't like to see *each other* more than once every century or so."

"So, you've just been hanging out here by yourself until this afternoon when Mrs. Pearl finally found you," I concluded.

"Is she the fat lady with blue hair? I was so upset. The first person I've had a chance to talk to in over twenty years, and she screams and runs away. Then half a dozen others did the same."

"They didn't mean anything by it," I said hastily, hearing the hurt creep back into his voice. "It's just that nobody expected to find a dragon in the basement, not even in this neighborhood."

"I'm glad *you* decided to talk to me," he said warmly.

"Well . . . it's my pleasure."

"You'll come back again and talk to me now and then?"

"Sure. Of course I will." What else would I say? The poor thing was so lonesome, so grateful for a little companionship. And Fluff was really pretty pleasant company, to be honest. More so than Lloyd had ever been. "Of course, I have to admit I'm not much of a chess player—"

"Oh, that's okay. I have lots of other games," he assured me, trundling over to the other end of his cavern. "Checkers, Monopoly, Trivial Pursuit, Pictionary, Life. . . ." His voice trailed off and he obligingly blew out a stream of fire so I could see his hoard—an enormous pile of games, old sports equipment, clothing, vases, pottery, books, magazines, handicrafts, and more kinds of jumbled junk than the Eleventh Avenue Thrift Shop had, even right after Christmas.

"My God, what is all this?" I breathed, astonished that this had been down here without our knowledge.

"My treasure," he said proudly. "Dragons are the guardians of splendor."

Although some of the stuff was clearly very old, I noticed a few items he must have collected just recently. "Hey, this is mine!" I grabbed the T-shirt that I thought the washing machine had eaten and waved it in his scaly face. "How did you get this?"

"I can't tell you that. Trade secret." He sounded a little smug.

"And all this other stuff," I murmured. "You really have sticky claws."

"I told you, I collect things. That's my job. Dragons are hoarders. But the treasure's been getting very big, since I've been living all by myself for so long with no one to share it with." He gave me a toothy grin, and I fell back a step despite myself. "But now it's all yours."

"Mine? Why?"

"Because I choose to give it to you. We collect treasures, and then we give them away to mortals who do us a favor or make us happy. Or sometimes even to mortals who need something and just ask politely." He blew out some smoke in a derisive snort. "But no one seems to understand the custom anymore."

Not wanting to offend him, I said carefully, "Thanks, Fluff, but it's such a lot of stuff, and my apartment is so small."

"Oh, I'll keep guarding it for you," he offered eagerly. "That's often part of the bargain."

"Then I'll just keep this T-shirt, and you can guard the rest. Oh, and do you happen to have a quarter, by any chance?" It would be a lot easier to explain things to Mrs. Pearl if she got her quarter back.

"Of course! I have hundreds of thousands of them!" He scooted a little further into the darkness and dragged an enormous, ancient wooden chest toward me. "I found this chest floating in the East River one night, about twenty-five years ago. Isn't it *amazing* what people will throw out?"

"Amazing." When he opened it though, I lost my casual manner and dropped my expression of polite interest. The contents of the chest gleamed beneath Fluff's fiery breath. Nickels, quarters, dimes, pennies, gold rings, sparkling earrings, and strands of pearls filled it to the brim. "I don't believe it," I whispered.

"I have lots more stowed away back there," he said, his scaly chest expanding with pride.

"This is fantastic." I looked at him questioningly. "People drop dollar bills, too."

He snorted again, causing me to jump back a little. "Dollars aren't pretty at all," he said contemptuously.

Although some of the jewelry was certainly fake, a few pieces looked pretty real to me. I'd have to have them evaluated. "Uh, this is all mine, too, Fluff?" I asked hesitantly.

"Of course," he said.

Believe it or not, I hugged him. "I'll pay my rent, I'll put a little in the bank for emergencies, I'll get my mother a birthday present. . . ." I looked around. "You know, Fluff, this isn't a bad place you've got down here, but it really needs a few things. Things that don't fall through cracks in the sidewalk or end up floating in the East River."

"Like what?" he asked excitedly.

"A color television, for one thing. Ricardo knows all about hooking up to cable without paying for it. And we'll get you nice blankets and some fresh flowers, and we'll have some good produce delivered so you can stop going all the way downtown for it. And you definitely need a few lights so you don't have to breathe fire every time you want someone to see something." I patted him on the wing. "Everything's going to be fine from now on."

"But the others," he said hesitantly, "do you think they'll like me?"

"Of course they will," I assured him. "But let's keep this part of the treasure out of sight, agreed? And there's no need to mention it to them, is there?"

"Not if you don't want to, um . . .?"

"Esther," I supplied.

We played a few rounds of checkers, and then he beat me at Monopoly. Dragons are hoarders, after all, and I spent my paper money as recklessly as I spend the real stuff. It was very late by the time I heard Arnaud's voice on the stairs. "Esther? Esther, are you there?"

"Oh, Christ!" I jumped to my feet. "They've been waiting for me all this time. They probably think I'm dead or something." I called through the open door, "I'll be there in a minute, Arnaud."

I heard him shout, "She's alive!" A faint cheer seemed to echo down from the first floor.

"I've got to go, Fluff. I'll talk to Ricardo about setting up a television right away," I promised.

"And you'll come back soon?" he asked, making a brave little effort not to sound pathetic.

"I'll be back before you've noticed I'm gone."

"Esther." His voice stopped me when I had nearly reached the top of the stairs.

"Yes?"

"Before you go, isn't there some wish I could grant you?"

"That's right, I'd forgotten you said you could grant wishes."

"Well?"

I shrugged. "I've got an audition tomorrow. Think you can get me the part?" The silence went on for so long, I prodded, "Fluff? Is something wrong?"

"It's just ... well, couldn't you ask me for something hard?"

Visions of playing Scarlet in the sequel danced in my head, but my mother had taught me not to be too greedy. Not right away, anyhow. "Oh, let's start out small. We have plenty of time to get really ambitious."

"If you say so. Good night, Esther."

"Good night, Fluff."

"Esther?" he called again, just before I was out of earshot.

I returned to the doorway under the stairs. "Yes?"

"It's so nice having someone to talk to again."

I felt my throat get tight. Poor Fluff, all that solitude must have been just awful for such a sociable creature. "It's really nice knowing a dragon like you, Fluff," I said at last.

"Thank you, Esther." He sounded pleased to the point of embarrassment.

I turned away and climbed the stairs back to the first floor.

"Well?" said Arnaud, as he and the others en-
circled me.

"There's a dragon in the basement," I said.
"Everybody be nice to him, he's been very
lonely. Ricardo, I'll get a T.V. for him tomorrow.
Can you please hook him up to cable for me?"

"Do you have my quarter?" Mrs. Pearl
demanded.

"Are you insane?" Arnaud demanded.

"I'm definitely renewing my lease," I said.
"Goodnight, everybody. I've got a big day ahead
of me tomorrow."

As I climbed the stairs to the second floor, Ricardo said, "Hey, man. New York. You gotta love
it."

THE HIDDEN DRAGON

by Barbara Delaplace

Sarah remembered exactly when she first saw the dragon. It was just a glimpse out of the corner of her eye, and vanished as soon as she turned her head to look directly at it, but she was sure of what she saw all the same: a flash of rust-colored scales on a snaky, spike-fringed tail that disappeared amongst the shrubbery.

It was a mistake turning her head. James was in the middle of one of his lectures and immediately noticed her innattention. "I expect you to listen to me when I'm talking to you, Sarah. It's not time for another lesson in courteous behavior, is it?"

She instantly focused on him again, the all-too-familiar chill running down her back. "I'm sorry, James. I shouldn't have let myself be distracted. It's just something I saw out in the yard. It was so odd—" She bit her lip and stopped. Better not to have said anything at all. James was a practical man, as he often said. He

135

had no time for fantasy or metaphysical mumbo jumbo.

"What do you think you saw?" His tone was reasonable, controlled, and her anxiety began to grow.

"Nothing, James, really."

"You must have seen *something*, Sarah. You turned away from me. It must have been something very unusual for you to suddenly ignore me like that." His voice was becoming harder.

"I thought I saw a deer." She didn't dare mention what she *really* thought she'd seen. "It must have been my imagination. I'm sorry, I won't let it happen again."

"A deer is hardly odd out here, Sarah. Our home is isolated and we see them fairly frequently. I think you're lying to me." His eyes were cold as he looked at her. "I won't stand for that."

The sessions in the bedroom were always worse if he accused her of lying. Better to tell the truth.

"It was just out of the corner of my eye. For a moment . . ." she paused.

"Yes?" His patience was an ominous presence.

"For a moment it looked like . . . like the tail of a dragon. But it couldn't have been." It *couldn't* have been. "It had to have been a deer, and I just imagined the rest. I'm sorry. I know better."

She'd appeased him, slightly. His face wasn't as terrifyingly frozen. "You have an overactive imagination, Sarah. We both know that. It's something we have to work on together. Might-be's and what-if's are simply a waste of time. I think we'd better discuss it in the bedroom." He turned away.

"Yes, James." He was right; he always was. It must have been her overactive imagination. She steeled herself and followed him.

Her back was too painful to let her sleep. So she waited until the sound of James' breathing became slow and even—he always slept deeply after an evening session spent correcting her—then slipped quietly from the bedroom.

Once she reached the living room Sarah relaxed, alone and safe. For now, at least. The armchair was out of the question because of her back, so she settled cross-legged on the floor in front of the huge picture window overlooking the flower beds and the stream. The scene was so peaceful in the moonlight, as always. She sighed with pleasure. When she was alone and it was quiet and she could sit undisturbed—that was the best time of all.

She glanced across the lawn to the vegetable garden. She loved watching the deer that came to the brook to drink, but they were a constant threat to her salad greens and she kept a watchful eye on—

The dragon was there. Crouched quietly on the smooth lawn, neck gathered into a compact sinous curve, tail looping away in a graceful arc past the garden.

"No," she whispered. There weren't any such things as dragons. Maybe she was dreaming? But she could feel the shaggy texture of the rug under her hands, smell the cool freshness of the night air whispering in through the half-open window, hear the breeze rustling the leaves just outside. Her dreams never had this sharp reality of the senses.

The dragon uncoiled its neck and stretched out its head, seeming to test the air for some exotic scent. Moonlight shimmered off its scales, stealing away their daytime hues. Sarah watched the creature's supple movements, her startled fear briefly forgotten as the massive head quested to and fro, then swung back toward the garden. It nosed gently among the herbs bordering the garden's edges. She had an absurd impulse to shout at it to leave her favorite lavender alone, when it came out of its crouch and moved toward the house.

Sarah scrambled to her feet as her fear rushed back over her. She *had* to be imagining this! She backed away from the window, ready to run— where? part of her mind laughed hysterically. What protection was a window or a wall against a thing the size of a dragon? *But it wasn't real*, another part of her mind shouted. She backed into the coffee table and lost her balance, reached out a steadying hand—

—and when she looked up the dragon had disappeared. The lawn was empty. Somehow that was even more discomfitting. She knew she should go to the window—that's what James would do. No, he'd go outside, flashlight in hand, firmly resolved to show her the reality of the situation. There would be no dragon if James was here.

But she wasn't James, and it was very late. She was tired and confused; her back throbbed dully. There were painkillers and sleeping pills in the bathroom. She decided to make use of them to get some sleep—then she wouldn't have any more visions of mythical beasts in her yard.

The next morning James remarked solicitously on her wan appearance. "You should look after yourself better, Sarah—you're not getting enough rest."

"I feel fine, James."

"All right, then. I'll see you tonight." He gave her an abstracted kiss, his mind already on the demands of his job in the city, and was out the door.

She heard the car drive off as she finished her coffee and sighed. She'd slept, but the dragon seemed to lurk in one corner of her mind, and her slumber was restless. Somehow she got the impression it was a sentinal, watching for something. . . . Enough of this! she thought briskly. It was only a dream. Or hallucination. Or something. What she needed was a friend to talk to.

James didn't seem to appreciate how lonely she was out here. The place had been a good buy and was a good investment. But there were no neighbors, and she had no car to enable her to visit the city. ("After all, we really only need one car and I have to use it to get to work. Besides, you have lots to do, keeping the house and the garden ship-shape. You don't have time to waste gossiping with idle women.") And somehow since their marriage, she'd lost track of her old friends, until now all she had, really, was her husband.

Oh, but this was self-indulgent nonsense, as James always said. He was right—she did have lots to do. And it wasn't going to get done if she just sat here drinking coffee. She picked up the dishes, and headed for the sink. Time to get started on the "lots to do."

She'd fully intended to start in on the dishes and the other housework, but when she glanced out the window and saw the dewy freshness of the morning, she couldn't resist the temptation. She could do the housework later—now was the time to enjoy the garden.

Sarah loved growing things. Fortunately, James felt a well-kept garden added to the value of their home, so she could indulge in her love with a clear conscience. The warmth of the sun, the droning of the bees, the green and the fragrant scents, all combined to soothe her spirit and leave her in a tranquil frame of mind. She knelt to inspect some lambs' ears. They were coming along nicely, and she stroked the soft furry leaves with pleasure.

She stood up and was about to go to the vegetable garden when she noticed a depression in the smooth expanse of grassy lawn. And there was another, some feet away from it. Muttering "moles" to herself, Sarah went over to inspect them. Each had several gouges in front of it, and there were a few dead leaves scattered about, their rusty-red color standing out sharply against the green background. She bent over to sweep them into her hand and realized she'd never seen any quite like these: long narrow ovals which gleamed dully, like leather. They were leathery in texture, too. Now what sort of plant would have leaves like that? A cactus, maybe? But cactus didn't grow around here; there was too much rain. And conifers simply didn't have needles like this. . . .

Then Sarah stopped deceiving herself and knew the depressions were footprints. And the leaves were scales.

So the dragon was real. Here's evidence I can hold in my hand. She felt a strange sense of relief. *I'm not out of my mind, thank God!* she thought. *I really did see it.* But of course that led to the next questions: *Where did it come from? And why is it here?*

Though she pondered all morning as she watered and weeded and pruned, she couldn't seem to make sense of it. One thing she *did* know— there was no question of telling James about this, even though she had solid, tangible evidence of the dragon's reality. She *couldn't*; she didn't know why. But something within her rose so strongly in protest that she didn't dare even question the assumption.

By noon Sarah was finished in the garden. Her muscles ached; she was more than ready for a break. And the gurgling of the stream was a seductive reminder of how good the water would feel. Taking her cap off and wiping her perspiring face, she walked down the slope of the lawn to the brook. At the edge, she sat down and removed her sneakers.

"Ahhhhhh," she sighed as she dabbled her bare feet into the cool water. "Just what the doctor ordered." She leaned back but decided she'd be more comfortable on her stomach; the bruises on her back were still too sensitive. She rolled over and rested her chin on her forearms. It was so relaxing just listening to the sounds of the stream, not having to worry about anything. *Not even James' demands*, said a tiny voice within.

The fugitive thought made her start guiltily. Why, James didn't demand much. And it wasn't as if she had anyone else to worry about, what with no children. Compared to the workload so many women carried these days, she was fortunate indeed that all she had to worry about was James.

She realized she was hearing more than just the sounds of the stream—there was also a sound of crunching or snapping, as if something was being broken in half. And it seemed to be coming from James' workshop.

The workshop was some yards away from the house and shaded by several towering evergreens; an insulated line was strung from the house to provide electricity. Squirrels lived in the evergreens and had made both the workshop roof and the power line part of their personal elevated highway. Probably one of them was simply working its way through a lunchtime pinecone, but Sarah thought she'd better check just in case it had decided to gnaw through the power line instead—a couple of the trees' inhabitants had developed a regrettable taste for electrician's tape. She got to her feet and picked up her abandoned sneakers, then walked back up the slope.

She was halfway up the hill when she realized the sound wasn't coming from the roof of the workshop but rather midway between the two buildings. And it was too loud to be made by a snacking squirrel. Squirrels didn't hiss to themselves either. Tension tightened her stomach as she reached the top. She had an uneasy feeling she knew what might be making the sounds.

Her premonition was right. The dragon had returned.

Its head lifted and turned sharply toward her as she appeared, and Sarah stepped back nervously. But it made no move toward her and simply regarded her calmly. As in her dreams, it gave a sense of purpose, of watching for something.

She noticed the creature seemed to have brightened in color since that first glimpse yesterday. Its body glowed a rich mahogany red, while the crest of spikes that ran the length of its neck and back were copper-colored in the sunlight. So were the powerful claws on each foot.

Sarah gasped in dismay when she realized what was between those front feet: one of James' fly fishing rods, now a splintered ruin. Obviously that was the source of the snapping noises that had first attracted her attention. But how had the dragon gotten hold of it? Her glance darted to the workshop, where James kept his fishing tackle. Several rods leaned against the wall, while others were scattered about in the grass. Now she remembered; he'd been working on them yesterday evening. Keeping a watchful eye on the dragon, she went over and restored them to order.

But she wouldn't be able to explain the broken rod to James. What could she do? Fear welled up inside her as she thought of what *he* might do. The only thing she could think of was to hide the remains of the rod in the garbage, and pretend—convincingly, she desperately hoped— that she had no idea what happened to it when he noticed it was gone. She knew he'd notice; by malicious chance the dragon had destroyed the one rod he'd be sure to miss, his favorite black graphite.

This was assuming the dragon would move away from what was left of the fishing rod, of course. Something that large moved when *it* wanted to, she thought wryly. But to her amazement, the great beast backed carefully away from the splintered bits, then turned and moved away into the trees.

Sarah didn't wait to question her good luck. She swiftly gathered up the broken pieces and took them into the house. There, she wrapped them up in old newspapers before disposing of them in the trash can.

She was on tenterhooks when James came home, but this time chance was with her. He'd brought home work from the office, and immediately after dinner he became immersed in it, only emerging when it was time for bed. Sarah breathed a grateful prayer for escaping—thus far—and went to bed herself. But she didn't sleep well.

For several days James continued to be occupied by work. But one evening he came home early. She was in the kitchen, busy with a new pastry recipe, when he swept in, caught her up in a hug, and announced, "All finished up! And I'm taking a few well-earned days off."

She hugged him back. "That's wonderful, James. You've been working so hard."

"That's what Peter said when he told me to

take the time. And I know just what I'm going to do—a little fishing."

Somehow she kept the smile fixed on her face, even though her stomach tightened. "Just what you need, some time to outwit a few trout."

He didn't seem to notice her tension. "I'm going to change and go out to the workshop to get my gear ready. Pine Lake, here I come!" He released her and went into the bedroom to change out of his suit.

She was glad her voice sounded so natural. "I'll call you when dinner's ready."

"Fine!" A minute later, he came through the kitchen and headed out the back door toward the workshop.

Anxiety gnawed at her while she finished the pastry and prepared the salad and vegetables for the meal. But there was no sound of the workshop door slamming, no outburst of cursing. She started the meat cooking, then went out onto the front porch. Perhaps looking out over the stream would calm her down.

It didn't. The dragon was coiled up on the front lawn. Her fear increased sharply. James mustn't see it! *Why not?* an inner voice asked. *Just* what *would he do about it? What* could *he do about it?* But it didn't help her unreasoning certainty that she couldn't let him see the dragon. It *had* to go away. *So what are you going to do? Shoo it away with the broom? Get the Dragonsbane from the medicine cabinet?*

Without stopping to think how bizarre—or

146

dangerous—her behavior appeared, she stepped off the porch and walked toward the beast. It watched her approach with unblinking eyes. Her steps slowed as she got nearer, until she stopped a few yards away.

She hadn't really realized how big the dragon was, until now. With the body curled up, it was difficult to tell its length, but its head alone was as big as her torso. And she noted with surprise that it had blue eyes. *I never heard of a dragon with blue eyes*, she thought. Of course, now that she thought of it, none of the stories she'd read about dragons mentioned their eye color at all. And there was something else about its eyes. Something about them was strangely familiar. . . .

With a start, she remembered why she was out here: to somehow get the dragon to go away. As if it heard her unspoken thought, it uncoiled its body, and she backed hastily away. It paused for a moment to yawn, and Sarah felt her blood go cold at the glimpse of the daggerlike teeth lining upper and lower jaw. Then the vast mouth closed again. The creature regarded her steadily for another moment, then glided away into the trees. She watched it go with enormous relief, then returned to the kitchen and dinner.

James came into the house just as she was about to call him, his face puzzled. "Sarah, have you seen my graphite rod?" he asked.

Her anxiety returned in a sudden rush, but she kept her voice steady. "Why, no. I haven't been inside the workshop for a long time, you know."

"Yes, yes, I know that. You haven't run into it anywhere else, by any chance?"

Her heart in her mouth, she replied, "No, I haven't."

"Neither have I. It must have been one of the ones I loaned to Peter. It figures, now that I want to use it. I'll have to ask him about it Monday. You can serve now." And with that, he sat down at the table. To her relief, there was no further mention of the missing fishing rod.

Sarah didn't sleep well again that night. Between worrying about whether James would discover she was lying and wondering about the dragon's continued presence, she tossed and turned through the dark hours.

In the morning James noted her pale, tired face. "You've been looking run-down the last few days, Sarah."

"I haven't been getting much sleep lately, that's all."

"I think you should take it easy today while I'm gone. It'll do you good."

"Well, perhaps after I get the housework done."

"That'll be fine." And giving her a peck on the cheek, he hurried out the door to finish loading the car for his fishing trip.

After he left, she'd intended to start in on the housework, but the singing of the birds in the morning air lured her outside and down to the brook. The grassy bank, warmed and fragrant, invited her to lie back and bask in the sunlight. And she was so tired. She'd just close her eyes for a moment. . . .

"Sarah!" James' angry voice snapped her awake. He was standing above her, furious. She blinked, glancing about hastily, and realized from the angle of the sun how late it was. Why, she had been so weary she must have slept all day! "Sarah! You're not listening to me!" She realized James was still talking to her and scrambled to her feet. "I come home and what do I find? The breakfast dishes still undone! Dinner not started!"

It must have been because she wasn't fully awake that she was so reckless. "But James, it's not as if the dishes *had* to be done. I'll do them tonight. And I'll start dinner right away and we can eat in half an hour."

"I don't expect to have to wait for my dinner because my wife has been wasting the day sleeping!"

"But you said I should take it easy today, that I wasn't getting enough rest. . . ." Her voice trailed away as she saw his face.

"Are you contradicting me, Sarah?"

She lowered her eyes and replied in a low voice, "No, James."

"It certainly sounded to me like you were. No

wife of mine contradicts me. I'm going to have to correct you for this."

Fear, her familiar friend, returned. "I'm sorry, James."

"That's too bad, Sarah. Apologies aren't enough. You seem to delight in thwarting me, and I'm going to punish you for it. Come along." He turned and started up the sloping lawn to the house.

And once again, out of the corner of her eye, she saw the dragon. It seemed to shine red-gold in the rays of the late afternoon sun. She hastily focused her attention on James' back. Right now she had more important things to worry about. Dutifully she followed him.

Once they were inside the house, she turned toward the bedroom, but his voice stopped her. "Where do you think you're going, Sarah?"

Timidly, she answered "I thought you wanted to. . . ."

"I want you to fix my dinner first. We'll deal with your laziness and insubordination later."

Dread ran through her. But what could she do? "Yes, James, of course. I'll start it right away."

And as she drearily started her preparations, she could hear James in the bedroom making his preparations for after the meal: the sound of a limber rod whipping through the air and smashing down on the pillow. The sound sickened her.

The next morning she hurt so much she didn't want to move; her back, buttocks and thighs throbbed with pain. But James, as usual, behaved as if nothing at all had happened the night before. "Good morning, Sarah. It's a beautiful day. Why don't you get up and we'll have breakfast together out on the lawn?"

Her voice was muffled. "I'm afraid I don't feel very well, James. Thank you all the same, but I think I'll stay in bed for a while."

"Can I bring you something to eat? Or some juice or coffee?"

"No, thank you. I'll just rest for a while."

"Whatever you wish." He finished dressing and left the room. Once alone, she managed to roll out of bed and moved unsteadily into the bathroom. She opened the cabinet and took out a bottle of pain-killing tablets. It was safe to take them now—James didn't like to see the damage he caused during the sessions in the bedroom. Then she walked stiffly back into the bedroom and lay down again in her customary postion, on her stomach, waiting for the pills to ease the pain and make her drowsy. She was dimly aware of James coming in to brush his teeth, telling her he'd be out in his workshop. Then she drifted away into the arms of sleep. And seemed to feel the presence of the dragon at the edge of her mind, watching, waiting.

By the following day, she didn't hurt so much and was able to move around fairly easily. James was still asleep when she stepped into the bathroom and shut the door, so the sound of the water filling the bathtub wouldn't wake him. She stripped off her robe and turned so she could inspect the back of her body in the mirror. Well, at least it no longer looked quite so raw. With resignation, she poured baking soda into the lukewarm water, turning it into a soothing bath. She glanced at the mirror again, and the sight of the wounds striping her body suddenly enraged her. *What* right *had he to do this to her?* But just as quickly she pushed the mutinous thought down. James was her husband; she'd married him for better or worse, till death parted them. She took those vows very seriously.

She turned to face the mirror. *Count your blessings*, she told herself wryly. *At least he doesn't hit you in the face. No black eyes for Sarah.* Her eyes were one of her best features. She played up their blueness with ... her thoughts stopped abruptly as she stared at her reflected face. The dragon had eyes exactly the shade of her eyes— *that's* why they looked familiar! That would give anyone a shock—seeing a part of themself transformed into a monster like that.

Seeing a part of themself transformed. Suddenly she remembered how the dragon had twice done what she wished it to. How it had nosed at the lavender, her favorite of all the plants in the garden. How it had known which fishing rod was James' particular pet rod. How it appeared whenever she was particularly upset and frightened, when James ... no! *No!* Coincidence. It *had* to be. *It* had *to be!* Such a monster couldn't

152

have *anything* to do with her! She was a gentle woman, a dutiful and loving wife. James once told her it was her gentleness that had attracted him most of all. Something that powerful and dangerous couldn't be *any* part of her! *It wasn't her!* There was a startling clash of breaking glass. She realized she'd smashed her clenched fist against the mirror, sobbing aloud.

"Sarah! Are you all right?" James pulled the bathroom door open, shock in his face as he surveyed her tear-stained face, the broken mirror, her bleeding hand.

"No! Get away from me!" she sobbed, throwing on her robe and brushing past him.

"Sarah! Come back here! Sarah!" He was coming after her, and she couldn't bear to face him, not right now.

"Leave me alone!" She ran into the kitchen, then the living room, her heart racing.

"Sarah, come here! Now!" He was getting closer.

"Go away!" she cried.

"Are you defying me, missy?" His voice was loud and angry, and as he entered the living room, she saw he was infuriated with her.

She ran out onto the porch, down the steps, to the lawn. If she could only get away— She stumbled over the edge of a flower bed and fell to the ground. She could hear his footsteps, his harsh breathing, and rolled over to face him, ignoring the fierce ache in her back and buttocks. His face was flushed and he reached down to grab her arm, jerking her up to her feet—

—there was a roar behind them. James turned, disbelief and fear on his face when he saw the dragon, glowing fiery red, rearing above him. It roared again, mouth gaping wide, those vicious teeth gleaming in the morning light. The great head snaked down and the jaws closed around his torso. He screamed in terror and agony as the monster effortlessly lifted him high in the air. Sarah watched in horror as he struggled feebly in the dragon's grip, screaming again and again until the jaws crunched closed, cutting the awful sounds off. Then with terrible ease, the neck corkscrewed sideways as the dragon flung the body away.

Sarah sank to the ground, shaking. It seemed deathly quiet now. The dragon curled up, watching her quietly. It no longer glowed red but was its original rusty color.

She sat there for a long time, until the dragon had gone and the shaking stopped.

She'd have to call the police. She'd tell them she'd heard the sounds of a bear, a grizzly, that it attacked her husband, that she'd heard the screams. She—they—didn't own a gun, so the police wouldn't expect her to be able to rush to James' defense. "No, we didn't hunt, officer," she could hear herself saying. "My husband enjoyed fishing, but—" she could hear the break in her voice that would come there.

They'd believe her. Really, there was no other

possible explanation, was there? And they'd be nice to her. A new widow who had just lost her husband thanks to the attack of a wild beast? They'd treat her gently. That would be a nice change after the way James treated her.

They'd *better* be nice to her. After all, if they weren't, the dragon would come back. . . .

TAKE ME OUT TO THE BALL GAME

by Esther M. Friesner

"Explain it to me again, O Master," said the dragon. With a single golden claw it prodded the mystic deck spread out before it. Curls of violet smoke crept from its nostrils to wreath the images of lewd and diabolical beings unscrolled against the walls of the wizard's chamber.

"It's simple," replied the mortal who, despite his puny size and unassuming appearance, was undisputed master of the great Worm's every action while residing in this bubble of a here-and-now. A scholar's hand—soft, womanish, the nails badly bitten and begrimed with ink—jabbed down to pinpoint one specific effigy from among the many similar pasteboards laid at the dragon's feet. "This is Billy Jim-Bob Borden, number eight for the Mets. When he comes out of the bull pen to pitch against the Cubs, you eat him."

"Cubs," the dragon mused, stroking the orange barbels depending from its scaly chin. "I have

156

eaten cubs before this, of many sorts: Wolf, bear, lion, gryphon. . . ."

"No, no, no! Not the *Cubs*! You don't eat the *Cubs*! It's the Mets I want you to devour, dammit!"

"What? All of them?" Beautifully articulated five-toed paws folded themselves across a belly luminous as the full moon and nearly as vast. "Even in my greedygut youth I could not manage to consume more than three princesses daily without getting a case of the Jabderi Turnabouts, and I have no idea if these creatures you call Mets are more or less digestible than royalty. I fear I will be ill if I obey you, O Master, and I assure you, even a mage of your doubtless powers would not be happy trying to command an ailing dragon." Something in the way the beast's eyes narrowed when it said that left little space for debate.

Very patiently the wizard explained, "I don't want you to eat *all* the Mets; just a *few* Mets."

"Fewmets?" The dragon's indignation and revulsion flared up with a corresponding augmentation of body heat, causing paint to peel from the walls. "Am I summoned to this miserable ratfart world that I might use my gifts for the processing of mere sewage? Fewmets, forsooth!"

"Oh, jeez, I didn't mean—I just want you to—the *pitcher* for the Mets!" the wizard groaned. "That's all I want you to eat, okay? Just the pitcher, see?"

"I see." The dragon made a face. "Will it be crockery or metal?"

"Will what be?"

"The pitcher. The one you want me to eat. I pray it be not glass, which repeats on me like a curse. If you could see your way clear to arranging matters so that it is porcelain, O Master, I would be eternally grateful. And I do mean eternally."

The wizard jammed his Chicago Cubs cap down hard over his eyes, flung himself on his bed, and began to sob. The dragon observed this display with scarlet eyes made dispassionate by the inexorable roll of countless centuries and ate a Metallica poster off the wall.

"I never said it was going to be easy, Larry," said the wizard's apprentice from her place by the PC. She was a whole lot better-looking than the usual run of *aides-de-grammarye*, and had a way of making her sigil-strewn robes pooch out in a manner that had caused Wizard Larry to forget about the Cubs' league standings for all of fifteen minutes at a stretch. This was not one of those times.

"Yeah, Shannon, but you said it was going to *work!*" he countered. A bitter man is not a pretty sight, but one who has had his innate bitterness refined by long years of backing the Cubs is about as ugly as a Gorgon with PMS.

Ever reasonable (and for that very quality Larry vowed to kill her some day) Shannon replied, "I said the *incantation* would be easy. Did

I lie? It was easy as pie, once we got that virgin's blood."

For some reason, at mention of the blood, Larry turned sullen. More sullen.

"There, there, O Master," the dragon said, helping itself to a big glossy of David Lee Roth. A titanic paw patted the wizard's back with enough companionability to dislocate several vertebrae. "I'm sure you have a great personality."

"*You* be quiet!" Larry roared at the monster. "And *you*—" he whirled on Shannon "—you mention that vir—vir—that blood stuff one more time and I tell Rover over here to warm up by eating *you*! You got that?"

The dragon dipped its horned head until those leathery lips were within whispering distance of Shannon's delicate ear and confided, "No wonder he can't get a date." Shannon just nodded. "What's a nice piece of ya-ha like you doing wasting your time in this blob-tail's company anyway? Apart from needing a dependable source of virgin's blood."

"Oh, he's okay, really," Shannon responded. "You should've known him in college, the way I did. With a good job like he got—computers, of course—why he ever had to move back in with his mother—"

"Since college?"

"Four years ago, yup."

The dragon was dumbfounded. "He has known

a morsel of your evident relishability for at least four years and he is still a vir—?"

Before Shannon could respond, Larry picked up his genuine replica St. Louis slugger with the authentic ersatz Mickey Mantle autograph decal and poked the great beast hard amidships. Well, hard for Larry. The dragon barely noticed the impact until the little wizard screamed, "Hey! Pay attention to me! I'm the master here!"

Shannon's adorable mouth curved into that most goading of female expressions, the skeptical smile. "So you keep telling us. Okay. Master something. But before you start throwing your cosmic weight around, Larry dear, just remember this: You're in charge on *my* sufferance. *I* showed you the book." Here she patted the right hip pocket of the designer jeans now peeping from beneath the silky folds of her robe. "*I* suggested ways we might modernize the incantations. *I* cleaned up after you wet yourself at the thought of actually trying to summon a beast from the Beyond. *I*—"

"I did not!" Larry protested. He leveled a badly shaking finger at Shannon's smug face. "I never wet myself! You were here—" he appealed to the dragon. "You saw. I struck fear into your heart with my very presence! I was superb! I was commanding! I was—I was masterful! I was—I was—" His voice and his certainty drained away with equal rapidity. "Wasn't I?"

The dragon sighed and fumbled around the many creases of its iridescent hide until, from some bizarre, biological equivalent of a pocket, it withdrew a much-crumpled parchment. "Look, O Master, all I know is you were the one who uttered the key phrase of summoning, and it says right here in the regs (paragraph XVII, section C, subheading 83f) that my end of the deal is to appear and fulfill your desires for the span of fifty-two *uribets*. Once that span has passed, if you have not already dismissed me by the potency of your sorcerous spells—" here the dragon did its best to conceal a sarcastic snort, "—anything goes. Including you. Now, would you care to get *on* with it?" An ominous ticking filled the bedroom, although no timepiece was visible. The very rock-star posters on the walls seemed to pulse with the regular, inexorable beat of passing *uribets*.

"How long is that in real time?" Larry inquired with understandable concern.

Dragons lack shoulders and cannot shrug effectively, yet the Worm still managed to convey the sentiment *beats the hell out of me* without recourse to speech. "What good would it do you did you know that, O Master?" He waved the parchment about so that it rustled loudly. "As any fool can see, paragraph LXIV, section G, subheading 6i, codicil t4 expressly forbids me from giving you that information."

In the great tradition of the otherwise resourceless, Larry whined, "But that's not *fair*!" His appeal to good sportsmanship cut no tofu with the dragon.

"*Que voulez-vous? Quien sabe? Cui bono?*" the beast replied, showing off the fabled encyclopedic wisdom of Worms everywhere. "*Nu?* Is it fair for lowly vermin such as yourself to yank beings of my grand and immortal breed from the pressing business of our normal lives, just to feed your piddling egos and do your scutwork? Therefore, that the greedy may know and tremble, the regs do decree a finite timespan to our servitude, yet keep full knowledge of that span from you. Thus you must use our powers judiciously and quickly, lest the allotted time pass and we munch your—"

"Point taken, point taken." Larry shooed the dreadful thought away. "Hey, I'm no time waster. Haven't I been trying to make you understand what I want for the past hour?"

"Greed," opined the dragon, "is sometimes less of a problem than incompetence. Neither, however, is *my* problem. I do what I am told. Now, you said there was this flask full of bear-cub fewmets you wanted me to—"

"Don't scream like that, Larry," said Shannon. "Your mother will come upstairs to see if I'm having my will with you." The look on her face added a silent *you wish,* with perhaps a hint of *I wish, too,* thrown in for honesty's sake. She tossed the dog-eared paperback onto the bed. "If you'd done your homework, you'd see that there's no reason to go to pieces over this. It says right there that dragons are very old and very wise. And very acquisitive—treasure hordes, and all that—but that's beside the point. Because they're so wise, they never undertake a task until they understand it fully, and because they're so old, they've got all the time in the world to figure it out. You want fast service, you're going to have to explain things carefully, completely, literally, and in detail."

"Super," Larry grumped. "Explain everything there is to know about baseball? The season will be over by then."

"The alloted *uribets* may be over even sooner," the dragon mused.

"Ah, shoot, it'd be easier to—to—"

A frightening expression slowly spread itself across Larry's sallow features, a look of revelation and renewed zeal that signals danger in a sane man and absolute Armageddon-a-brewin' in a diehard Cubs fan. Shannon saw, and knew, and trembled.

Somewhere, somehow, someone was going to have to pay the price for Larry's unheralded brainstorm.

"Why did *I* have to pay for the tickets?" Shannon growled as they sidled their way into the stadium seats.

"Because I'm the wizard and you're just the apprentice," Larry returned smugly.

"It was *my* book. It was *my* idea."

"And it was *my* blood. As you keep reminding me every chance you get. So I might as well get some satisfaction out of it."

"The day you get any satisfaction . . ."

"Don't snarl, Shannon." Larry was practically beaming. "Next time I'll let you do the summoning."

Shannon's dangerously glittering eyes could have forewarned Larry that any dragons his lovely apprentice summoned would be given one command right off the bat, and it wouldn't be one he'd live to appreciate. But for the nonce, Larry wasn't in a reflective mood. His step was light and his heart was high. He was about to give the dragon a paws-on lesson, as it were, in the Great American Pastime. And then there would be no linguistic confusion whatsoever when he issued his "devour" directive. Billy Jim-Bob Borden didn't know it yet, but he was as good as Worm Chow right now.

"Excuse me. Pardon me. Oh, was that your foot? A thousand pardons," said the dragon, wriggling its scaly rump past the other spectators in the row until it reached its seat. A gusty sigh, garnished by whirlwinds of pale purple steam, escaped through the creature's nostrils as it plopped down and remarked, "So this is baseball. I like it."

"You ain't seen nothing yet," Larry promised it.

That much was true. It was a clear, hot July day at Wrigley, perfect baseball weather. The teams hadn't taken the field yet, but the newscasters and sportswriters were already at their posts, ready to verbally bludgeon the upcoming contest into more-or-less immortality. An insert in the program book informed the Gentle Spectator that today's game was special in that a large delegation of Japanese businessmen would be present in the same box with the sportscasters and writers, honored guests of the Management. Whether they were there with an eye to buying Wrigley, the journalists, or Chicago itself remained to be seen. No one with an ounce of business acumen ever dreamed they were there to purchase the Cubs.

The crowd was enthusiastic, even if more of their optimistic spirit sprang from the huge paper cups of beer in their hands than from any hope of seeing the Cubs win one. The smell of hot dogs was heavy on the air. Larry felt a drop of something thick and wet soak his shoulder. He looked up and saw that the dragon was drooling.

It was while the dragon was stuffing the fourteenth red-hot-with-everything down its gullet that Shannon leaned over and whispered, "They really don't see it, do they?"

Larry shrugged. "They see it enough to hand it a weiner and charge it admission."

"You know what I mean by *see* it!" Shannon snapped. "And they don't. How come?"

"Beats me. You could look it up. It's *your* book," Larry reminded her nastily.

"The book tells about the characteristics of dragons and how to summon them from one plane of reality to another. It doesn't say much about their effect on people, aside from the section on diet and digestive problems. Ogres give them the colic."

"So we won't let it eat any Republicans." Larry rested his miniscule chin in his hand, thinking over the rest of what she'd said. "Maybe people just see what they want to," he concluded. "If it doesn't make sense to them, they refuse to admit it's real."

"You mean 'I'll believe it when I see it' really ought to be 'I'll see it *if* I believe it'?" Shannon asked. Larry nodded. With rather needless malice she added, "Like the Cubs winning a game."

That smarted. Larry shot her the briefest of stink-eyes, then threw himself back into explaining baseball to the reptile with renewed zeal.

The problem with such a state of spiritual frenzy is that certain details often go unexplained as being too obvious for elucidation. This most egregiously overlooks the fact that there is no such thing as *too obvious* to a dragon, with the exception of . . .

"Diamonds?" The fringed skin of the creature's brow ridges rose. "It is played on diamonds?"

"Yeah, right, like I just said. Anyway, that mound in the middle of the field—"

"A field of diamonds . . ." the Worm breathed, and closed its glittering eyes in reflective ecstacy.

By the time the Cubs and the Braves got out there ("This is a battle of the giants, ladies and gentlemen!" shouted ace sportscaster Gregory Hughes. The Japanese were the only ones present polite enough not to laugh out loud.) the dragon was well enough versed in the gentle art of horsehide slamming for Larry's purposes.

Or so Larry thought.

"That is the pitcher?" the dragon asked, indicating the young man occupying the mound.

"That's Carl Watson, pitcher for the Braves. You don't wanna eat him."

"I don't?" Only one brow ridge lifted this time. "Why don't I? I'm hungry."

"Because he's no threat to the Cubs and if you're hungry I'll get you another foot-long with everything. Now *pay attention*! You will eat the Mets pitcher and the Mets pitcher only. To be more specific, you will eat *this* Mets pitcher." He flipped a baseball card out of the pack he always carried in his shirt pocket, tucked in snugly right behind the calculator and the leaky Bic pens.

With surprising delicacy, the dragon took the card between two claws, the better to examine it. "Your pardon, O Master, but full sunlight does not suit my vision." It brought the pasteboard to the very tip of its nose, only to have the constant curls of violet smoke emanating from its nostrils obscure it. Out of patience, the dragon snorted to clear the air and sparks flew, several coming perilously near the card.

"Hey! Watch it! That's valuable!" Larry squawked, wigwagging his arms.

"What is?" asked the dragon with what Shannon might have recognized as dangerous interest. Shannon, however, had gone to the ladies' room and, if the lines were as usual, wasn't expected back that decade.

"That card, you 'gator farm reject."

The dragon regarded the sputtering little man that an ungenerous Fate had made its temporary Master, then glanced back at the card. "It's paper," it commented. "Not even of the sort your kind use for currency, debauched and metal-poor creatures that you are. It is *not* valuable. I should know. Valuable is my life."

"Oh, for—! Look, I admit it's not as rare as a Honus Wagner card, but there are plenty of people out there ready and willing to pay five bucks cash money for a Billy Jim-Bob Borden card in good condition."

"Bucks?"

Larry leapt in quickly to untangle any linguistic snarls that might compel the dragon to ask about does, fawns, and other non-negotiable cervines. "Dollars. The green paper we use as currency. Enough to buy you a couple more red-hots-with-everything, at least."

"With everything?" The dragon licked its chops. "For this?" It tilted the card this way and that before its beady eyes. "And how many red-hots might I obtain for this Honus Wagner you mentioned?"

"Red-hots? Ha! A Honus Wagner is worth— it's worth—" Larry groped for the hot-dog-equivalency-table value of the most prized baseball card of all time and failed. "A Honus Wagner's worth a blipping king's ransom!"

The dragon was telling Larry that where it came from, kings did not blip, when Shannon came back, bearing beer.

"I sneaked into the men's room. How's it going with the education of Godzilla Kaplan?"

"Who?" asked the dragon.

"Not bad," Larry admitted. "I think we're halfway home."

"Home plate," said the dragon, and Larry beamed. The beast handed him back the card. "So that is my meal-to-be. And when may I have the pleasure—?"

"When he steps out onto that mound right there to pitch against my Cubs exactly one week from today. Got that?"

"Got it." The dragon helped itself to Shannon's beer and guzzled it noisily, dribbling most of the brew down onto poor Larry. "Sorry," it said. "It's difficult to be neat when you don't have lips."

"I dated someone like that once," Shannon mused, hailing the vendor for refills across the board. The dragon did for five more measures of the foamy; its belch rattled windows up and down the length of Michigan Avenue.

"Oh, great!" Larry threw his hands up in disgust. "I bet that Richter Scale ripper knocked everything I've already told you clean out of your narrow little skull."

169

The dragon took umbrage. "It did not. I have my orders. I am to devour one Billy Jim-Bob Borden, pitcher for the Mets, on this very site in one week's time. That *is* all you wish me to do for you, is it not, O Master?"

"Yes, yes, thank God *yes!*" Larry let his head droop with relief. "That's it, that's all, that is absolutely the whole shebang, my one and only desire, after which you may take yourself back to whatever backed-up drainpipe of reality spawned you."

"Good," said the dragon. "You have spoken, O Master, and I shall obey." Whereupon it spread its huge, leathery blue wings, caught a wayward breeze off the lake, and soared into the clouds. It returned in a swoop of such glorious grace that its sheer immanence caused the whole of Wrigley Field's audience to rise to their feet and collectively accept the fact that yes, Chicago, there *was* a real dragon.

The fact that it ate Steve Donahue, the lead hitter for the Cubs right off the bat, as it were, was also pretty darned persuasive.

"What is it doing? What-is-it-*doing*?" Larry shrilled, ripping the Cubs cap from his head and following it with several handfuls of hair.

"Well, it *did* ask you if all you wanted it to do was eat Borden in a week's time, and you *did* say yes, it was your sole desire," Shannon reminded him. "So I guess it figures that until then, it's a free agent."

Panic. Turmoil. Lots of shouting in Japanese.

The scene down on the field and up in the stands was that uncomfortable amalgam of good old American survival instinct versus good old American rubberneckers' death-wish. Larry and Shannon both leapt up to stand on their seats, the better to avoid being trampled by the thundering hordes of escaping spectators, only to discover that none of the thundering hordes were in any hurry to escape. Not when it looked like there was a pretty good chance of making it onto the evening news.

"Henry! Henry, let's get out of here!" shouted one matron from her place a few seats down from Larry and Shannon.

"You nuts, Darlene?" her mate replied. "We're right in a line with that lizard and the T.V. cameras. Hey! Hey, up here!" he shouted, waving a huge green foam-rubber hand, index finger extended, at the gentlemen of the electronic press. "We're number *one*! We're number *one*!"

The newshounds could not have cared less. It was dog-eat-dog on the Wrigley turf, as well as dragon-eat-Donahue. After the initial shock cooled, old reflexes kicked in hard. Orders were barked in the press box, phones seized, backup videocams dragooned into service as the journalists descended, bag and baggage, upon the playing field. The cohort of Japanese businessmen came trotting after in closed phalanx, for reasons known only to themselves.

There was chaos in the trenches, for the dugouts had been transformed from congenial shelters sacred to ump-cursing and crotch-scratching into military strongholds. Feelings ran high among the Cubs, many of whom seized their heaviest bats and swore to avenge poor Donahue's death upon the dragon's very skull. Their manager, Tommy Adano, had his hands full trying to restrain them. On the other side, the Braves might have no such personal stake in matters, but with the cameras on them they were constrained to live up to their name, at the least, and rouse a monster-threatening rhubarb for the benefit of the fans back home.

As for the dragon, it gobbled up its prey in two squirty bites, spitting out Donahue's cleats and cap like watermelon seeds. Then it looked around at the milling throng surrounding it and shook its head as if deploring so many snacks, so little time.

"They're nuts," Larry said to no one in particular. "They're out of their minds. Why don't they run away?"

"They're media," Shannon answered.

"They're meat."

His words proved true, with benefit of dragon. The newsmen were intent on giving the public what the public wanted, and the only thing that all members of the public there present wanted was their fifteen minutes of fame. As they swarmed about it, the dragon watched their shenanigans with that fine detachment usually exhibited by patrons of the better class of dessert trolleys.

Its hauteur was deceitfully encouraging to the bolder newshawks as well as to the more war-minded among the players. They mistook it for the state of somnolent sluggishness that common reptiles display after gorging themselves. How tragic, such careless generalizations. How sad that they could not do the simple, lifesaving arithmetic to prove that a single ingested ball-player was hardly sufficient to glut even one of the dragon's bellies.

Carl Watson leapt from the dugout, brandishing a baseball bat to which he had affixed some especially sharp spikes. A frothing Tommy Adano pounded after, showing absolutely no concern for his star pitcher's morale to judge by the names he was calling him.

Gregory Hughes, with a fine "once more into the breech" spirit, led a head-on, mikes-foremost charge of two backup "color commentary" ex-jocks, three cameramen, and an assistant makeup girl who thought she was joining an escape party. Several of the Japanese businessmen jogged behind, perhaps under the impression that the Honorable Hughes-san was the closest thing they had to an official host and that it would be impolite to abandon him.

This turned out to be providential. The dragon was not full and ultimately not fussy, except when it came to munching electronic equipment.

Shiro Matsuhito managed to retrieve the rejected comm-unit and relayed the unfortunate news that the dragon was systematically consuming all comers.

"Yes, yes, yes!" he shouted into the mouthpiece. "He is doing what I tell you! Everybody, everybody he is eating, one after the next!"

"Waitaminnit," barked the harried anchorman still safe at Gregory Hughes' home station. "Slow down, okay? Where's Hughes?"

"Where I tell you!" Mr. Matsuhito insisted. "The dragon, it eats Hughes-san first, Watson second, and third—" he looked up to doublecheck "—Adano."

He wondered why the honorable gentleman with whom he spoke groaned so loudly. He marveled even more at the death-threats he received when he passed on the news that the dragon had just devoured the assistant makeup girl, whose name happened to be Tamara, and one of his own colleagues, the honorable Mr. Todai.

Up in the stands, Larry had gone so far as to tear his Cubs cap from his fevered brow and fling it down amid the puddles of spilled soda pop and crushed hot dog stubbins. "Gimme the book!" he bellowed at Shannon.

Dutifully she passed him the dog-eared paperback guide to matters occult. The price sticker from that strange little used-books store in Schaumberg still covered over part of the words *For Funne & Prophette* in the title. Larry flipped through the pages like a madman until he found the section he was looking for.

" 'To Banish Ye Dragonne . . .' " he read aloud.

"Thank God!" With the look of a man possessed, or at least determined, he jammed his Cubs cap back on, settled it at a this-means-business angle, and stalked down onto the field. Shannon remained behind in nearly the same pose as a thousand pink-gowned princesses on a thousand fairy tale battlements. Her expression, however, was less *My Hero!* than *We're All Going to Die, and You First, Larry, Which is Kinda Too Bad Because I Kinda Like You and I Wish You Didn't Live with Your Mother.* Then she sighed, shrugged, and trotted down to the field herself, the better to pick up the pieces.

She did not reach the diamond as quickly as he did, owing to a slight touch of myopia that made her very cautious when confronted with large quantities of descending stairs. She held onto the railings and for the most part kept her eyes fixed on her feet, with occasional upward glances to see how things were going. Halfway there, she thought she heard Larry's shrill voice shouting, "Let me through! I'm a wizard!" Three-quarters of the way down she caught sight of the crowd parting so that he might approach the monster. She paused only long enough to see him raise a commanding hand at the dragon while the other thumbed awkwardly through the book. A series of eldritch and arcane syllables thundered from lips never meant to thunder anything—a sound quickly swallowed by the sonic boom of a dragon laughing. Shannon didn't know whether to redouble her pace to reach the field and stand by her man, or just give the whole thing up as too little, too late. When she had no more than a handful of steps left, there came the unmistakable *vroosh*! of flame and a nasty, burning smell. It seemed as if her decision had been made for her.

Strange to say, there were no Bits-O'-Larry to pop into a body bag, but his Cubs cap was a goner. The little man staggered into Shannon's arms and collapsed. She cradled his head in her lap and reflected that he looked rather sweet when barbecued. The layer of charcoal on his person was about analogous to that on a piece of Mother's Day breakfast toast as made by an ambitious three-year-old. A few fingerlings of smoke wafted up from his singed hair. A quick triage on Shannon's part revealed that the dragon was indeed a lizard of exceptional control and an artist among its kind. The damage to Larry was purely superficial, done more for dramatic effect than earnest destruction.

Oddly enough, the dragon's assault on Larry had effectively put its other plans for extended carnage and havoc on Hold. The great Worm yawned, snorted at the milling throng, curled up on the pitcher's mound and went to sleep with its forepaws hugging some particularly gory leftovers. From outside the stadium came the sound of police sirens approaching, but the dragon paid them no mind. It could fricassee Chicago's Finest before they were halfway through reading it its rights, and it knew it.

Shannon took advantage of the lull to tend to Larry. She found a half-empty cup of beer and used it to bring her knight in Extra Crispy armor around. "You're alive," she told him when he opened his eyes.

"The hell you say," he replied, sitting up suddenly, and kissed her so long and hard and true and honest that for a moment Shannon wondered as to the wisdom of letting nice guys read Hemingway. Then she settled down to enjoy it.

When at last the liplock let go, Shannon managed to pant, "So ... the incantation didn't work?"

"Does it look like it did?" Larry returned. "Dragons are worse than kids when it comes to holding you to your word. Uh—you did say you wanted to have kids, didn't you?"

"Three," Shannon affirmed.

"Okay, one of each, then. Anyway, *it* said it'd gotten its assignment and if it could fulfill it before the *uribets* hit the fan, or whatever, then it was free to do anything it wanted until then because *I'd* said eating the Mets' pitcher was the only thing I wanted it to do. I had, in effect, waived my power over it in all other matters, including the consumption and/or incineration of other baseball players, reporters, and digestible bystanders."

"What if the time-limit runs out before it can eat the Mets' pitcher?" Shannon asked. "Can you banish it then?"

Larry held up a wad of blackened, curling

sheets of paper that still smelled faintly of sulfur, chili-dogs, and beer. "It was your book. How good is your memory?" Shannon groaned; Larry comforted her. Thoroughly.

"If we survive," she said after awhile, "I'd like a church wedding."

"We might not," Larry reminded her, a canny look in his eye. "Care to cut to the honeymoon? It's not as if we're ever going to need any more of my blood—except to get the marriage license, and they don't care if I'm still a vir—"

"Here?" Shannon was scandalized. "You want us to make love *here*? On a field where the *Cubs* play?" The lady's resentment was understandable. "And you said I was special!"

But Larry chuckled. A brush with flaming death often wields transforming powers, and for some reason nerds cook up better than most other folk, developing a much-needed layer of crust where lesser men crumble. "But this isn't just a field where the Cubs play, darling," he said. "I'll bet there isn't a more priceless *lit d'a-mour* anywhere in the world than this field right here. If you believe the dragon, I mean."

"Larry, baby, I love you," Shannon remarked. "And because I love you I feel compelled to point out that I think the dragon sizzled up a great big dollop of your gray matter."

"I'm not nuts, Shannon. I'm just saying that the reason the dragon isn't going anywhere is that when I told it baseball is played on diamonds, it took it literally. Now it's convinced that under that dirt—"

"Astroturf," Shannon corrected. "I think."

"Whatever. Anyway, *under* it are the *real* diamonds. And you know how dragons are about sleeping on treasure. It told me it's not going anywhere, not even after the fifty-two *uribets* are up."

"You're kidding! I mean, I can understand relocating to Chicago, but voluntarily choosing to stay anywhere near the Cubs—" Shannon spread her hands, helpless to comprehend the ways of Worms.

"A nice, comfy bed to sleep on, a populace with no licensed or experienced dragon-slayers, and the equivalent of room service meals? Yeah, I think the greedy son-of-a-suitcase knows what it's doing." Larry looked thoughtful. "Greed . . . One thing I do recall from your book, Shannon is where it said that dragons are very old, and very wise, and very acquisitive. Which is a nice way of calling them just as big pigs as us."

"So?" Shannon inquired.

"So . . ."

So, some time later, as the remains of three police cars smoldered on the outfield and the dragon sat picking its teeth with a nightstick, Larry once more sallied forth onto the turf. He had driven home, showered and picked up a change of clothes, but no weapons, sorcerous or mundane. Most of the spectators had retreated far from the line of very real fire, although Authorities demanding that they vacate the stadium were ignored. It mattered not that the dragon had given a whole new twist to the term Sudden Death Overtime. They had paid their money and, by God, so long as they had a fighting chance of living through this, they were going to get their money's worth.

"Ahem," said Larry.

The dragon put down the nightstick. "Yes?" it drawled.

"Shouldn't that be 'Yes, O Master?' " Larry prompted.

"Hardly." The dragon's jaws gaped in a mammoth yawn. "You stopped being my Master about two *uribets*, seventeen-and-a-half *divblas* ago."

"Yeah? Well, you still owe me *something*. What about eating Billy Jim-Bob Borden?" Larry asked, pretending great annoyance.

"So sorry, O Former Master. Had the opportunity presented itself within my time limit, I would have been pleased to oblige you. Now, however ..." Unable to shrug, the dragon was not all hampered when it came to giving the old Bronx cheer. When done with a forked tongue, it was twice as messy.

Larry wiped dragon-spit from his face. "You never said that my desires had to be fulfillable within your time limit."

"You never asked me."

"If your time is up, why are you still here?"

"I like it here," the Worm replied, and enumerated the very same reasons Larry himself had elucidated for Shannon's benefit earlier. In conclusion it said, "So you see, you risk more than you know in coming along and bothering me this way now. Nothing compels me to obey you at all, and you remain unscalded where you stand only upon my sufferance. Call me a sentimental fool, but when a Former Master has as many strikes against him as you do, I just can't bear to finish him off."

"Strikes against me? You *did* say strikes against me?" Larry beamed. "I may not be a great wizard, but at least I managed to teach you a thing or two about baseball."

"Lovely game," said the dragon. It was caught off guard by a sudden belch and a Cubs cap flew out of its mouth. "I am very fond of it. But I am fonder of the diamonds upon which it is played. Diamonds by themselves, however, do not make for an entirely satisfactory bed. If you want real sleepable softness and slumber support, you need an assortment of gemstones plus the more popular precious metals. As soon as I have rested I intend to issue an ultimatum to the citizens of this town."

"Oh?"

"Yes; they must bring hither all their gold, jewels, and other valuables at once, to add to my bed, else see their city burned to the ground around them!"

"It's been done already," Larry said. He reached into the left pocket of his chinos and took out a blue disposable butane lighter. "By a cow." He flicked it on. "Belonged to a Mrs. O'Leary." He reached into his right pocket and took out a something thin, flat, oblong, and fairly fragile-looking. "Or so they say." He held the little pasteboard three inches above the flame.

"What's that?" the dragon asked.

"A baseball card," Larry said in an offhanded manner. "Nowadays they come in waxed paper-wrapped packs, just the cards alone. Before that, you had to buy them with bubblegum that was so bad, chewing the cards was better. But 'way back when, you got 'em with cigarettes. Smoking's a filthy habit, don't you think?"

The dragon gave a suspicious growl and sent up small, involuntary puffs through its nostrils.

"Okay, so you disagree. But there was this one ballplayer back then who didn't. He wasn't a smoker himself and he thought tobacco was a health hazard and he figured that having his picture used as a promotional gimmick for cigarettes was wrong, so he demanded that the company withdraw it at once. Only a few of those cards ever went public, which is what makes them so valuable."

The dragon's eyes lit up like furnaces at the v-word.

"Yessir," Larry went on, letting the lighter rise about an inch nearer the pasteboard. "You sure have to admire that Honus Wagner for being a man of principle."

Dawn hit the dragon right between the eyes. It uttered a horrified shriek, made all the more terrible by the fact that so few things can horrify a dragon. "That's a Honus Wagner!" it cried. "By the Egg, be careful, you mortal fool! Its value is incalculable!"

"I know how valuable a Honus Wagner is," Larry replied. "I was the one who taught you that, remember?"

"And you will burn up such a treasure?"

"Right before your beady little eyes, yup."

The dragon snarled. "Do so and die."

"How?" Larry smirked. "By fire?"

The dragon's snarl went deep into its chest and rumbled loud its helpless frustration. A huge paw armed with fearsome golden talons raised itself above Larry's head, but the little man just brought the card close enough to the flame so that any impact strong enough to jostle him would mean its immediate, fiery destruction. The paw lowered, the talons drummed an angry tattoo on the playing field.

"All right; it's your card," the dragon grumbled. "Deal."

"It's simple. I give you the card, you leave our world and return to your own."

"Agreed," said the dragon a trifle too readily.

"*And* you swear by whatever oath you hold most sacred that you will never, never, *never* come back here!" Larry plugged the obvious loophole solidly.

The dragon's head drooped. "I cannot promise

183

that. Some powers are greater than my own. What if you summon me here again?"

"I'd call the odds on that mighty slim. You smashed the book, remember? And I don't think Waldenbooks or B. Dalton's has it on permanent re-order."

"The book?" A glimmer of cunning came into the dragon's eye. "Oh, but a mage of your inherent gifts does not need all that folderol to summon a Worm. In truth, you have but to speak aloud the cantrip—" here the dragon lowered its voice and whispered a short series of syllables which, by a happy coincidence, just happened to be the easily remembered brand names of Larry's favorite chocolate syrup, deodorant, and steak knives not available in any store "—let fall the requisite five drops of virgin's blood, and I shall appear to do your slightest bidding."

"What makes you think I'm dumb enough to make the same mistake twice?"

"No mistake, O Potential Master, if your first request is that I give you the mystic words to send me home again once our business is done. Think of all I could do for you. Think of the wealth I could fetch you, the enemies I could slay for you, the power I could bring you, the bevies of beautiful, sloe-eyed women I could deliver to your doorstep, piping hot." The dragon showed more teeth than a platoon of life insurance salesmen and said, "Trust me."

"I'll think about it. Meanwhile, do we have a bargain?"

The dragon raised its right forepaw. "I do swear most mightily by the sacred Egg of my forebears; we do." Larry handed over the card, which the dragon snatched up eagerly. Holding it near its eyes, the Worm remarked, "Honus Wagner looks rather young."

"Clean living," Larry supplied. "And just think: If a Honus Wagner card is worth so much *here* for its rarity, imagine how valuable it'll be in your home world where they don't have any baseball cards at all!"

"Say, you're right!" The dragon actually wagged its tail. "And to think that old Gryth-phulc was lording it over the rest of us because *he* owns the bones of a pedigreed albino swordsman! I can hardly wait to see his face when he beholds my Honus!" Gloating nastily, the dragon launched itself skyward until, reaching the proper altitude for such things, it vanished.

It was in a lull between press conferences, civic banquets, parades, and his induction as an honorary member of the Baseball Hall of Fame that Larry was finally able to steal a few moments alone with Shannon. The rendezvous took place in his room because, as his mother reminded him, receiving the plaudits of a grateful city was no excuse for not cleaning out his closet.

"Maybe I should call the dragon back," Larry grumbled. "Let *him* clean out the closet."

"And the rest of Chicago for lunch, while he's at it." Shannon kicked off her shoes. "Dragons are sly. No matter what he promised you, he'd find a way to get out of it if you bring him back. And once he's back, how long do you think it'll take before he finds out that was no Honus Wagner; that was a wallet-size fake baseball card of you when you played Little League? Boy, talk about dead meat!"

"Oh, yeah? Well, maybe it'd be worth the risk. Just a few fast magical words, five drops of virgin's blood, and next thing I know I'll have wealth, power, more hordes of gorgeous women than I'll know what to do with—"

"Probably true." Shannon sighed and yanked him out of the closet by the neck of his honest-to-sweat Cubs shirt. "Absolute power corrupts. I can see I've got my work cut out for me."

"What work?" asked Larry as she shoved him in the direction of the bed.

"Saving you from corruption." She sat down beside him. "By removing the temptation to re-summon the dragon." She threw her arms around his neck. "By removing the means to re-summon it."

Later, Larry's mother pounded on the door and demanded what on earth he was thinking of, making all that racket.

"Baseball scores, Mom!" he shouted back. "I'm thinking of baseball scores!" Well, he *was*.

THE DRAGON'S SKIN

by Ruth Berman

In Le Rozier a new dairy was going up, with plenty of space for making cheese. The sheep and goats that pastured up the steeps of the limestone heights gave milk, said the townfolk, of unutterable sweetness. Besides, with a good many years of peace inside the borders of the kingdom under Charlemagne, there was time for putting up things other than strongholds.

Bradamant helped pass stones up to the workers on the roof, which was gradually rising beehive-round over the base. She thought that working on the dairy would lead easily and pleasantly to asking about the trade that came through town of pilgrims on their way to Saint James, and from the pilgrim traffic she could go on to ask about the nearby shrine, and the whispers she'd heard that the rueful Saracen returned there to guard it. But somehow her questions fell flat.

Well, Le Rozier was off the main line of the

187

pilgrims. The best road went just a little to the west, through Millau and south over the Larzac Causse, not over the Black Causse that shadowed Le Rozier. The high limestone tablelands of the Causses were barren country, offering a little pasture, but no farmland, and their very barrenness made them easier to travel than the rivers, too steep and swift in the highlands to be a useful guide. So pilgrims went over the Causses, where the footing was easy, and the traffic spread out to wherever there were interesting shrines to visit and villages to offer guides and guards against bandits, and why wasn't Le Rozier getting its fair share, and why didn't anyone seem to think the Saracen's shrine was interesting?

Bradamant worked a while longer, keeping silence, then said she was hungry. A couple took her into the shade of a chestnut tree, its leaves bright green above the blackness of its wrinkled bark. The two brought her a meal of cheese and nutbread and some of the local wine, mixed with water. She drank thirstily, for the air was growing hotter as the sun rose higher.

The woman said abruptly, "If you're on pilgrimage, Lady, you'd best ignore the chapel here. Go south."

"No, I mean to see the chapel."

The woman frowned, but her husband's face suddenly brightened. "Are you here to take care of the Saracen, Lady?"

"What needs doing?"

"He needs killing, I think," said the man.

"—unless you could get him to go away home," said his wife. "But then we'd need to be sure he'd stay away. The other time he left, they said he'd gone to join the battle, and we thought he died there. But back he came with new scars, and up he went. Didn't seem to matter then. All he did was keep watch, peaceful like. But now— Lady, if he wants to batter everyone who comes near him, let him do it somewhere else. We have sheep and goats to pasture."

"Everyone?" said Bradamant.

"Everyone who goes up on the causse," the man said.

"But why?"

"Who knows? He started—oh—this last winter when the rains were so cold and heavy."

"No, he was getting odd and quiet before that," said the woman.

"No, that wasn't—well, perhaps. Saracens don't all go off their heads when they meet with bad winters, do they?"

"No," said Bradamant.

"It's warm enough now," said the woman. "Can you help us, Lady?"

"I'm not sure. Maybe," said Bradamant, feeling confused. The villagers should have sent for help before. Evidently they did not much like their lord, and probably they'd hoped to keep their share of the pilgrim trade by not admitting that there was much the matter. But what did Rodomont think he was up to?

When he had first begun mourning Isabelle's death, his way of expressing it was to fight and slay all knights who passed by. Bradamant had beaten him in combat, and he had given up mourning to assume his command in the war against the Franks. Now it seemed he was back, and making matters worse. Bashing herders was no way to do penance.

Up on the causse it was hot. There were no trees there, and no shade. The tallest things growing there were the juniper bushes. Under the heavy gold of the sun, the juniper and the scrubby lavender bushes filled the air with tangy smells, as of things being preserved. Where the limestone came to the surface, the bald outcroppings swelled up, glowing many colors in the light, red and amber, white and grey and blue.

The grass was not as dry and slippery as it would turn in the high summer. The footing was not bad, and the broad-brimmed straw hat given her in the village helped against the sun.

When she came out on the tableland, the stone stretched its colors out before her. In the distance she could see the little chapel with its tower and beyond it the towers of the city that was no city, Old Montpellier, the town of limestone crags, castles of solid rock.

The chapel was made of limestone, and inside lay the gilded body of Isabelle, who had tricked

Rodomont into killing her rather than let him rape her.

Bradamant set out across the field of stone.

When she was halfway to the chapel, she caught sight of Rodomont, coming out the door. She waved, and he came running to meet her. As he ran, he drew his sword.

Bradamant frowned. "I just want to talk!" she called, but he didn't slow down. She clicked her tongue, drew her sword, and swung her shield forward.

Rodomont was not carrying a shield.

There was something odd about his pace. It was heavy, and a little slow. As he came nearer, she could hear his footsteps crashing on the stone, and soon she could feel the sound of them, shuddering in the ground beneath her feet.

The dragonskin armor passed down to him over centuries from the hunter Nimrod still shone bright blue and green. It glittered as he came near. Under the dragonhood she caught a glimpse of his face for a moment. It glowed dark amber, except for the gray scars, where her husband had struck him down in single combat in the war and left him for dead.

Something warned her—the look of his face, or the weight of his tread. As he swung on her, she leapt aside instead of taking the blow on her shield. His sword cut through air, and she could tell by the feel of the wind that the strength behind it was too much for a man. If it had landed on the shield, her arm behind it would have cracked.

She closed in to fight him, so that he could not strike a round, free blow at her with that unreasonable power. For some moments they traded blows, as he tried to go over or under her shield before it was raised or lowered against the blade.

Bradamant's chainmail was well made, but it was not invulnerable, as the dragonskin armor was. Any blow that Rodomont landed had a good chance of damaging her. She needed to strike him under the hood, or on the buckles of his armor.

She got one buckle open at the knee, and next chance hit him there again.

The sword clanged against his leg and chipped off a fragment—surely not of flesh. Her hand and shoulder felt numb with the impact. For a moment she stood, gaping.

He howled in rage and struck her on the side. Her armor held, but she was knocked off her feet and fell clattering on the hot stone.

He came running after, but she was too quick for him, rolling over and scrambling to her feet. His attempt to strike off her head as she lay fallen on the ground only removed her hat. He trampled it as he followed after her.

It was time to retreat. Back over the side of the causse? No, he might stand there and wait for her to reappear. Instead she ran toward the chapel.

Rodomont followed.

She leaned against the back wall, midway between the corners, catching her breath. When he came around one side, she retreated round another.

Going past the door, she could see, inside, Isabelle's coffin, carved in her likeness, and covered with goldleaf for her skin and hair, jewels for her eyes and lips and headdress. Dark lines of lead set off the sheen of gems and metal.

Rodomont came round a corner again. This time she retreated beyond the chapel, to the gorge, a long, deep crack running through the limestone. A bridge of limestone slabs built over a wooden frame went across it. There were no railings.

She had just time to pull up the bucket that reached into the cold water running in shadow far below. She gulped down several mouthfuls of the bitter water. It tasted of the metals in the rock it had gone through.

Then she retreated to the middle of the bridge.

The last time she had been there, she and Rodomont had tilted, and she had beaten him, tumbling him off his horse and into the gorge. She wished they had horses this time, instead of fighting on foot like bandits. She wished she had Galafrone's spear back, too. How was she going to get through that armor without magic? Still, invulnerable armor would not help him climb out of the gorge if she could tumble him into it—preferably without being thrown over herself.

But Rodomont came running heedlessly onto the bridge. It creaked beneath his weight, but it was strongly built and did not give way.

Bradamant could not stand up to the charge, and there was no room to dodge. She fled, without even trying to trip him or slice at a buckle, and made for the crags of Old Montpellier.

Inside the rocks, in spite of the shade, the air was hot, shimmering between the bright colors of the rock towers.

Old Montpellier gave her an eerie feeling, on its own account, apart from the oddness of the game of armed peekaboo she had to play. Many of the stone buildings looked familiar. There were some like palaces in Paris, and some like tents in the desert. One was like the magician Atlante's castle of cold iron perched on a mountain. The boulder beneath it gave the replica a mountain of its own to rise from. And one was like Rodomont's chapel, tower and all. Were they really so much alike, or was it illusion, or had Rodomont been shaping it?

Rodomont came round the corner of the tall pink obelisk next to it, and she advanced to meet him. The "street" was too narrow for him to swing with his whole force. With the advantage of greater speed, Bradamant chopped open some more buckles. One blow landed on his knee, where she had nicked him before, but he did not seem to feel it this time. She got several of the fastenings chopped open before he realized he was losing and retreated backward down the street.

She followed, still chopping at him. "What's happened?" she said, in between blows. "Why are you doing this?"

He made no answer.

The street opened out into a junction. Rodomont grinned and swung in a wide arc.

The blow fell on her shield and smashed her down against the square purple tower behind her. Bradamant rolled over and caught hold of a knob projecting from the tower to pull herself to her feet, leaving her shield behind.

It hurt to breathe.

She hid herself again in the mazes of Old Montpellier, stumbling and wheezing. She couldn't get enough air inside her to run. She stopped at last and leaned against a fiery pillar.

The heat weighed on her shoulders like a cloak. Colors wavered, glistening on the stones. She wanted another drink of water.

The pain about her chest grew easier. She must be badly bruised, but she did not think she had cracked any ribs. What she needed, she thought, was an advantage. What was there to work with? Stones, and cracks in the stones were about all there was in Old Montpellier.

She clicked her tongue and went looking for an aven. She had passed one or two already, but in the maze was no longer sure where they had been. The one she finally found was not, she thought, one that she had seen before. It lay at the foot of an amber minaret.

After a look up and down the street, she knelt and put her head into the aven. She couldn't see anything, but when she called out, the echo was enough to show that the hole underneath was large and deep. It was easy to understand how in old times people thought they led to Avernus, the old hell. She stood up and hopped cautiously. The stone quivered beneath her. Rodomont would not think that an aven led to Avernus, but he would still have to treat it with respect.

When he came that way, stalking her, he did not see her. She was up in the first balcony of the minaret, her bruises rather the more painful from the effort of the climb. He came near the aven.

"Hold still!" Bradamant called. "Stay where you are, and talk to me, or I'll jump." His weight and her weight landing from above would certainly break through the crust and drop them into the aven. It would probably be harder on her than it would on him. She hoped he would not put it to the test.

Rodomont stayed where he was, and looked up at her.

"What's happened to you? Why are you doing this?" she said.

He stared up at her, and the hood of his armor fell back. His dull eyes were wide with astonishment. "To be safe," he said, forming the words with difficulty, as if he had not spoken in a long time. He thought it over, nodded, and thumped himself on the chest, as he repeated, "Safe." He thumped his chest again, thought some more, and struck himself with his sword across the knee she had nicked.

The sword broke.

"Safe," he said. He turned and marched away, back toward the bridge over the chasm.

Bradamant shivered, in spite of the heat. She did not like this magic, born of Old Montpellier and Nimrod's armor. She climbed over the edge of the balcony and went down the slender tower, groping about with her feet for the rough bits where she could get hold. The quilting under her armor stank of sweat, and the iron links gave off a hot, rusty smell.

She followed after Rodomont. He left Old Montpellier, and headed back to the chapel beyond the bridge. Bradamant did not try to catch up to him. At the bridge she took another drink of the bitter water and found a smaller rift nearby, where she turned aside to relieve herself, then went back to the bridge and stepped onto it.

Rodomont was in sight again, coming back from the chapel, but not alone. He was carrying the gold effigy.

Bradamant tried to hold the bridge against him, but he brushed on by, knocking her over with the effigy's feet, without bothering to try to push her over the edge. He seemed to have given up on the chapel he had built and the dangerous open spaces of the causse. He was heading for the replica in Old Montpellier.

She got to her feet stiffly and followed after him.

If he really meant to shut himself up in Old Montpellier, it would be small loss to anyone. He had been a disastrous king for his own people, leading them into war. Le Rozier had found him a difficult neighbor. He was her enemy. And yet somehow she did not want to leave him to the city on the causse.

She caught up to him and cut open the remaining buckles as they went. The coiled tail spread out behind him, undulating on the ground as he walked, and the cuffs flapped around his hands and feet. She tried to trip him, but without success. And all the while she kept trying to persuade him of the benefits of life. There were plenty of women left alive in the world, if not Isabelle, and there were gentler ways to woo them. There was his kingdom in Africa to rule. There were notable warriors he could test his skill against—not so many as before Roncesval, but she did not tell him that. There was a rosetree in Le Rozier coming into bloom.

Rodomont paid no attention, but flapped along to the duplicate of his chapel, in Old Montpellier. He stood the effigy against the wall and stuck his fingers into the crack that looked like a door ajar. He pulled, straining, and the crack split a little wider open.

"It isn't too late," said Bradamant. "Take off the armor and you can still be healed—I think."

He set the effigy inside.

Bradamant caught him round the waist and squeezed in between him and the wall to face him. Rodomont and the wall felt much the same. She kissed him, trying to soften his lips.

Her feet went numb.

She let go of Rodomont.

Rodomont pointed to an octagonal castle down the street. "You could have one," he said. He stepped over her shield, where it still lay in the street, and went into the chapel.

Bradamant stuck a foot in the door. He tried to close it, but the pressure did not hurt her, and he could not close the door with her there. He raised one foot, balancing himself against the darkness of the inner wall, to kick her out.

"I can move faster than you," Bradamant reminded him.

He stopped and waited for her to explain what she wanted, if it was not a castle of her own in Old Montpellier.

"Take off the armor," she said. "You could still be—"

His chest moved slightly, as if letting out a sigh. "No," he said. "Couldn't."

He shrugged off the armor and dropped it on her. He banged one hand against the wall, with a boom that damaged neither. "Safe," he said.

Bradamant pulled herself and the armor free of the chapel. She tried to stand up, but it was hard to balance on her numb feet. She fell, sprawling in the street, with the armor spread out before her.

Rodomont slammed the door, closing himself in with his golden Isabelle.

The door was gone. There was no break in the limestone wall.

Bradamant hitched herself out of the sunlight into the shade of the wall and sat up to pull off her boots. Her feet were gray and stone-hard. She wanted to scream, but was afraid it would hurt her bruises. She forced her eyes away from her feet and looked at the dragonskin. It was a powerful prize. She could still hear the scrape of the chapel door closing to disappear.

Something moved at the top of the pink obelisk beside the chapel—moved and came slithering down, spiraling round and round the tower, and moaning softly as it went.

Bradamant stretched out and pulled her shield to her.

It was a dragon.

A pink dragon.

She tried to get her sword into her hand.

The pink dragon stepped gingerly onto the ground, balanced her tail above her back, and ran on tiptoes to the skin. "That's mine," said the dragon. Her French was clear, although the accent was peculiar, with a whistling, throaty tone.

The dragon stretched the skin out wide, then,

with little grunts of pain, crawled under it and tried to fit into it. The head and front legs went in easily enough, but the hind legs and tail kept getting twisted. The delicate underskin was getting scraped against both the stones of the ground and the scales on the outside of the skin. The grunts turned to groans, and at last the dragon stopped, and peered out through one eyehole at Bradamant. The other eyehole had gotten hitched over the brow ridge.

"Help me!" said the dragon, thought a moment, and added, "Please."

Bradamant gaped at the dragon. "I can't let a dragon loose on the world!" she said.

The dragon, with a little squeal, got both eyeholes into place and reached up one front claw, preening the ears into place. "By 'world,' I think you mean the homes of the two-legged creatures like yourself. Two-legged child, it was not the dragons who were loosed upon the 'world,' but the 'world' that was loosed upon the dragons. There are not many of us left. Help me."

Bradamant hesitated. "Do you promise not to harm people, if I do?"

"I have lived in terror of my life for more centuries than you can count, child, tracking after mine own—and I have survived, while dragons who thought themselves safe died. Of course I will not harm your people. Credit me with a little sense!"

"People say dragons are not to be trusted."

"How dare they!" The dragon gave a blurt of

fire that hissed against the stones and died away. "Are those truly the stories you have heard, two-legged child? Dragons do not lie. Two-legs lie." The dragon shrugged. "Dragons only mislead."

"I've heard that," said Bradamant.

"I tell you: I will not hurt your people."

"But—what do you eat?"

"Meat, of course. But why bother with meat as dangerous as a two-legs? There are pigs on the earth, and goats, and wild-ox, and antelope, and elephants—" The dragon seemed ready to spend ages recalling the delights of food, but pulled up and interrupted herself regretfully, "—when possible. But it usually isn't possible, unless the elephant is old or ill, and not worth the eating. Do you have any meat with you?"

"No."

"Will you help me?"

"And you won't harm people?"

"I will not," said the dragon, with exasperation.

Bradamant crawled over and straightened out the skin, then helped the dragon get tucked into it.

It was rather like getting her son ready to go outside on a cold day, when he was small. Of course, the dragon was larger than her son, even fully grown.

She helped pick out pebbles that had gotten in and were chafing the dragon.

The dragon rolled over on her back, licking and smoothing herself like a cat. The slit down the middle of the skin kept pulling open, but each time the dragon licked it the belly scales held together a moment, and it seemed as if each time the moment was slightly longer. The scales flashed blue and green.

Bradamant, on her hands and knees, watched in fascination. A hole she had made fighting against Rodomont before, with a magic spear, was visible on one flank.

The dragon stopped suddenly. "Two-legged child, why do you go like the beasts of the field, and the dragons? Is that courtesy?"

Before Bradamant could answer, the dragon had thrust her snout forward and was sniffing at the stony feet.

"Oh, I see," the dragon said. "Well, I am clearly in your debt and owe you a favor." The dragon let out a burst of fire. The flames played over Bradamant's feet.

Bradamant cried out in fear, but stopped. The fire did not hurt, or not at first. The heat began to hurt her legs, and she moaned. Then suddenly her feet were burning, and she screamed.

The dragon's jaws snapped shut, cutting off the flames. The dragon sniffed at her feet again, swallowed, and coughed, giving off a smell of sulfur. "Those burns will heal," said the dragon, and went back to rolling and preening. "Do you have such a thing as a gold solidus about you?"

"No."

"Never mind." The dragon licked the hole in

her flank. "I have some about the right size in a hoard." The dragon rolled some more.

"How did you lose your skin?" said Bradamant.

The dragon stopped rolling to shudder at the memory. "Have you heard that Nimrod was a mighty hunter, child?"

"Yes."

"Well," said the dragon, "He was." The dragon lifted her head, sniffing the wind, and then dropped it to set one ear against the ground. The dragon sniffed again, and listened again. "There are advantages," said the dragon, "to life unarmored—although not many." The dragon listened again and finally was sure of what she heard. "The villagers are coming to see what has happened. They will help you off the hill. Farewell."

The dragon was off, winding between the tall rocks, a streak of blue-green brilliance where the light reached her from the lowering sun. The scales flapped around the long belly, but without slowing the dragon's pace.

The air was a little cooler.

"Farewell, dragon," said Bradamant. She called once to the stone chapel, "Rodomont?" There was no answer from the seamless wall. She said a prayer for him and another for Isabelle.

She did not want to walk on her scorched feet, so she pulled her shield over, pillowed her head on it, and waited for the villagers to find her.

SHING LI-UNG

by Tanya Huff

"Donna. Your grandmother has asked to see you."

Incipient panic thrust Donna Chen up out of the chair and nearly pushed her voice over the edge to shrill. "Me?" She waved an agitated arm toward the backyard where her three cousins were playing a subdued game of croquet. "What about them?"

Her Aunt Lily, her mother's younger sister, stepped back out of the family room and shook her head. "You're the oldest. And besides, she asked to see *you.*"

Donna recognized the tone; her mother had one just like it. Ears burning, she stood and headed for the stairs. With her aunt marching close behind, she felt as though she were being escorted to her own execution. *There's someone dying in my house. That just doesn't* happen *in the suburbs.*

Just outside the master bedroom, she paused,

resisting the pressure of a small hand between her shoulder blades. "What if she dies while I'm with her?"

"Oh, for heaven's sake, Donna, you're almost eighteen; you're not a child. And you'll be in a lot more trouble if she dies before you get there. Now go."

The bedroom had been her parents until eight months ago when her grandmother had fallen, broken her hip, and been unable to live alone any longer. She had been frail then. Now, with eight months of pain behind her and death so near, she looked ethereal, no longer real.

To Donna's surprise, the curtains were open and, instead of the gloom she'd been expecting, the afternoon sun filled the room with golden light. Father Xiangao, the priest from Our Lady of Sorrows, sat to the right of the bed, her mother to the left. She paused just inside the door but her grandmother saw her and, murmuring something in Mandarin, beckoned her forward. Determined to make the best of a bad situation—given that she had no choice—Donna moved to the end of the bed and paused again, her knees pressed up against the mattress.

"Yes, grandmother?"

The bird-claw hand beckoned her closer still.

Eyes on the neutral landscape of the yellow blanket, its surface barely rippled by the wasted body beneath, Donna shuffled past her mother's knees and jerked to a stop when fingers of skin and bone clutched suddenly at her wrist. Heart

in her throat, she somehow managed not to pull
away.

"Chun Chun, woh yu ishi don-shi ne shu-ino."

Although her grandmother spoke fluent English, in the last few months she had reverted
solely to the language of her childhood. As
Donna spoke no Mandarin, Father Xiangao
translated.

"She wants to give you something. She brought
it with her from Kweilin. It carries very powerful . . ." he paused and asked a question before
continuing. "It carries very powerful
protection."

Donna allowed her hand to be pulled forward
and, curious in spite of herself, leaned down for
a closer look. Although she didn't understand
the words, she understood the tone. Her grandmother considered this to be very, very
important.

Three inches long and about one high, a red
and gold enamel dragon on cheap tin backing—
the kind they sold for less than a dollar at most
of the junkier Chinatown stores—lay on Donna's
palm, still warm and slightly damp from her
grandmother's hand. This was it? Donna turned
it over. Meant to be worn as a broach, the pin
had been bent and straightened more than once
and rust pitted the clasp that secured it.

"Shing Li-ung."

Startled, Donna glanced over at the priest.
Maybe she was missing the point of this.

"That's its name," the priest said softly. "It means, Shining Heart."

Donna could feel her mother's presence behind her and knew what was expected. "Thank you, Grandmother." It could have been a lot worse.

The grip the old woman had on her wrist relaxed a little and then surprisingly, convulsively tightened again. Her eyes opened very wide and she appeared to be staring at a patch of sunlight on the ceiling. Then thin lips curved up in a wondering smile and, just for that moment, Donna realized that this woman had once been eighteen, too.

She breathed out the name of her husband, long dead, and never breathed in again.

Trying very hard not to freak, Donna pulled her hand out of the circle of slack fingers as Father Xiangao reached over and gently closed the old woman's eyes. The imprint of the death grip clung to her wrist. Frantic scrubbing against her jeans did nothing to erase the feeling.

Then behind her, over the drone of the priest's prayers, she heard her mother crying. Puzzled, she turned. She had seen her mother cry before but never like this. Understanding came slowly. The dragon dropped to the blanket, momentarily forgotten, as Donna drew the older woman's head down to her shoulder and held her tightly while she wept. Her own tears were not so much for her grandmother as for the sudden knowledge that someday, *she* would be the daughter who grieved.

"So this is the family heirloom, eh?" Bradley grinned down at the dragon and then up at his sister. "Boy are you ever lucky that you're the oldest and it went to you. I mean, this must be worth, oh, seventy-nine cents."

"Very funny."

"Maybe you should rent a safety deposit box. Wouldn't want it to be stolen . . ." He rubbed a thumb over the enamel. "Hey, it looks kinda sad."

"What are you talking about?" Donna took the dragon pin back and frowned down at it. It did look sad; its eyes were half closed and its great golden mustaches appeared to be drooping around the downturned corners of its mouth. Its whole posture spoke of melancholy. "Yeah, I suppose it does. Do you miss grandma, Shing Li-ung?"

"Shing Li-ung?" Bradley repeated.

"That's its name."

"Oh, great. You've got a piece of junk jewelry with a name." He reached out one finger and stroked the red scaled curve of its tail. "So, grandma didn't mention she had a pair of ancient family chopsticks or anything for me to guard and revere did she?"

"No." Donna sighed. "Just one seventy-nine cent dragon."

"For you."

"I was there."

"Yeah, well, if you don't want old Shing Li-ung, I suppose I'll take it."

She stared at him in surprise. "You'll what?"

"I'll take it." He looked disinterested in his own words—the way only a young man almost seventeen could. "It'll look kinda cool on my jean jacket. Very ethnic. And besides, Chinese dragons are supposed to bring you luck."

"Grandma said it was for protection ..." *And she died giving it to me* ... Just for an instant Donna felt the clasp of dead fingers around her wrist. "I think I'll hang onto it." She scooped her canvas shoulder bag up off the floor and forced the pin through the thick fabric. "Besides, I'm the one who's starting university in six days; I'm the one who's going to need the luck."

"Suit yourself," Bradley shrugged, his expression unreadable, and slouched out of the family room.

"Shing Li-ung?"

Three inches had become thirty feet; thirty feet of shimmering scarlet and gold in constant flowing motion. Tooth and claw gleamed; strength and power in every curve, in every edge, in every point. Its eyes were deep and black and the light from a thousand stars shone in their depths. The air around it smelled strongly of ginger and when she drew it into her lungs, it burned just a little.

It was frightening but she wasn't frightened—which made perfect sense at the time.

Then it bent its great head and asked her a question.

She spread her hands. "I don't speak Mandarin."

It frowned and asked again.

"If you don't speak English, how about French?" She felt it sigh, the warm wave of its breath rolling over her, sweeping her away until the dragon was no more than a red and gold speck in the distance.

And then she woke up.

The red and gold speck remained and for a moment the dream seemed more real than her bedroom. But only for a moment, as normalcy fell quickly back into place. A narrow beam of light from a streetlight at the curb spilled through a crack in the curtains and across her shoulder bag propped on the top of her dresser. It illuminated the pin, igniting the enamel into a cold fire.

Pretty but hardly mystical, Donna decided, and padded across the room to twitch the curtains closed. With one hand full of fabric, she paused, frowned, and took a closer look at the dragon. Shing Li-ung no longer looked sad.

It looked disgusted.

"Hey Bradley, have you seen my bag, I had it when I got home this afternoon but I haven't seen it . . . oh, there it is." She moved her brother's feet and scooped the bag up off the end of the couch. "What are you watching?"

"Television."

"Very informative." A quick glance at Shing Li-ung showed it still looked disgusted. Its expression hadn't changed in the last four weeks and Donna was beginning to believe she'd imagined the whole thing. Although, considering that it had just spent three hours pointed at prime-time programming, it had reason for looking disgusted tonight. "This show any good?"

"It's crap."

"Then why are you watching it?"

"What else am I supposed to do?" Bradley jabbed at the remote. The new program didn't look significantly different; same dizzy blonde, same square-jawed hunk, same disgustingly cute kid.

Donna sighed and sat down on the arm of the couch. Always prickly, since Labor Day Bradley had been developing a noticeable attitude. "Is everything all right at school?"

"Why shouldn't it be?"

"I don't know, you just seem kind of, well, cranky." Not the right word but she couldn't think of a better one.

"Cranky?" He spat it back at her. "Little kids get *cranky*."

"Look, I just wondered . . ."

"Well, you can stop. You don't know shit anymore about what's going on with me."

She should have remembered. He'd been impossible when the year between them had left him behind in junior high. God only knew what he'd get into now. And now, he was old enough to get into things that could have serious consequences. She *was* the oldest. He was, to a certain extent, her responsibility.

"So," she tried again, "how's Craig?"

"How should I know?"

"But he's your best friend."

"Was. I have other friends now."

Great. "Bradley . . ."

"Kae Bing."

Donna blinked, brought to a full stop. Finally she managed a weak, "What?"

"Kae Bing. It's my name."

"But you hate that name, you never let *anyone* use it. You told Aunt Lily it sounded like a chicken puking."

"Maybe I changed my mind. Maybe I want to get in touch with my Chinese heritage."

"Bradley . . . Okay," she raised a hand in surrender, "Kae Bing, that makes as much sense as black guys in the seventies calling themselves Kunta Kinte."

"African-Canadian."

"What?"

"Nobody says 'black guys' anymore. You're the *oldest*, I thought you would have known that. Everybody has a hyphen now. Oh, pardon me, everybody who isn't white has a hyphen now."

The laugh sounded forced, even to her. "Oh,

come on, we live in Don Mills, the definitive sub-urb, you can't *get* any whiter than that."

He didn't smile. "Looked in a mirror lately, Chun Chun? Well I hate to break this to you, but you aren't white. *You're* what's known as a visible ethnic minority. And what's really disgusting, you go out of your way to fit the stereotype." He began ticking points off on his fingers, the edge in his voice sharpening with every point. "You're quiet, you're polite. I've never seen you lose your temper. You don't smoke, you don't drink, you probably don't even kiss with your mouth open. You're a dutiful daughter, a good student—especially in all those subjects us Asians are supposed to be good at like math and physics. You even play ping pong, for chrisakes."

Donna opened and closed her mouth a few times, but all she managed to get out was, "What's wrong with playing ping pong?"

"Not a damn thing. It *is* the only sport we slants excel at after all." He threw the remote to the floor and flung himself up onto his feet. "Well, you can keep playing by their rules if you want to, Donna . . ." He weighted the name and threw it at her as he stomped out of the room. ". . . but I quit."

"But Mom, you should have heard him. He was really angry."

"Young men his age are always angry."

"Not like this." Donna paced the length of the kitchen, trying to think of some way to make her

214

mother understand. "He wanted me to call him Kae Bing."

"It is his name."

"But he hates it!"

"He's just looking for something to believe in. That's common enough."

"But he's hardly ever home anymore and when he is he spends all his time sulking in front of the television."

"Leave him be, Donna. It's harder for boys."

"What is?"

"Finding out who you are."

"I know who *I* am."

"You're a girl. And, you're the . . ."

". . . oldest. Yeah, I know."

"But Dad, what do you know about these new friends of his?"

"Your brother is almost seventeen years old, Donna. He's capable of choosing his own friends."

She couldn't believe she'd heard correctly. "You wanted to know the family background of every person I ever spoke to."

"You're a girl. Boys need more freedom."

The habit of being a dutiful daughter closed her mouth on the reply she wanted to make, but only just.

"Was that all, honey? I really have to get this report done for tomorrow."

"That's all, Dad. Good night."

If they wouldn't listen, what could she do?

*   *   *

It moved like fire and air and water all at once and its beauty brought a lump to her throat. It lowered its head until she could see into the diamond strewn blackness of its eyes and it asked, "WHAT IS EVIL?"

Shing Li-ung seemed to have learned English in the last month. She hoped it hadn't picked up any bad habits from all the television it had been exposed to.

It didn't seem to mind having to wait for an answer.

"Evil is hurting someone else," she told it at last.

"SO," golden brows drew down and light glinted off a thousand pointed teeth, "BY YOUR DEFINITION IT IS SOMETIMES NECESSARY TO DO EVIL."

She had a sudden vision of taking a baseball bat to the side of her brother's head. "To prevent a greater evil, yes."

It cocked its head. "THE YOUNG LIVE LIFE SO SIMPLY," it said thoughtfully.

"And the old complicate life with the past."

It laughed then and the sound vibrated through her body, shaking blood and bone and tissue. While not exactly an unpleasant feeling, it wasn't one she was in any hurry to repeat.

"YOU ARE WORTHY," it told her, twisted back on itself and disappeared.

"Well, whoop de do," she muttered and fell deeper into sleep.

*   *   *

Donna had taken the special eight week night course at Victoria College over her parents' objection and would have thrown that small act of defiance in Bradley's face—except she never saw him any more. She left early every morning for the long transit ride downtown and, as Bradley had no classes until ten, she was gone before he got up. He was never home in the evenings, having suddenly acquired more freedom than she'd ever been allowed.

She'd seen his new friends only once when they'd dropped him off late one Saturday—or early one Sunday—and the noise of their talking and laughing had woken her up. From her window, she'd seen the red glow of a trio of cigarettes and heard how "they wouldn't be allowed to take over our town. They can just fucking get back on the boats and go back where they came from." She didn't care who "they" were; she wasn't impressed.

"What?" Bradley had demanded the next day when she'd approached him. "You think they're not good enough for me 'cause I don't have an accent? 'Cause they know what it's like to be Chinese? 'Cause they're living with their heritage, not hiding and pretending?"

"No one except you cares that you're Chinese!"

"My point exactly," he sneered and flicked the dragon pin with a fingernail. "You think you're so smart. . . ."

"No," she snapped, "but I think Dad's going to kick your butt if he finds out you're smoking. You know how he got about it after Uncle Karl."

Uncle Karl had been a two pack a day smoker and had died at fifty-one, both lungs eaten away by cancer.

The new friends never dropped him off at the house after that, but Donna was sure nothing else had changed. Maybe next year, when he'd pulled even with her again and was at university, too, they'd be able to talk. Meanwhile, she could only hope he didn't get into anything he couldn't get out of.

She was thinking of transverse vectors, not her brother, when she came down the steps of Victoria College and realized that, except for her, the night was empty. What had happened to the other thirty-seven students in the class? She'd stayed to ask a couple of questions, but she hadn't stayed *that* long. Had she? The echo of a stereo drifted down from the student residence to the east but the paths were deserted and dark and the subway a long, lonely distance away.

I'm being ridiculous. She settled her bag more firmly on her shoulder and clamped it securely down with her elbow, the edge of enameled tin cutting into her upper arm. The soles of her shoes made a soft squelching sound against the mat of fallen leaves that covered the pavement as she started toward Queen's Park Circle and the security of street-lights and traffic. *Once I get out onto the street, everything will be. . . .*

Will be. . . .

Between her and the street, a shadow moved. It could have been the trees, tossing in the wind. . . .

One foot lifted to step forward, she paused, and turned and started moving quickly along the darker paths that cut between the university buildings. *I'm being ridiculous,* she told herself again but she couldn't make herself believe it.

"Hey, China doll."

The voice came from behind her, from the way she had so suddenly decided not to go. Her legs moved faster; not running, not yet. The buildings around her were locked and dark. The only safety lay three hundred twisting meters away where the paths came out onto the blaze of light that was University Avenue. Three hundred meters.

She started to run.

A hand grabbed hold of her jacket and jerked back hard. She went down, arms flailing wildly in an effort to keep her moving forward. Moving away. Moving to safety. Then a larger, heavier body landed on top of her.

"Hey, China doll, I don't want to hurt you. I just want us to have some fun."

The hand he clapped over her mouth when she opened it to scream smelled of deodorant soap and the cuff button of his leather school jacket dug into her cheek. He was blond. He was clean shaven. He was smiling. His breath smelled like peppermints and beer. He shifted his weight, grinding her head through the pad of dead leaves and into the concrete.

"Now, we can get something going here if you'll just stop. . . ."

She didn't so much stop fighting as stop moving. In fact, at that moment, she doubted she was capable of movement. Her eyes were open so wide they hurt.

"Hey! What're you staring at?"

Red and gold it towered up behind his shoulder. Beautiful. Terrible. Impossible.

Real.

Blood splashed against her face as talons dug deep and lifted him skyward. He twisted against their grip for a second, staring down at her in disbelief. Then he screamed.

Donna screamed with him. And when he stopped, she went on screaming.

"ARE YOU HURT?"

The voice rang through her head like a gong, impossible to ignore. "I, I don't think so."

"THEN WHY DO YOU MAKE SUCH A NOISE?"

"I, uh, I. . . ." She got slowly to her feet, head craned back, eyes still open painfully wide. It was like sitting too close to the screen in a movie theater; too much to take in all at once. The smell of ginger made her want to sneeze. *I'm not afraid,* she realized. *I was, but now I'm not.* She took a step back, and then another, and then, in the red/gold light that came off the dragon, caught sight of the broken body crumpled across the path, one massive taloned forefoot still resting negligently across its back. "Oh, my God, you killed him!"

"YES."

Her exclamation had been purely instinctive. Shing Li-ung's placid confirmation transferred her growing sense of wonder into outrage. "You can't *do* that!"

It cocked its head to one side and regarded her with mild curiosity. "WHY NOT? I HAVE PROTECTED YOU AS I PROTECTED YOUR GRANDMOTHER."

"You just can't kill somebody like that!"

It looked down at the body. "YES, I CAN."

"Well," she threw her shoulders back, "if that's the kind of protection you offer, I don't want it."

Great golden brows drew in. "BUT I MUST PROTECT THE HOLDER OF THE TALISMAN."

"Do you have to *kill* people?"

"I MUST PROTECT YOU."

"But you don't have to kill people!"

The shrug rippled the full thirty foot length of Shing Li-ung's serpentine body. It didn't look convinced. "YOU HAVE BEEN GIVEN THE TALISMAN."

"Then you must obey me?"

"NO. I MUST PROTECT YOU."

"I don't believe this," Donna muttered and brushed her hair back off her face. It came away damp and sticky. Her heart back in her throat, she held it out and in the dragon's light she saw it smeared with blood. "I don't believe this!" But this time the words were wailed as whatever cocooning the dragon's presence had offered peeled away.

An echoing wail came from behind the surrounding buildings, from the street.

The sound brought a new panic.

"The police! Someone called the police."

"YOU WERE MAKING A GREAT DEAL OF NOISE," Shing Li-ung observed.

"But what do I do? He's dead!"

"ARE YOU IN DANGER?"

Her laugh hung on the edge of hysteria. "I am if I stay here. I'll end up in the psycho ward. I didn't kill him, Your Honor, my grandmother's dragon did."

"IF YOU ARE IN DANGER, I MUST PROTECT YOU."

In the next instant, she stood on the front porch of her parent's house in Don Mills, safe in the suburbs, miles away from the savagely murdered body of a young man. *And barely a month ago I was freaked by my grandmother dying peacefully in bed. . . .*

Her hands shook too violently for her to open the door so she leaned against the bell.

"Keep your pants on, jeez, I'm . . . Donna?"

"Mom? Dad?"

Bradley dragged her inside and managed to hang onto her as she sagged against him. "Mom's at Aunt Lily's and Dad's working late. Christ, Donna, you're covered in blood!"

"Not mine."

"Not yours!?" His voice which hadn't cracked in years shifted an octave on the second word. He lowered her onto a chair and gripped her shoulders so tightly she squeaked in pain. "What happened to you!?"

"What happened to me?" Donna shrugged his hands away and dragged the canvas bag down onto her lap, turning the dragon pin into the light. The tiny golden claws were red. "What happened to me?" she repeated, just barely holding on to coherency. "Oh, nothing much happened to *me*."

". . . and then I was home."

Bradley sighed, a long exhalation that released all the interruptions he wanted to make but hadn't throughout her story. She wouldn't let him touch the dragon, so he sat and stared at it as she turned it over and over between fingers puckered by almost thirty minutes in the shower.

She looked up at the sound and waited for him to speak, wondering what he was thinking. Would he think she'd gone crazy? Had she? But he didn't speak and she couldn't read his expression. The silence lengthened until she broke under the weight of it. "Well?"

"I need a smoke."

"No, you don't!" The response was automatic older sister and it snapped her past some of what she supposed had to be shock. She sighed in turn and felt the knot in her stomach begin to ease with the wavering breath. "Bradley, please. . . ."

He spread his hands. "I want to believe you," he said simply.

And he did. Donna recognized his expression now. Hope. A desperate hope. She thought she'd done all the crying she could in the shower. She was wrong.

"Jeez, Donna, don't. I mean, you're all right, right? Like that guy didn't hurt you and you're okay. You said, Shing Li-ung came in time. I mean, jeez, please Donna, stop crying."

Because it was upsetting him, she tried. It took a few minutes. "Why don't you believe me?" she asked when she finally regained control.

He shrugged, watching her nervously in case she should break down again. "Well, I mean . . . a dragon?"

She rubbed her nose on the fuzzy purple sleeve of her old bathrobe. "You're the one who's always going on about Chinese heritage. Dragons are a part of that."

"Yes." He turned that over, accepted it.

"And you know I never lie. Not even when it would keep me out of trouble. Even when it would keep *us* out of trouble. You always said it was one of my most annoying habits. If I never lied before, why now? And why about something so . . . so extreme."

"Why indeed?" His sudden smile illuminated

the room. "Donna, this is awesome. A dragon, a real dragon."

"No, Bradley. . . ."

"Kae Bing and what do you mean, *no*?"

"It isn't awesome, at least not like you mean . . . that boy is dead."

"So?"

"Dead!" she repeated. "And Shing Li-ung killed him."

"He deserved to die."

"It's not that simple," she began, but she saw suddenly for Bradley, for Kae Bing, it was that simple. "Look, you can't just go around saying that some people deserve to die."

"Can't I?" He jerked to his feet, hands balled into fists. "Well, maybe Saint Donna can't, but I can. Get some sleep and forget about that round-eye punk, he got what he deserved." Half out of the room, he paused and looked back. "Oh, and I wouldn't tell Mom or Dad about this. *They* wouldn't understand."

Then to Donna's surprise he bowed to the bit of enameled tin she still held in her hand.

The boy's name had been Alan Ford and all three city papers had a full report of his death. The tabloid even had color pictures. Not one of the papers mentioned a thirty foot long, scarlet and gold Chinese dragon although all of them mentioned multiple knife wounds.

To her parents' relief, Donna dropped out of the night school course and unless she had a crowd of friends around her, she stayed off the paths in the daytime as well. But even crowds couldn't stop her reaction to blond hair and leather university jackets.

Shing Li-ung stayed at home on her dresser, watching its own reflection in the mirror. Donna had no intention of being responsible for releasing the dragon again.

"I MUST PROTECT YOU."
"No!"
"WHY DO YOU FEAR ME?"
"Because you burn too brightly."
"I MUST PROTECT YOU."
"Get out of my dreams!"

"Mr. Chen?"
"Yes, I'm David Chen. What is it, Officer?"
"Are you the father of Bradley Chen?"
Donna came out of the family room, one finger holding her place in a physics text, heart beating so loudly she was certain the two police constables at the front door must hear.
"I'm Bradley's father, yes."
"Your son has been injured, Mr. Chen."
"Injured? Bradley? How?"
Standing just behind her father's shoulder, Donna saw the look they exchanged. *How much do we tell him?*
"There was a gang fight, in the Dragon Mall, on Spadina. . . ."
"And my Bradley got caught in it?"

No, Dad.

"No, Mr. Chen. Your son was part of a Chinese gang attempting to force a Vietnamese gang off their turf."

"That's impossible!" She could feel the indignation coming off him in waves. "My son would never get involved in something like that."

"There's no doubt about his involvement, Mr. Chen."

"Well, you're wrong!"

No, Dad.

"We're sorry, Mr. Chen, but. . . ."

"You said he's injured, where is he?"

"He's been taken to Wellesley Hospital."

"Well, I'll go to him. I'll talk to him. You'll see. He wasn't involved in this. You're wrong."

Again, Donna saw the silent exchange between the two constables.

"Dad, I'm going with you." She knew without looking that the dragon pin would be missing from her dresser.

Bradley had remained quiet and unresponsive throughout their father's questioning. He had admitted being part of the gang, his lower lip thrust out in what looked to Donna like a defiant pout, but he had refused to cooperate any further. Finally, the police took their father aside for a private discussion and Donna was left alone with her brother.

He had a hundred and thirty-seven stitches, mostly in his right arm and side. She thought the bandages and the tubes made him look ridiculously young and she couldn't think of what to say.

Bradley finally broke the silence.

"It's in the drawer."

She pulled the pin out of the jumble of personal effects—the contents of his pockets, his watch, an earring; *when had he gotten his ear pierced?*—and brought it back to the bed.

"You really sucked me in." His voice had the rough rasp of unshed tears behind it.

"What?"

"I believed you. Believed your stupid story about the dragon. There isn't any dragon. There never was."

Donna closed her fingers so tightly around Shing Li-ung the edges cut into her palm. Anger she could have dealt with but not this black despair.

"Oh, stop crying. I've learned my lesson."

"Good." Donna drew in a long shuddering breath and swiped at her cheeks with her empty hand. "So you'll come home and stop seeing these people and stop this gang stuff. Bradley, I. . . ."

"Kae Bing!" He spat the name at her. Now, the anger showed. "Shall I tell you what I've learned. I've learned that if we're going to make a place for our people in this country, and hold it, we're going to have to do it one drop of blood at a time." He couldn't move his right arm, but his left came up off the bed and his fist punched the air. "If they use knives, we'll use knives. If they use guns, we'll use guns."

"You sound like a bad remake of *West Side Story*." She couldn't believe she was hearing this. "You haven't learned anything."

"I learned the lesson your *dragon* taught me; we can't count on outside help. We have to do this ourselves." He turned his head on the pillow. "Now get that piece of junk jewelry out of my room. I'm tired."

"Bradley ... I mean, Kae Bing, I want to help."

The glimmer of silver between his lids was her only answer. She watched one lone tear roll onto his pillow then, slipping the pin in her bag, she left the room. She didn't know what else to do.

"Why didn't you protect him?!"

"I WAS NOT GIVEN TO HIM."

"But you were with him! And he only acted so foolishly because he thought you'd protect him."

Shing Li-ung looked somewhat taken aback. "YOU DO NOT KNOW THAT."

"I do know that. You inspired his recklessness."

"I DID NOT."

"You did."

"DID NOT."

"Did. And now because you didn't show up, he's convinced that the gang answer is the right answer."

Tanya Huff

"THE YOUNG CAN CONVINCE THEM-
SELVES OF ANYTHING."

"Well, you should have protected him against
that, too!"

"THERE IS NO PROTECTION AGAINST
YOUTH SAVE TIME. AND BESIDES, I WAS
NOT GIVEN TO HIM. I MUST PROTECT
THE ONE I HAVE BEEN GIVEN TO." It
snorted and the smell of ginger became almost
overpowering. "IF THAT ONE IS WORTHY."

"Oh, that's it. You didn't find my brother worthy so you let him almost die?"

"IT DID NOT COME TO THAT. I MUST
FIRST BE GIVEN." Obviously considering that
to be the final word on the matter, it twisted
back on itself and disappeared.

"Come back here! This is my dream and I'll
tell you when you can leave! Shing Li-ung! Shing
Li-ung!"

Her anger almost woke her, but she fought her
way deeper into sleep, searching for the dragon,
chasing a gleam of scarlet and gold.

Winter broke before Bradley left the hospital
and Donna suspected the weather, not his injur-
ies or the terms of his probation, kept him home.
He spent long hours on the telephone, talking,
she was sure, with his *friends* from downtown,
keeping the anger alive. It didn't help that most
of the kids at school considered him some kind
of hero.

Donna tried to understand what he was angry

Tanya Huff

"THE YOUNG CAN CONVINCE THEM-
SELVES OF ANYTHING."

"Well, you should have protected him against
that, too!"

"THERE IS NO PROTECTION AGAINST
YOUTH SAVE TIME. AND BESIDES, I WAS
NOT GIVEN TO HIM. I MUST PROTECT
THE ONE I HAVE BEEN GIVEN TO." It
snorted and the smell of ginger became almost
overpowering. "IF THAT ONE IS WORTHY."

"Oh, that's it. You didn't find my brother worthy so you let him almost die?"

"IT DID NOT COME TO THAT. I MUST
FIRST BE GIVEN." Obviously considering that
to be the final word on the matter, it twisted
back on itself and disappeared.

"Come back here! This is my dream and I'll
tell you when you can leave! Shing Li-ung! Shing
Li-ung!"

Her anger almost woke her, but she fought her
way deeper into sleep, searching for the dragon,
chasing a gleam of scarlet and gold.

Winter broke before Bradley left the hospital
and Donna suspected the weather, not his injur-
ies or the terms of his probation, kept him home.
He spent long hours on the telephone, talking,
she was sure, with his *friends* from downtown,
keeping the anger alive. It didn't help that most
of the kids at school considered him some kind
of hero.

Donna tried to understand what he was angry

about, but it seemed directed at being Chinese—
not because he didn't want to be, but because he
did. Her own anger she reserved for her family,
who seemed to think that by ignoring the problem, it'd go away.

She buried Shing Li-ung in her underwear
drawer.

In March, when the snow stopped and the air
began to warm, the patterns of the previous au-
tumn reappeared.

"Say, Donna, isn't that your brother?"

If it was, he'd skipped his afternoon classes
again. "Where?"

"On the corner, with those other two guys. I
didn't know he smoked."

"He doesn't."

"He is."

The other two guys were all angles and edges
with slicked back hair and muscles pulled tight
over bone. Inside their expensive clothes and
heavy jewelry, they moved with the boneless
grace of alley cats anticipating a fight. What
bothered Donna the most was not how different
Bradley looked, but how much the same.

"I'd better go over and talk to him."

"He doesn't look like he wants to be bothered."

"Tough." But by the time she got across the
street, they'd already begun to move and she had
to hurry to catch up.

". . . be there tonight."

"I'll be there." Bradley tossed his cigarette in

the gutter. "Jade Garden Night Club Restaurant. One-thirty in the am."

"Why don't you just tell the world?" hissed the taller of his companions.

Bradley's laugh scraped at the hair on the back of Donna's neck. "We'll have the guns," he pointed out. "Who's going to stop us?"

That's my cue, Donna thought, feet suddenly rooted to the sidewalk as the trio pulled ahead and turned the corner onto Beverly without ever seeing her. Jade Garden Night Club Restaurant. One-thirty am. We'll have the guns.

I could tell the police; if nothing else, Bradley's breaking probation. Except that he was her brother and, as much as it was the sensible, right thing to do, she couldn't do it.

I could tell Mom and Dad, and they'd say boys will be boys and insist he's given up all that gang nonsense, that he swears he's given it up. "And it would never occur to them that someone who gets into knife fights in shopping malls could be lying."

"What?"

"Nothing. . . ." She flushed and started walking, ignoring the worried looks shot her way by the two elderly women who'd heard her talking to herself. Their parents expected both her and Bradley to fit neatly into the lives they'd devised for them. That she did made it even harder on Bradley who didn't. The incident last fall had shaken their belief in the system only for a moment.

So. It looks like it's up to me. She fought with a sudden irrational desire to rip open her jacket and yell, "This is a job for Shing Li-ung!"

If the dragon deigned to make an appearance. It had already refused to rescue her brother once.

And what are you going to do if Shing Li-ung doesn't show? Donna asked herself later that night, emotions trembling on the edge of hysteria. *Stick the bad guys with the rusty pin and hope they get tetanus?* She'd told her parents she had to go back downtown to use the library. It was the first time she'd been out after dark on her own since. . . .

A tall young man across the subway gave her a speculative look. Donna jerked her head away and stared fixedly at her reflection. *Don't try anything, buddy. I've got a dragon in my pocket.*

She stayed at the library until it closed at eleven and then closed down the coffee shop across the street at twelve. The Jade Garden Night Club Restaurant was on Baldwin between Beverly and McCall, right in the heart of Chinatown. The library—and the coffee shop—was only five blocks north—five short blocks—so she arrived just before twelve thirty, the dragon clutched in a sweaty hand, heart leaping into her throat at any and every noise.

The restaurant was locked although she could see people moving around inside, lifting chairs onto tables, sweeping the floor.

Am I too late? Has it happened?

Moving slowly and carefully, trying to see everything at once, she backed to the edge of the sidewalk. The health food store across the road had large empty plywood bins out front, a perfect hiding place if she wanted to watch and wait for Bradley, then ... then ... then what? She still didn't know.

This is ridiculous. I should have told someone. I don't know what I'm doing here.

But she went and hid in the bin anyway, crawling through the open back, trying to ignore the rotting bits of vegetable on the pavement. She was the oldest. He was her responsibility. Just for an instant, she envied Bradley his ability, or at least his attempt, to break free of the conditioning they'd faced all their lives. *But if I break free, little brother, where does that leave you?*

The car pulled up at twelve fifty, when only one light remained on in the restaurant and most of the staff had left. It cruised by not two feet from where Donna knelt, turned into the alley way beside the store, and cut the engine.

No.

It hadn't happened.

This was it.

The silence thickened until it lay over the street like a fog, enclosing it, isolating it. The steady traffic on Beverly, only two short blocks to the west, sounded muffled and distant. She wouldn't have heard the car doors, or the footsteps approaching, had she not been listening so desperately for them.

"He's still inside. That's his car down the street."

They were leaning on the outside of her bin. Donna peered through the crack where moisture had warped the boards apart. Her brother looked like a stranger, all angles and edges.

"Remember, full automatic. Don't worry about accuracy. We've got to do them and get out of here."

"Them?" She could see the curve of a black tube cradled in Bradley's arms. It took her a moment to realize it was part of a gun. She'd never seen a gun before. "What do you mean *them?* I thought we were after Bui? We take out the leader of the most powerful Vietnamese gang and the gang falls apart. I mean, that was the plan."

"Hey, Kae Bing, chill out. Bui owns this place and the guy who manages it for him is in gang business up to his balls. He launders the gambling money, stores the dope, pimps for the whores. We do him, too."

"Besides," the second of Bradley's companions took a long pull on his cigarette, "they'll come out together. It's all or nothing."

Nothing, Donna prayed. *Please God, nothing.* Her brother's jacket brushed up against the bin. She could slip the dragon pin through the space between the boards and drop it into his pocket. Give *him* the dragon. There was nothing she could do about the two men in the restaurant, but at least Bradley would be safe.

"What's taking them so long?"

"You scared, Kae Bing?"

"Fuck you."

He was scared. She could hear it in the bravado. Holding Shing Li-ung by the very end of its tail, Donna pushed the other end at the crack. There'd be just barely enough room—if only there'd be enough time. Then the clasp caught on a sliver of wood and jerked the dragon out of her grip. It twisted back on itself, hit her shoulder, her knee, and rang against the pavement under the bin.

"Hey, what was that?"

She froze, too frightened even to blink.

"What was what?"

"I heard something under here." Bradley slapped his palm down and the wood over Donna's head boomed.

"Probably a rat. Or a cat, or something."

"Well, I'm going to look."

"No time. Here they come."

It suddenly didn't matter if they heard her. She pressed her face up to the boards as the door to the restaurant opened and three people came out onto the step.

"Hey wait!" She saw Bradley's arm go out, stopping the surge forward. "There's a waitress with them."

"So?" They shook free of his restraint. "Come

on. We've got to do them before they reach the bottom of the stairs."

"You can't shoot her!"

"Wanna bet?"

Donna, eye tight against the hole, saw her brother break into a run toward the three figures on the steps and knew without a doubt what he was going to do. Desperately, she scraped the pavement with her fingers, searching for the dragon.

He'd gone four steps when she found it.

Six when she threw herself out of the bin.

Seven and the guns came up.

Eight, he grabbed the terrified woman by the arm.

Nine, he threw her out of the way.

On ten, they opened fire.

"No!" Donna's scream got lost in other screams, in the spitting roar of the pair of sub-machine guns, in lead impacting with flesh. She didn't feel the pavement rip through her jeans and into both her knees as she flung herself down by Bradley's side. Two crimson rosettes blossomed and spread across his chest and a line of them stitched color down his leg.

But he was breathing. And conscious.

"Donna?"

"Shut up!" She snatched his hand up off of the ground, forced the bent fingers straight, and pressed Shing Li-ung into his palm. "Here, this is yours now, I'm giving it to you."

He blinked. Tried to focus on his hand. Couldn't do it. "Wha. . .?"

"Fucking stupid, Kae Bing."

And the world came back.

"You just signed your death warrant, you know." The quiet conversational tone was infinitely more terrifying than an attempt to terrify would have been. "You *and* your girlfriend."

"My . . . sis . . . ter."

"Rough luck for your folks," said one, shaking his head.

"Say good-bye," said the other.

The guns came up. Donna saw their fingers tighten on the triggers and afterward, although she knew it was impossible, she swore she saw the first bullets emerge.

Then the street between them became filled with thirty feet of scarlet and gold dragon.

"Ho . . . ly . . . fuck."

Shing Li-ung bent its massive head down until its golden mustaches brushed the pavement and just for an instant Donna saw her brother reflected in the starlit depths of its eyes. "YOU RISKED YOUR OWN LIFE FOR ANOTHER," it observed. "YOU ARE WORTHY."

"Awe . . . some."

The dragon smiled. "YES."

Then it turned and faced the gunmen.

Donna closed her eyes. The wail of a police siren snapped them open again. She should have realized. Fifty-two division was barely four blocks away. They must have heard the shots.

"Shing Li-ung! Look out!"

Then she was looking through red and gold after-images at a police car and an empty street. Two submachine guns lay by the opposite curb and a rain of bullets dropped harmlessly to the pavement between. An Asian police constable stood half out of the car, staring wide-eyed at the space Shing Li-ung had been, murmuring *Tien Lung* over and over.

"Jesus H. Christ!" His partner obviously saw only the bodies and the blood.

The next little while became a kaleidoscope of flashing lights, loud voices, and the lingering scent of ginger. Gently, but firmly, the ambulance attendants moved Donna away from her brother and she found herself standing beside the young woman whose life he'd saved.

Cold fingers clutched at her arm. "The dragon can't let him die."

"It doesn't work like that."

"Then tell me his name, I'll pray to the Buddha for him."

Donna closed her hand around the enameled pin that had slid to the pavement, the curved loop of Shing Li-ung's tail cutting into her palm. It took a moment for her to find her voice. "His name," she said, swallowing tears, "is Kae Bing."

The graveyard was still and quiet, the only sound a cicada high in one of the surrounding trees. Donna laid Shing Li-ung down on top of the tombstone and dug a stick of incense out of her purse, her hand a little unsteady as she bent and pushed one end into the grass.

She stepped to one side as Kae Bing knelt and pulled out a disposable lighter.

"Not very traditional," he muttered, "but it'll have to do."

Donna slipped a hand under his elbow to steady him as he stood. Over a month in hospital had left him weak and pale, tiring easy, still in pain, but alive. His trial was scheduled for October sixth, over thirteen weeks away, but everyone concerned seemed to think his dramatic change of heart combined with a willingness to cooperate would keep him out of prison.

No one mentioned the dragon.

The bodies of the two gunmen still hadn't been found.

"Are you sure this is going to work?"

"Look," Donna sighed and pushed her hair back off her face, "we agreed that Shing Li-ung is too much for one person to handle."

Kae Bing patted the warm marble of the tombstone, brows drawn down. "Grandma managed."

"Grandma knew who she was. She had centuries of history behind her. What do we have? We're not white, we're not Chinese...."

"But we have a dragon." Shaking off the melancholy, her brother grinned. "Let's get on with it."

They each gripped one corner of the dragon

pin between thumb and forefinger and held it over the rising column of blue-gray smoke.

"If this doesn't work, we're going to feel like idiots," Kae Bing pointed out, nervously licking his lips.

"If this doesn't work," Donna reminded him, squinting through the smoke, "we've got something much bigger to worry about."

"Yeah. About thirty feet bigger." His brows dipped down again. "I wonder where it came from."

"Maybe, it came from where we're sending it."

He blinked and shook his head. "Deep, Donna. Very deep. So let's do it on three."

Their unison sounded a little ragged and, over her brother's deeper, measured tones, Donna could hear her voice shaking.

"We give Shing Li-ung, Shining Heart, to the spirit of Chinese-Canadians so that spirit might be protected."

They'd argued for weeks about the wording.

The colors of the pin began to move; to throb to the beating of a pair of hearts; to swirl about in a pattern too complicated to understand.

And then all they held was memory as the smoke from the incense rose over their heads and disappeared.

Kae Bing swallowed audibly. "Holy shit. It worked."

"Yeah." Donna stared down at her fingertips then slowly raised them to brush at the tears trickling down her cheeks. She didn't know why she was crying. It wasn't as though they'd actually given the dragon away.

"Uh, Donna? We forgot, I mean, how are we going to know if it considers them . . . us . . . worthy?"

"Mommy! Look at the kite! Look at the dragon kite."

A number of people at the First Annual Chinese Heritage Festival squinted skyward, heads turned by the piping cry of the child. High overhead, far above the other kites, a scarlet and gold celestial dragon gleamed iridescent in the sunlight and danced with the wind. It swept over the crowd, then rose on a hundred breaths exhaled in wonder.

Donna, her fingers white around the frame of the kite she carried, felt as though her ribs were suddenly too small to contain her heart. Faces all around her seemed lit from within. Even her parents, pulled protesting out of the suburbs by the determination of both their children, watched the dragon with a new awareness shining from their eyes. Kae Bing lifted one hand to the sky in salute.

She bit her lip, afraid she might cry out. *So, Shing Li-ung,* she gave the thought to the wind. *Does this mean we're worthy?*

From deep within, and from high above, and from all the people around came the answer.

DID YOU EVER DOUBT IT?

CONCERTO ACCADEMICO

by Barry N. Malzberg

The first dragon entered orchestra hall and moved gracelessly, a three ton package, toward the podium just as the Tarrytown Symphony was beginning the third movement of the Vaughan Williams Ninth Symphony. Glassop, in the third chair of the seconds, on the outside thanks to the oldstyle antiphonal seating that gave the seconds their own arch opposite the firsts, was among the first to see it but he kept very calm, bowing only slightly disturbed by the entrance of the green beast, slithering now down the aisle. Fulkes, the conductor was, of course, unaware of the dragon at this point and Glassop did not see fit to enlighten him. In the dim light of the auditorium, no artificial illumination being turned on for a day rehearsal; the beast looked like a floating, cleaned-up crocodile. Glassop had seen pictures in the children's books, knew at least what he was looking at. He was no dummy. The beast was definitely a dragon and it looked most determined, as if it had a mission. Glassop hit the pizzicatos, listening to the theme crawling from the bassoons, tried to concentrate upon the notes. You had to stay calm in this business, if you got caught up in the moment by moment stuff, you could be destroyed like Nikisch throwing the baton on his toe and dying of septicemia in the days before antibiotics. And Toscanini, of course, taking out a violist's eye with a flung baton. "Excuse me," Schmitt, his seatmate said, "but is that a reptile coming down the aisle?" Schmitt had played in the Oslo Philharmonic, second stand firsts he had complained to Glassop, before he had decided to join his daughter and spend his pension in America. He was a dour Scandanavian and not such a good violinist, but Glassop knew that he was observant.

"It's a dragon," Glassop said. "Like in the forest or maybe with the queen."

"I know what it is, dummy," Schmitt said. "But where does it come from?"

Glassop shrugged. Sometimes no answer was the best answer. The dragon paused midway between the back doors and the podium and seemed to paw the ground, fixed the woodwinds on risers of the Tarrytown Symphony with a dim and preoccupied pair of eyes. Fulkes banged the baton on the empty music stand, said "Woodwinds, woodwinds!" until all of them stopped. Glassop rested his violin on his knee, looked at the middle-aged conductor whose life was edged in disappointment, Glassop supposed, married to an heiress and conducting a semi-professional orchestra in Westchester when his real ambitions lay somewhat to the south. Once as an assistant conductor of the New York Philharmonic he had filled in for Boulez at a children's concert, but that was a long time ago.

"Woodwinds," Fulkes said, "that is not the way that this very sinister passage is played. You must make legato, must lead the way toward the flugelhorn!"

"Dragons," Schmitt said. "They were rumored to be in the forests of Riga when I was a young man. Of course I am not a young man now, my friend. Do you smell that beast?"

Glassop inhaled delicate draughts of air, thinking of his grandson, Zeke, and what he would make of a dragon in the orchestra hall. Probably the boy would be as matter of fact as Schmitt or perhaps as oblivious as Wilkes. Children nowadays were exposed to too much sensation, murders on the MTV, dragons were nothing to them. The one at issue pawed the tiled floors and then sat gracelessly on its haunches, fixing Fulkes' back with an insistent and compelling expression. It might have been holding an oboe for the degree of attention it now showed.

"This is a *most* sinister symphony," Fulkes said. "Vaughan Williams composed it in 1958, in the last year of his life. He was 86 years old and not feeling very well and he looked, in the words of Colin Davis, like a sack of bricks. We must acquaint ourselves with a man who thought of himself as being on friendly terms with death, who saw death, so to speak, as a disheveled guest in his own home, perhaps an elderly acquaintance who himself looked like a sack of bricks. Later on it is time for the middle strings to plumb the nature of the north region, but now the woodwinds must gracefully usher the old fellow in. Do you understand?"

Glassop shrugged, and stared over at the fourth stand firsts where, on the inside, sat Gertrude whom he loved. Gertrude had come to the Tarrytown Symphony only as a means, she said, of filling up the hours while her children slowly dismantled her life but Glassop thought that he knew better, that he could look deeply into her very soul. Thirty years younger than he and most of the string section of this orchestra of refugees from Communism or decadence or retirees from capitalism, she had she said a mature and loving heart and no prejudice at all against second violinists or older men. If her husband and children were only to die, she had told Glassop once in the sacramental confines of the rear booth at the college coffee shop, she would genuinely consider his offer, his aching need. Of course this was not likely at any time in the foreseeable, but then again you did not know.

Gertrude looked over at him, said something. *Dra-gon*, Glassop lip-read expertly. *Do you see the dra-gon?* She made a circle of her right thumb and forefinger, gripped the bow, raised it, pointed to the far aisle. *Am I cra-zy?* Glassop lip-read. *Is that a dra-gon?*

No, Glassop motioned with his head, then nod-ded yes. No, you are not crazy. Yes, that is a dragon. He did this twice to make sure that the message could not be confused. Gertrude sighed, shrugged, raised the bow again. *Are we the only ones?* she said. *To see it? To see the dra-gon?* Glassop shrugged. Who knew? It was enough to manage your own perceptions, let alone account for those of others. *I don't know,* he mouthed back to her. Now it was her turn to shrug, and then turn a page of the score as if in dismissal. Well, that was what the emotion of pure love got you at 67. If he were lucky he would, with the Greek philosopher, have the beast taken from him soon enough. In the meantime, he had the assurance from Gertrude who was the recipient of his earnest if unavailing passion that he was not mad, that he had indeed glimpsed a dragon in the aisle. Perhaps others had, too. Perhaps the entire orchestra had grasped the situation but was remaining very calm. That was the nature of the Tarrytown Symphony. These were people who had, most of them, been through a great deal, much displacement, the fulcrum of dispos-session had had its way with two out of three of them and a dragon in orchestra hall was at this time among the lesser of their concerns.

"That is good enough," Fulkes said. "We try again now. From the beginning of the movement, please. Remember, should we get that far that the last movement is *attaca,* you must make the audience feel the transition rather than see it. Vaughan Williams died just three weeks after the premiere and the night before Boult made the recording. We will endeavor now not to do the same."

Glassop put the fiddle under his chin, listened to Barnett's snare drum, watched Leonard Zeller put the clarinet through the opening phrases. What was it like for Vaughan Williams in that last year? Glassop wondered. Eighty-six years old, still writing symphonies, did *he* see dragons? English music was full of moats, castles, knights and unicorns, surely there must have been room for a dragon there. The Czechs had goblins and water sprites, dour Scandinavians like Schmitt were concerned largely with dwarfs. But dragons were kind of hard to place, not really nationalized in the way that most myths were. Glassop followed Fulkes' baton, was cued in, played his way through the grim answering theme.

The dragon rose suddenly to all fours and bellowed, then raised its front legs to rear to a surprising height, perhaps half the distance to the roof of the orchestra hall. The sound was surprisingly high, fluted, not what one would associate with a menacing beast. However, it stopped the woodwinds cold and broke down Solomon before he could raise the flugelhorn. There was no question now of the visibility of the dragon or the attention of the Tarrytown Symphony. The players were indeed fixated upon the situation. Fulkes turned, stared into the auditorium, then whirled back and faced them. "Oh, my," he said, "oh, my, it is very large." He grasped his chest, pounded it in an odd rhythm, then dropped the baton. "I think I am going to faint," Fulkes said. "It is a great, a surprising strain."

The dragon wandered toward the edge of the stage, perched on the floor then right under the second violins, closest to Glassop. At the fourth stand on the outside, Glassop had the most privileged of vantage points, he could stare the animal down eye to eye and at the same time maintain some perspective. "Oh, my," Fulkes said, lunging to the right, then the left. "I have never seen anything like this." He fell to his knees, crept around the podium, found the baton and lurching into a half-crouch fled the podium, lunging through the firsts at hobbling speed and exiting behind the curtain. There were sounds of consternation among the bassi and two of the firsts at the rear stand rose to follow Fulkes, possibly to check upon his health, but otherwise all remained calm. Glassop stared at the dragon, an elongated and amiable crocodile with large, fixed eyes and a peculiarly generous expression around the mouth. The beast exhaled and the smell of flowers wafted its way to Glassop, filling his nostrils with sweet and ancient odors.

"Oh, what a grand circumstance," Schmitt said, entranced, holding his violin with two hands against his belly and looking at the engaging beast beneath them. "Magic," Schmitt said as if having returned from the land of the fiords that very morning. "It is magic."

Glassop put his violin slowly, firmly on the floor. Magic, he thought, Schmitt was right. The quality was of magic. Seen from this angle the beast was enormous yet somehow accessible. Peacefully it exuded its floral scent and then, as Glassop extended his hand to touch a scale, the dragon licked Glassop's hand with the greatest and gentlest of attention. Glassop felt a strange and wondrous peace filling him.

He stood carefully, making sure that he did not bump his violin, a simulated machine-made Amati worth perhaps twelve hundred dollars but of some sentimental meaning and went to the podium, mounted it slowly and stiffly. The Tarrytown Symphony—old men, older men, middle-aged women, a few people of indeterminate age and of course his beloved, harried Gertrude—stared at him. The rear stand first violinists had followed Fulkes and there were a few gaps in the woodwinds and bassi but the body of the 73 member orchestra remained on stage. Glassop found himself filled with an odd and persuasive joy, something unlike anything he had felt in these many years. He looked at the dragon—which was now submitting to Schmitt's scratchings and whispered confidences—for courage and then he looked at Gertrude who gave him her most attentive and dedicated coffee-shop smile and then he addressed the orchestra.

"At eighty-six," Glassop said, "Ralph Vaughan Williams, the great British composer who Colin Davis described as looking in his dotage like a sack of bricks experienced wonders, knew wonders, composed in that eighty-seventh year of his the greatest of his nine symphonies and lived to hear its premiere. He heard wonders, saw dragons, saw lovely and mythical beasts against the screen of his consciousness, wrote a fierce and humorous commentary. Can we do less? In our own near-dotage can we ask less of ourselves than did Ralph Vaughan Williams?

"Come," Glassop said, feeling massive, solid, feeling the full *locality* of himself and basking in the sudden and expanded breath of the dragon. "We will make music together. In E minor we will make such sounds as Ralph Vaughan Williams heard from the fen, as he moved toward the far region. Gertrude," Glassop said, "I truly love you, wreckage that I am, I confer upon you the benison of my understanding and my simple, unadorned, insubstantial passion." He raised the baton. "From the very beginning," Glassop said, "we will start the E Minor symphony from the beginning with its earnest, descending theme and then we will move on and on through its thirty-seven minutes of steady grandeur. Celli, prepare to lead."

Glassop, no longer a refugee, raised his hands. The music sighed from the celli. Behind him

Glassop could hear the sound of the dragon's heart as it opened its joyous mouth to emit fire, the pure fire ascending from its living breath and in the arch of Gertrude's bow Glassop dreamed that he could see the mysterious fen, the walking stick of Ralph Vaughan Williams, the splendid old man himself as riding the fire of the dragon he sped toward eternity.

—*in memory of Sir Adrian Boult*

DRAGON'S DESTINY

by Josepha Sherman

High in his cold mountain stronghold, his cave far above the realms of men, the dragon-sorcerer Gorynich sat in man-form—all sleek, sharp angles, yellow-gold of skin and hair and slanted, narrow eyes—and cast the carven scrying sticks again and yet again. Those sticks had once belonged to a northern shaman, who had seen his own death in them, a prophesy fulfilled when Gorynich had come flaming down out of the sky to steal them. (The shaman had dared defy him in those last few moments of life, dared shout that Gorynich knew only the cold, empty gathering of Power, not true strength—what weak mortal foolishness!)

Staring down at the pattern of the sticks, Gorynich hissed, refusing to accept what the omens showed him. The flame: himself. The star: a *bogatyr*, a warrior-knight, falling athwart the flame. And falling with it: moon-tears, fatal silver. This warrior, this foolish *bogatyr,* would be his destiny or his death—

"No!" Gorynich snapped, springing to his feet, prowling restlessly about his cave. It was a natural cavern, smooth-walled with the passage of time, and nearly empty, save for the stone niches in which he stored those gems he'd hunted over the ages to amplify his magics, the one chest that contained what few clothes it pleased him to wear in man-form—he, who felt neither cold nor heat—and the occasional small piles of stone littering the floor from when he'd accidentally chipped them from the walls when he'd worn dragon-form. There were no signs of mortal comfort, neither chair nor bed; a dragon-sorcerer hardly needed them.

Gorynich turned sharply back to the scrying sticks. He hadn't come so far, risked so much, to meet death by some ignominious little human's hand. Granted, once, he dimly remembered, he, too, had been human, merely that, one small mortal sorcerer mocked by the stronger, the more important, one small nothing aching with the need for Power till at last, despairing, he'd called upon the Primal Dark. And been answered. Slowly, painfully, the change had come, and if there'd been a time when he'd regretted, when he'd been terrified of humanity, warmth and joy slipping away ... No. Power and the wielding of Power was all there was, all there need be.

Gorynich flexed his sharp-clawed hands again,

glancing down at the lean, sharp, no longer human lines of himself with cold approval: no mortal weakness here, no soft, foolish, easily shattered body, only this strength, this Power. Power that no human would destroy, no matter what these foolish sticks might claim.

"His name," the dragon-sorcerer hissed to them. "Tell me this *bogatyr's* foul name."

He read the answer, saw the image behind the name, and smiled a knife-sharp smile. Destiny or death, was it? His destiny, perhaps—but *not* his death.

Rising, Gorynich blurred, shifted. His shriek tore the still mountain air as he rose on dragon wings in sleek, sharp, deadly dragon-form, yellow-gold and lean, and soared out from his mountain cave, hunting.

Bogatyr Dobrynya, a tall, well-muscled, pleasant-faced man not quite young, not quite old, rode peacefully along the river bank, far from the golden courts of Kiev, only the sword and dagger at his side and the silver-hilted riding crop slung from his red leather saddle marking him as anything more than peasant farmer. His plain brown tunic and trousers were of common linen weave, and on his yellow hair sat his old Greek hat, the despair of courtly servants, disreputably shapeless and stained dark by time but comfortable and wide-brimmed against the warm sun of late spring.

Dobrynya smiled. Courtly life was all well and

good, and he was honored to be one of Prince Vladimir's own chosen warriors, but there were times when the glitter and closeness of it all nearly stifled him.

The air was rapidly turning outright hot. "What say you, horse?" he murmured to the animal, grinning to see an ear flick back to catch his words. "Think the water's warm enough for a swim?"

This wasn't his war-stallion, but it was trained to stand, hardly stirring a muscle as Dobrynya dismounted, slinging his swordbelt over the saddle's pommel, tossing off hat and tunic.

But as he was sitting to pull off his soft leather boots, Dobrynya felt a cold shadow pass over him. As his horse shrilled in terror, the *bogatyr* glanced sharply up. For a nearly fatal moment he froze in sheer disbelief, staring wildly at the dragon gleaming coldly golden in the sunlight, plummeting down at him. Impossible, his mind insisted wildly, there weren't any such things as dragons (though it was true this one was smaller than the stories told, barely larger than a tall man), no dragons except of course for dragon-sorcerers, those magicians who surrendered their humanity to Darkness, and they were only myth, of course—

Then he was about to be roasted by a myth. Dobrynya scrambled to his feet, snatching for his sword. But dragons were far beyond any horse's endurance. Training or no, his panic-striken mount was galloping off as fast as it could run—taking his sword with it!

The dragon screeched in fury—or triumph?—and hurled a bolt of white-hot flame at Dobrynya. The *bogatyr* threw himself into the river, diving as deep as he could, feeling the fire heating the water over his head, wondering, *How long can the creature keep hurling flame?* At last, lungs aching, Dobrynya knew he couldn't stay under any longer. He surfaced, gasping for breath, ready to dive again if he must, looking frantically back over his shoulder. The dragon was gone, and in its place stood. . . .

"Ah. Dragon-sorcerers aren't myth, are they?"

The tall, lean, golden figure on the river's far bank stared back at him with flat, reptilian eyes. "No more than are *bogatyri*. You are Dobrynya."

Dobrynya fought down a shudder at the sound of his name spoken by that cold, cold voice. *How could he know—Ah. Of course. Sorcery.* "I am. What do you want of me?"

"Your life. And that, I shall have."

It was a ridiculous time and place for defiance, bobbing in the middle of a river with a dragon-thing ready to scorch him, but Dobrynya replied as coolly as he could, "When you catch me, then you can boast. And so far Dobrynya isn't in your . . . ah . . . hands."

Those hands had already become claws. Dragon once more, the sorcerer sent a new blast of fire searing toward him. Dobrynya hastily filled his lungs with air that was already uncomfortably warm and dove once more, just barely in time, heat prickling all about him.

I can't keep this up forever! But how can I fight back without weapons?

Wait . . . he still had his dagger, there on the riverbank with his tunic, a small blade, but good sharp iron. Before the dragon could catch enough breath to hurl more flame—Dobrynya hoped— the *bogatyr* scrambled out of the water, seeing out of the corner of his eye that ha, yes, the sorcerer had to regain man-form between each blast! With any luck, he wouldn't have time to cast a spell either. Dobrynya snatched blindly for the dagger, found his hand closed about the edge of his old Greek hat instead. No time for thought—the *bogatyr* scooped up a hatful of damp, heavy sand. As the sorcerer lunged at him in mid-shift (hideously no longer quite man, not yet quite dragon), Dobrynya swung his hat with all his strength, and felt the heavy weight of it hit his foe right between the eyes. Stunned, the sorcerer slid slowly to the ground, oozing back into full man-form as he fell.

He won't stay stunned for long. My dagger, where's—ah.

Before the sorcerer could stir, Dobrynya was astride him, iron blade at his throat. For one heart-stopping moment he felt the lean golden body shift beneath him, bones and muscles writhing sickeningly, and was sure he was about to be torn apart by the dragon. Then he managed to get out, almost calmly:

"Try it, and I'll cut your throat."

The flat eyes stared hatingly up at him, but the sorcerer fell obediently still. "Let me go."

"Oh, I'm not such a fool!"

"Let me go. I . . . will not harm you now."

"But you will later?" Dobrynya asked wryly. "That's not exactly what I had in mind. Who are you? And why in the name of all that's holy were you trying to kill me? I've never done you any harm—I've never even seen you before!"

The sorcerer's smile was a quick, cold, sharp thing. "That is not your concern. And do you think to gain power over me by learning my name?" He added scornfully, "Know, human, I am Gorynich."

"So. Gorynich. What's to keep me from killing you?"

"Why, you are a *bogatyr!*" The words dripped with irony. "A man of honor."

"I'm also, I repeat, not a fool."

But Dobrynya was wincing inwardly. Gorynich, unfortunately, was quite right; he couldn't kill even such a perilous foe in cold blood. Still, he wasn't about to let said foe loose, either! Bluffing wildly, Dobrynya set his face in a true warrior's grimace and tightened his grip meaningfully on the dagger.

"Prepare to die."

Evidently dragon-sorcerers didn't understand bluffs. Gorynich tensed in genuine alarm, eyes gone wild. "You really mean to— Don't kill me!"

"Why not?"

Plainly hating himself for this weakness, the sorcerer muttered reluctantly, "Because I . . . give you back your life."

"That's kind of you, considering I'm holding the knife. Swear by . . . by your Power and Warm Mother Earth. Swear that if I let you go, not only will you stop trying to kill me, you will also do no harm of any sort, ever, to me or anyone in the land."

The golden eyes chilled with hate. After a long, long moment, the sorcerer grudgingly spat out, "Done."

"And . . .?"

"And," Gorynich continued in a muttered rush, "may Power fail me and Warm Mother Earth swallow me if I lie. Now let me go, curse you!"

Dobrynya hesitated. Warily, wondering if he was making a fatal mistake, he backed off—only to be bowled over by the sudden surge of man-to-dragon. Before the *bogatyr* had time to think, *I'm dead,* Gorynich had lunged up into the air and was speeding away in a thunder of golden wings.

"By Heaven, he kept his vow."

Dobrynya sat where he had fallen, and let out his breath in a long, weary sigh of relief.

Gorynich tore through the sky, raging. How could he have given in to such human weakness? Granted, he'd been sure the prophesy of the scrying sticks was about to come true. Even so, though, how could he, *he,* ever have sunk to begging for his life? How could he ever have let that—that *human* overcome him?

Gradually the cold winds of the upper air cooled his frenzy. An oath sworn under duress was surely no oath at all, never anything to bind such as he.

Yes, but merely slaying the *bogatyr* was no longer enough! Now the memory of humiliation must be erased. The man must suffer disgrace. Even as Gorynich himself had suffered. But . . . how? Was there someone close to Dobrynya, someone who could be stolen away, destroyed? Akh, no, the scrying sticks had already hinted that the man had no family to be harmed, no close kin.

Wait, now . . . if Gorynich stretched his memory back as far as it would go, back to those hazy, dimly recalled human days. . . . Men such as *bogatyri* held honor in their sworn allegiance to . . . to princes, yes, that was it, even as this *bogatyr* belonged to the court of . . . ha, yes! Gorynich snapped dragon fangs together in satisfaction as the missing bits of information suddenly came to mind. The current prince was Vladimir, Vladimir the Golden, and *he* surely had kinfolk, kinfolk who could be used. The dragon-sorcerer cried aloud, a harsh, cold sound, dragon-laughter. Oh, yes, indeed!

Dobrynya slowly got to his feet, hardly able to believe, now that Gorynich was out of sight, that the whole fantastic scene had really happened. But his hands trembled slightly as he dressed and sheathed his dagger, and the *bogatyr* shook his head and went in search of his horse. The animal hadn't gotten too far, having snared itself firmly by reins and saddle leathers in the underbrush. Ears flat, coat wet with sweat, it cocked a nervous eye back at him as he, murmuring soothing words as he worked, disentangled it.

"*You* know all that really happened, don't you? Poor beast, I wish I could give you a good rubdown, but I'm afraid that will have to wait till we're both safely back home." He swung into the saddle, glad for the comforting weight of the sword once more strapped to his side, and the horse stepped out enthusiastically down the long road toward the royal court. "Too bad we came out this far. Dragonly vows of safety or no, I'd really prefer to have a brace of archers around us right now!"

Still, nothing unusual happened during that ride. By the time they'd reached the high wooden palisade surrounding the royal city, allowing only tantalizing hints of red tile roofs and gilded domes, Dobrynya was almost relaxed, calling out his usual amiable greeting to the gatekeepers.

But to the *bogatyr's* bewilderment, when the gates swung open, he found himself facing a troop of grim-faced warriors in gilded mail, the prince's own guards, his royal *druzhina*.

"No further, traitor," one of them snapped.

"Traitor! Yuri, what in the name of. . . ."

Dobrynya's astonished cry faded into silence as he saw Vladimir, tall and golden of hair and beard, eyes fiercely blue as a clear winter sky, sitting his horse among those guards. "My Prince? What is—"

"Don't play the innocent, traitor. Enough men saw the dragon-thing come plunging down upon us, the sorcerer! Enough men saw him swoop and . . ." Vladimir's proud voice faltered slightly, ". . . and snatch away my sweet Zabava."

For a stunned moment, Dobrynya could only stare. Zabava was the prince's niece, a pretty, golden-haired young woman just barely out of girlhood, dear to the as yet childless Vladimir as a daughter. If Gorynich had stolen her— Of course it had been Gorynich, who else could take dragon-form, but—

Seeing the pain in the prince's eyes, Dobrynya stammered out, "He—he won't harm her," realizing how naive that sounded, praying he was right, "he can't, he swore a vow!"

"We know of that vow, traitor." The words were knife-sharp. "We heard the sorcerer boast of the pact he'd made with you!"

"But— No, I—"

"Wasn't *bogatyr* honor enough? Were you that power-mad that you stooped to Darkness?"

"I never—"

"Don't lie to me! We all saw the sorcerer, we all heard him! Come, come, what did you promise him? My treasures? My people? In exchange for Zabava and a throne—"

"No! My Prince, believe me, this is a trick, a—a—" But if Vladimir had a weakness, it was a terror of magic, and like most strong men, he was absolutely blind where that one weakness was concerned. Dobrynya stammered to a stop, knowing nothing he could say was going to sway the man. Vladimir was going to order him to prison. Or to the headman's block. Quickly Dobrynya added the only thing he could:

"I will go after Gorynich, my Prince. I will bring the Princess Zabava home safely to you. This I swear on my honor and my life."

Before anyone could move to stop him, the *bogatyr* turned his reluctant horse and spurred it into a gallop. If anyone chased after him, they'd almost certainly overtake him, because the animal was already weary from the long ride.

To his immense relief, there was no pursuit. That could mean his fellow *bogatyri*, whom he'd glimpsed there behind the wall of guards, were even now arguing with Vladimir in his behalf. *At least I hope they are. They surely can't all believe I would turn traitor . . . ?*

And then again, it might simply mean Vladimir was planning to follow him from afar, so as not to risk Zabava's safety.

Dobrynya slowed his horse to a gentle walk so the poor thing could catch its breath. Ah, merciful heaven, if he didn't keep his vow, he stood condemned in the royal sight, to be hunted down and slain by any honorable man. If he did keep his vow and went after the dragon-sorcerer—who, Dobrynya didn't doubt for a moment, meant for him to follow—he was almost certainly walking into a sorcerous trap.

"Gorynich, you treacherous hound, I still don't know why you've chosen me to hate, but I grant you this: you're a cunning foe!"

The dragon-sorcerer hissed in frustrated rage. Of all the humans he could have stolen, why had he taken this one? Oh, granted, he knew humans tended to act protectively toward their females, particularly those females who were young and of noble birth; he knew this had been a perfect chance to both discredit Dobrynya and force the *bogatyr* into foolish action.

But—why *this* female? She had looked so small and soft, so young and fragile there in the courtyard, a princess in a tale, a victim so perfect he'd had to fight a sudden dragonish impulse to crush, to feed. But from the moment his talons had closed about her, she had abandoned fragility, fighting him like a wild thing, struggling so savagely his body still ached, even now, in manform, with the effort he'd needed to keep them both aloft.

Gorynich clenched taloned fists. If he didn't need her as bait for his trap—

Ahh, look at her, glaring at him from the depths of his cave, her disheveled hair a wild

yellow cloud about her, her blue eyes fierce with
fear and defiance.

"Who are you, sorcerer? Why have you
brought me here?" Her voice fairly blazed with
regal rage. "What do you want of me?"

"Nothing. Be quiet."

"I will *not* be quiet!" Zabava brushed her hair
back with an impatient hand. "You've abducted
me, you whatever-you-are, you've brought me to
this—this wilderness, and now you try to tell me
I'm here for *nothing?*"

"Maybe I intend to eat you."

"Oh, don't be ridiculous! You wouldn't have
flown all that way to my uncle's court just for—
for dinner! What do you *really* want from me?"

Her shrillness was hurting his ears. "I told
you: nothing! Now *be still!*"

That last was shouted with all the Power in
him. She staggered and fell to the floor with the
force of it, too stunned—at least for the moment—to speak. Gorynich glared at her, then
turned to the intricate pattern of gems he'd ar-
ranged on the floor and crouched beside them,
trying to find the *feel* of Dobrynya's aura, willing
him, *come to me, come. . . .* But he could still feel
the woman's hot blue gaze stabbing at him, de-
stroying his concentration. Furious, he nearly
sprang to his feet. But what could he say? Stop
looking at me? She had already shredded his dig-
nity enough. He would ignore the creature, come
what may, until after the *bogatyr* had been
destroyed.

She was saying, very softly, "Was it worth it?"

That was so unexpected a question it pierced his resolve. The dragon-sorcerer turned sharply to look at his captive. "Was *what* worth it?"

She waved a plaintive hand, taking in the barrenness of the cave. "Was losing your humanity worth . . . this?"

"Material things are nothing. Only Power is important."

"But you don't really do anything with that Power, do you? You just gather it up, hoard it. Why, you're a miser!" she exclaimed. "For all your sorcery, you're nothing more than a lonely, sad old miser. You hardly needed to give up your soul for *that*."

Her words unexpectedly stirred old, nearly forgotten memories of warmth, of laughter, of . . . happiness. No! This was ridiculous!

"What I am or am not is not your concern," Gorynich snapped, and turned brusquely back to his magics.

Dobrynya stared up and up the weary height of the mountain before him. Far overhead, near the summit, he could make out the dark opening of a cave.

He's all the way up there. Of course he is. He wouldn't make things easy for me now.

It had been a long, exhausting ride through increasingly rocky, rugged country, and both he and his mount were tired and filthy.

"Time enough for rest and bathing," the *bogatyr* murmured, "when all this is over."

One way or another. Vladimir and his *druzhina* might have been tracking him, but there was no sign of them now, which (since they could hardly have missed seeing him during this ride in clear, sunny weather) hinted unnervingly of sorcery.

Sorcery. That the trail he had been following was a magic-tinged one, Dobrynya had no doubt; a flying dragon would hardly have left those tastefully placed claw-scrapes here and there along ground and rock alike, leading up to this mountain, if he hadn't wanted to be followed.

At least there hadn't been any signs that Princess Zabava had been harmed. Oh, no, she was surely the bait for this trap; Gorynich wouldn't risk harming her. Yet. Zabava had her uncle's courage and pride in full, untempered yet by the experience of age. Who knew how such a no-longer-human creature as the dragon-sorcerer thought. If Zabava—never the sort to cower in meek terror—said or did something to anger Gorynich. . . . Dobrynya dared not wait.

"So be it." By this point the *bogatyr* had outlasted any fear for himself. His horse could hardly manage the climb up there, so Dobrynya dismounted, tucking his riding crop through his belt. After a moment's thought, he removed saddle and bridle from the animal, just in case he didn't make it back. And then Dobrynya started the long climb up the mountainside.

Gorynich, cold-eyed and grim in human-form, was waiting for him at the top. "Why?" the *bogatyr* asked softly, sword in hand, stalling for time to recover his breath. "Why are you doing this?"

"It must be."

"What must be? That you try to kill me? Why *me*?"

"It must be," the sorcerer repeated. "We are each other's destiny or death."

The steadiness of Gorynich's gaze sent a cold little chill prickling up Dobrynya's spine. But as he stared, the *bogatyr* thought he saw lines of strain that hadn't been there before marking the sharp face, and forced a laugh. "Our fiery Zabava hasn't been an easy prisoner to keep, has she?"

The sorcerer's involuntary wince told volumes. "That is not your concern."

"Oh, it is. Come, she has nothing to do with this. Let her go, and you can have me instead."

"I already have you, *bogatyr*. You and your life. What's left of it."

"Don't be so dramatic," Dobrynya said wearily, and lunged.

Gorynich didn't bother with spells. Almost swifter than thought, he shifted forms, and Dobrynya's sword struck not a man but a dragon's hard scales. The good, strong blade which had served him faithfully all these years snapped in two like a child's tin toy, and Dobrynya nearly went crashing into Gorynich's side. He backed hastily away, staring in shock at the now useless hilt for a nearly fatal instant—then flung himself frantically aside as a blast of fire seared the ground where he'd just been standing.

Dobrynya hit hard, rock biting into his side, rolled, trying to get his feet under him, very much aware of the dragon looming over him, gathering flame, then twisted and threw the hilt with all his strength at Gorynich's fanged face. The sorcerer sprang back, frighteningly quick despite his dragon-form, and Dobrynya scrambled up, snatching out his dagger, trying not to think how useless such a little blade would be—

Aie! One taloned claw swiped out faster than human thought, smashing into his hand, sending the dagger flying. Panting, Dobrynya retreated, flexing his aching fingers, relieved that nothing seemed broken. But now he was weaponless!

No time to worry about it. He leapt aside as a second blast of flame seared out—only to realize he'd just cornered himself, rock walls on three sides, Gorynich on the fourth. As he saw the dragon gathering flame once more, the *bogatyr* knew he was doomed.

All at once Gorynich reared back with a startled roar as a rock caught him in the side. Dobrynya saw a second rock whiz by, connecting squarely with the sorcerer's head. *Zabava! She always did have good aim!*

No matter how brave the young woman was, she wasn't going to stop a dragon just by throwing rocks. Gorynich turned to her with murder in his cold eyes. Dobrynya realized the sorcerer no longer needed her alive, and searched feverishly for something, anything he could use as a weapon. If he lunged at Gorynich, he could—Could what? Strangle a dragon barehanded? Wrestle him into submission?

Something was digging painfully into his side, and Dobrynya reached down to find his silver-hilted riding crop still tucked into his belt. It made a ridiculously feeble weapon, but:

Better than nothing, he thought wildly, and charged. His first lash caught Gorynich harmlessly along the scales, but his second frantic blow, struck as the dragon was turning toward him, took Gorynich on the side of the head. *Ha, that stung!*

The dragon's fangs clamped shut on the end of the crop. Dobrynya, clinging to the other end, struggling to free it, found himself staring right into the hating yellow eyes, Gorynich's chill, alien scent filling his nose. If those deadly talons lashed out at this close range, he was dead. The *bogatyr* gave one convulsive tug, and the crop came free, but Gorynich's mouth was open, fangs glinting like so many daggers about to snap shut on him, and Dobrynya struck out in desperation. But at that close range, the crop twisted in his hand. He struck with all the force in his arm—but it wasn't the lash but the silver hilt that took Gorynich cleanly between the eyes. The dragon-sorcerer reared up, screaming, a long, shrill, terrible sound that seemed to go on and on and on. And then a great weight came crashing down on

Dobrynya. He heard, or thought he heard, Gorynich's voice, distorted by dragon-form, whisper:

"Moon-tears. My ... destiny ... has come upon me. . . ."

Then darkness swallowed Dobrynya, and silence with it.

He woke aching in every muscle, still pressed firmly against hard rock by that heavy something. Gorynich! It was Gorynich who had fallen on him!

But the dragon-sorcerer was dead, the yellow eyes glazed and empty. Dobrynya felt hands close about his shoulders. Zabava, panting, nearly sobbing, was struggling to free him.

"I—I can't!"

Dobrynya couldn't move, either. A fine hero, forever trapped beneath a dead dragon. "We are each other's destiny or death," Gorynich had said. Well, he seemed to have been Gorynich's death, all right, or rather, silver had done the job (and why oh why hadn't he remembered the stories that swore by the metal's power over sorcerers?), and now it was beginning to look as though Gorynich was going to be his death, as well, unless he could—

Ha, yes! Dobrynya wormed a hand free, riding crop still clutched in his fingers, and struck the cave floor as hard as he could with the silver hilt. "Hoy, old Mother Earth, Warm Mother Earth, you heard his vow, the vow of Gorynich the dragon-sorcerer: Let the earth swallow him if he lied. He lied, Mother Earth! Now fulfill your part of the bargain."

First he thought he was a fool for believing such peasant folklore. Then he thought he was a fool because if the Earth *did* answer, he'd probably be dragged down with Gorynich's body.

The Earth shook violently. Dobrynya felt the dead weight slide from him and scrambled to his feet, bruised and aching but unbroken, and caught Zabava's hand, pulling her against the side of the cave. The Earth shook once more, so roughly they fell to their knees, half-blinded by clouds of dust.

The Earth quieted. The dust cleared. Dobrynya and Zabava struggled back to their feet, staring, because Gorynich was gone, and only a thin crack running the length of the cave's floor remained.

"She answered," Dobrynya murmured in awe. "Old Mother Earth really did swallow him up."

"It—it was an earthquake," Zabava said firmly. "Only an earthquake. And I—oh, Dobrynya, I want to go home."

"So," the *bogatyr* agreed, "do I." He took a deep breath. "I . . . uh . . . doubt my horse stayed put. It's going to be a long walk back."

Zabava laughed, brushing back her disheveled hair. "Dobrynya, I've been carried off by a dragon-sorcerer, then nearly crushed by Mother Earth's tantrums. Do you really think I'm going to mind anything as dull and prosaic and safe as walking?"

Dobrynya burst into laughter. "Now that you mention it, neither will I. Besides, there's always the chance we'll be able to catch a ride from your uncle and his *druzhina*." He held out his arm to her. "Shall we?"

And, laughing together, comrades in arms returning from the battle, they started down the mountain for home.

BETWEEN TOMATOES AND SNAPDRAGONS

by Jane M. Lindskold

It may have been the planting of the tomatoes
by the snapdragons that did it, for surely this is
an unconventional arrangement. And the shooting star that landed in the garden may have con-
tributed its part. But, whatever the cause, one
hot afternoon when watering the back flower
bed, Jinny found a dragon's egg growing from
her tomato plant.

She had stopped, as was her custom, parting
the thick, downward-hanging, fernlike branches
of her Italian tomato plant to inspect the ripen-
ing fruit. As often as she did this, there was still
a sense of wonder that the little, yellow, starlike
flowers should become tiny green balls that gradually rounded and lengthened into a shape more
like an egg than a tomato. The plant seemed to
brood its fruit, nestling them under its fronds as
under the wings of a hen.

Still, she was surprised to find that one
flower—one that she had almost pinched off

since the bright yellow had been spotted with tiny red spots she'd thought were mites, but had left to grow out of pity—had actually produced an egg rather than a tomato.

The egg was pale green, a milky jade rather than the darker shade of the fruit around it. Like the flower, it had tiny red flecks. She had reached to brush the specks away one afternoon when the egg had grown to the size of the upper part of her thumb and had been unsurprised to find that they had stayed.

What had surprised her was that the skin of this odd tomato didn't feel like a tomato. It felt more like what she imagined a soap bubble would feel like if one could survive such a caress: cool, stretched tight over its contents, but infinitely fragile, not solid and rubbery like a tomato.

She thought, afterward, that this must have been when she started thinking of the odd fruit as an egg rather than a tomato.

Jinny lived alone and had for almost a year, so that there was no one to whom she could immediately show her find. Despite her love for her gardens, she belonged to no gardening clubs—the hospital simply didn't leave time—and after some reflection she decided against showing her find to her gardener friends. She would just let the egg grow, give it its monthly dose of Miracle Grow, and let it ripen in its course. After all, it had done fine so far.

And so the summer lengthened and the egg

grew slowly, more slowly than the tomatoes around it. These grew, flushed green-pink and then red, and then ended up picked and cut into a salad with garlic and olive oil or perhaps sliced onto a BLT.

Then, one night after coming home late from a particularly depressing day in the intensive care unit, Jinny went out into the yard to water the gardens. She had thought that the day would thunderstorm, as the air had been hot and heavy and so hadn't watered the plants, but the storm had blown over with barely a sprinkle. She set the hose on the beds nearer to the house and carried water to the farther beds, her gallon can in one hand and a large flashlight in the other.

She set the flashlight on the ground by the bed and poured water over the plants, soaking the roots well. Can empty, she reached for the light, and almost as an afterthought decided to check on her egg. Tilting the light up beneath the foliage of the tomato plant, she easily found the egg. It had grown larger than the usual Italian tomato, which usually topped at about six inches. But although the egg was at least eight inches long, it must have been far lighter than a comparable tomato, for it didn't bend the plant at all.

When she angled the light to directly shine on the egg she gasped in surprise, for the light went right through the shell and showed what was within as clearly as a picture from an x-ray.

Curled within the egg, its long tail curled

round and round the perimeter, was a small, lizardlike creature. It appeared to be sitting with its rump at the base of the egg, its bulging-eyed head at the top. As Jinny studied the image, the creature stirred, feebly moving its front paws as if to cover its eyes. Jinny quickly flicked the light off and crouched there in the dark, reflecting.

How a lizard came to be in her tomato didn't trouble her just then. What had caught her was that it was there and, from her experience with pediatrics, must be near hatching or its optic nerves wouldn't have been so sensitive to the light.

The next days passed in a pleasant fever of anticipation. She couldn't get away from the hospital. Rotation was too tight with summer vacations and what excuse did she have—"My tomato plant is about to hatch a lizard?"

So every day, after her shift ended, she would hurry home. When she could, she traded for night hours, feeling that when the egg hatched it would be in the daytime's heat. During the day, she set up a lawn chair and table in a shady spot in the yard, not too far from where the Italian tomato brooded. There she alternated napping and catching up on her paperwork. Often she caught herself talking softly to the unhatched lizard, letting out the frustrations that she never showed in front of her patients.

Her vigil was rewarded when one afternoon her attention was arrested by a rhythmic "tap, tap, tap."

Darting over, she dropped to hands and knees and carefully lifted the tomato plant's leaves. The egg was swaying slowly back and forth to the pulse of something beating against the shell. She restrained herself from breaking the shell, trying just to watch, and found that in her excitement she'd started the rhythmic breathing taught in Lamaze as if she was one of those participating fathers. Feeling a bit idiotic, she tried to breathe normally even when something the same pale green of the shell broke through.

It was vaguely pointed and reminded her of nothing so much as a chick's egg-tooth. The egg tooth was followed by a green snout, rather like that of a caiman alligator. This long nose thrashed around, breaking the egg further, so that a large chunk of shell fell to the ground. Through this aperture crawled the rest of the creature. It tumbled to the ground and sat there in the mulch, apparently confused.

Jinny studied it, afraid to touch it so delicate did it seem. But as she watched, it slowly shook itself, blinking away a protective film from its eyes and then looking directly at her.

It was beautiful, with none of the bumbling awkwardness of mammalian babies. Scales of pale jade covered the body, but the eyes and claws were bright scarlet flecked with gold. A long tail, twice the body's length, unrolled after it. As it moved towards Jinny, she could see, folded like wet hibiscus flowers on its back, what must be wings.

She lowered her hand then and the lizard crept onto it, the tiny claws bending, still too soft to gain purchase. Jinny drew it out into the sun and the little head lifted then, a crest with golden tips that she had not noticed before rising with what must be pleasure.

She carried it to a warm sunny rock where it quickly dried off, scales shimmering in the light. The wings that it unfolded, gently fanning them to dry as she had seen butterflies do, were translucent crimson and gold.

Enhancing the pleasure that she felt in hatching a dragon in her garden, for dragon this must be, was the fact that wherever she moved the bright ruby eyes followed her. If she moved too far away, the emerald tongue flickered out anxiously. Indeed, its first hesitant flight brought it to land on her outstretched palm where it sat on its haunches preening, absurdly pleased.

She was just wondering what infant dragons ate, when, as if anticipating her thought, the dragon soared into the air and landed on a hot Hungarian pepper, munching down its length with such intensity that it did not even shift balance when she pinched off the pepper. Carrying pepper and dragon into the kitchen, she tried various other foods, most of which it ignored, although it went into raptures over a sprinkle of cayenne pepper.

The hours passed quickly as she showed Cayenne her house and garden, too quickly really, because she hadn't figured out what to do with

him (the pronoun was a convenience as she had
no idea how to sex an infant dragon) when she
went on call. Experimentation showed that if
she left him, he would flutter after. If he was
locked away, he would peep, and, if she didn't
come, bash himself against whatever barrier separated them so persistently that she feared he
would injure himself.

Letting him out, she worried while he alternated soaring happily around her and swooping
down to lick cayenne pepper from a saucer. He
was poised on the edge of the saucer when at
the sharp sound of the telephone ringing, he suddenly vanished.

Jinny grabbed for the phone, staring at the
counter. Had the dragon gone invisible? Then,
as she told the telephone sales rep that no she
didn't want any new magazine subscriptions, she
suddenly saw. Cayenne was still there, but like
a chameleon he had changed his coloration to
match the surface he sat on. His head was the
red-brown of the pepper; his torso Delft white
and blue; his tail the butcher block pattern of
her counter-top.

As she hung the phone up, he slowly shifted
back, his green head remaining cayenne-colored
just a moment longer than the rest so that he
appeared to be blushing. With a chirp, he fluttered over to her.

"I wish I didn't need to scare you to get you
to do that again," she said, patting the slender
tail which wrapped around her fingers like a gar-

ter snake, "Then I could just take you with me to the hospital."

Cayenne looked at her, his red eyes fixing on hers, then, with a tiny hiss as of effort, he blended his colors to match her clothing.

"That's it!" she cheered and, with Cayenne barnstorming in front of her, she hurried to get changed.

The hospital where she did her residency was not very large, but, since it served over half of the town's population, it was usually busy. She made her rounds with Cayenne clinging to her shoulder, mostly tucked under her collar, his exposed portions shaded a gauzy white. She was aware of his whispers and sighs as he commented on the activity about them, his wordless hisses somehow an echo of the cadences of her own speech.

He revealed himself repeatedly though, but with curious perception he only showed himself to those who would be unable or unlikely to give away his presence. As Jinny performed an inevitably painful check on a little girl who was in for a marrow transplant, Cayenne suddenly leapt from her shoulder to dive and sweep in front of the girl with the abandon of a drunken butterfly. Distracted, the girl barely flinched as Jinny examined her, her eyes bright as she watched the dragon dancing on the air.

She took her medication without protesting, smiling as she did, "But I don't really need it, do I, Doctor? If I slept all through your checking me, I must be getting better."

"Did you sleep, Molly?"

"Uh-huh, and I had such beautiful dreams."

Jinny smiled and patted Molly's hand as the child drifted off to sleep. Back on his perch beneath her ear, Cayenne was muttering, his crest scratching lightly against her neck as he puffed himself out with pleasure.

Later, Cayenne crept out to study an elderly man in the last stages of terminal cancer. Jinny heard the dragon hiss with concentration and saw the old man's pain-killer bleared eyes suddenly grow sharp and bright. She watched as Cayenne hovered steadily in the air before the old man who watched him with greedy eyes. But Jinny wondered whether what the old man saw was a miniature red and green dragon, for his wrinkled lips managed a smile and a soft breathed "Martha" before he drifted off again.

There were other incidents of this kind before the night shift ended. Cayenne soothed the tired, the lonely, the pained, in a way that Jinny had only wished she could. In each case, after the little dragon's performance, the sufferer would drift off into a peaceful sleep. Yet, as if to prove that the dragon's dance was not a cure, the old man died a few hours after Cayenne's visit.

She left the hospital that morning with Cayenne still undetected on her shoulder. As she got to her car and unlocked the door, there was suddenly a cascade of peeping from Cayenne. He

burst into the air with a blaze from his wings
circled, and hovered in front of her. His ruby
eyes glittered wildly and his tongue flickered in
and out in what she had come to recognize as
distress. Worried that he might have picked up
something in one of the wards, Jinny held out
her hand.

He perched there, rubbing his nose vigorously
against her forearm and she could feel like a tangible thing his need to return to those who
needed him. Then, with a chirp that was both
apology and explanation, Cayenne took wing
again. She saw him rise, wheel away, and head
back toward the hospital.

She waited as he darted before the electric eye
and then between the opening doors. Then she
got into her car and sat with the engine running,
already missing him. Today, there would be no
dragon's egg in her garden, no dragon eating pepper in her kitchen. But as she pulled out, she
thought she saw a flash of scarlet and green from
the windows of ICU and was obscurely comforted to know that in counterpoint to the pain
and anxiety a dragon was dancing.

THE TRIALS AND TRIBULATIONS OF MYRON BLUMBERG, DRAGON

by Mike Resnick

Sylvia's always after me.

"It's a skin condition," she says.

"It's a wart," I say.

"It's a skin condition and you're going to the doctor and don't touch me until he gives you something for it."

So I go to the doctor, and he gives me something for it, and she makes me sleep in the guest room anyway.

"Myron, you're green," she says.

"You mean like I don't know the ropes, or you mean like I got ptomaine poisoning from your tuna salad?" I ask.

"I mean like you're the same color as the grass," she says.

"Maybe it's the lotion the doctor gave me," I say.

"It doesn't come off on your shirts," she says.

"So maybe it all dried up," I say.

"Maybe," she says, "but stay in your room when I have the girls over for mahjong."

"I told you not to smoke in bed," she says.

"I know," I say.

"Well, then?" she says.

"Well, then, *what?*" I say

"Well, then, why are you smoking in bed?" she says.

"I'm not," I say.

"Then how did your pillow get scorched?" she says.

"Not from the passion of your love-making, that's for sure," I say.

"Don't be disgusting," she says.

Then I belch, and out comes all this smoke and fire, and she says if I ever lie to her again she's going to give me a rolling pin upside my head, and then she walks out of the house before I can tell her I haven't lit up a cigarette in four days.

"It looks like a cancerous growth," she says.

"It's just a swelling," I say. "There must be a busted spring in the chair."

"You should see a doctor," she says.

"Last time you sent me to a doctor I turned green," I say.

"This time you'll see a specialist," she says.

"A specialist in swellings?" I ask.

"Whatever," she says.

*   *   *

"Well?" she asks.

"Well what?"

"What did he say?"

"He says it looks like a tail," I say.

"Hah!" she says. "I *knew* it!"

"I wonder if our insurance covers tails," I say.

"Is he going to amputate it?" she asks.

"I don't think so," I say. "Why?"

"Because even if our insurance covers getting rid of tails, it doesn't cover growing them," she says. "What am I going to do with you, Myron? We've got a bar mitzvah to attend this Saturday, and you're green and all covered with scales and you keep belching smoke and fire and now you're growing a tail. What will people say?"

"They'll say, 'There goes a well-matched couple,' " I answer.

"That is *not* funny," she says. "What am I going to do with you? I mean, it was bad enough when you just sat around the house watching football and reading *Playboy*."

"You might fix some dinner while you're thinking about it," I say.

"What do you want?" she asks. "Saint George?"

I am about to lose my temper and tell her to stop teasing me about my condition, when it occurs to me that Saint George would go very well with pickles and relish between a couple of pieces of rye bread.

*   *   *

It is when my arms turn into an extra set of legs that she really hits the roof.

"This is just too much!" she says. "It's bad enough that I can't let any of my friends see you and that we had to redecorate the house with asbestos wallpaper"—it's mauve, and she *hates* mauve—"but now you can't even button your own shirts or tie your shoes."

"They don't fit anyway," I point out.

"See?" she says, and then repeats it: "See? Now we'll have to get you a whole new wardrobe! Why are you doing this to me, Myron?"

"To *you?*" I say.

"God hates me," she says. "I could have married Nate Sobel the banker, or Harold Yingleman who's become a Wall Street big shot, and instead I married you, and now God is punishing me, as if watching you spill gravy onto your shirt for forty-three years wasn't punishment enough."

"You act like *you're* the one who's turning into a dragon," I complain.

"Oh, shut up and stop feeling sorry for yourself," she says. She holds out the roast. "It's a bit rare. Blow on it and make yourself useful." She pauses. "And if you breathe on me, I'll give you such a slap."

That's my Sylvia. One little cockroach can send her screaming from the house. She sees a spider, she calls five different exterminators. God forbid a mouse should come into the garage looking for a snack.

But show her a dragon, and suddenly she's Joan of Arc and Wonder Woman and Golda Meier, all rolled into one steel-eyed *yenta* with blue hair and a double chin.

"Where are you going?" she says.

"Out," I say.

"Out where?" she says.

"Just *out*," I say. "I have been cooped up in this house for almost two months, and I have to get some fresh air."

"So you think you're just going to walk down the street like any normal person?" she says. "That maybe you'll trade jokes with Bernie Goldberg and flirt with Mrs. Noodleman like you always do?"

"Why not?" I say.

"Well, I won't hear of it," she says. "I'm not going to have the whole neighborhood talking about how Sylvia Blumberg married a *dragon*, for God's sake!"

I figure it is time to make a stand, so I say, "I am going out, and that's that!"

"Don't you speak to me in that tone of voice, Myron!" she says, and I stop just before she reaches for the rolling pin. She pauses for a moment, then looks up. "If you absolutely *must* go for a walk," she says, "I will put a leash on you and tell everyone you are my new dog."

"I don't look very much like a dog," I say.

"You look even less like Myron Blumberg,"

she answers. "Just don't talk to anyone while we're out. I couldn't bear the humiliation."

So we go out, and when Mrs. Noodleman passes by Sylvia tells me to hold my breath and not exhale any fire, and then we come to Bernie Goldberg, who is just coming home from shopping at the delicatessen, and Sylvia tells him I am her new dog, and he asks what breed I am, and she says she's not sure, and he says he thinks maybe I am imported from Ireland, and then Sylvia yanks on the leash and we walk to the corner.

"He's still looking at you," she whispers.

"So?" I say.

"I don't think he believes you're a dog."

"There's nothing we can do about that," I say.

"Yes, there is," she says, leading me over to a fire hydrant. "Lift your leg on this. That will convince him."

"I don't think dragons lift their legs, Sylvia," I say.

"Why do you persist in embarrassing me?" she says. "Lift your leg!"

"I can't," I say.

"Whoever heard of a dragon that couldn't lift its leg?" she insists. "You don't have to do anything disgusting. It's just to show that know-it-all Bernie Goldberg."

I try, and I fall over on my side.

"What good are you?" demands Sylvia as Bernie stares at me, blinking his eyes furiously behind his thick bifocals.

"Help me up," I say. "I'm not used to having all these legs."

"Myron," she says as she drags me to my feet, "the situation is becoming intolerable. Something's got to be done before you make me the laughing-stock of the entire neighborhood."

"This is the last straw!" she says, ripping open the envelope.

"What is?" I ask.

"The state has refused to extend your unemployment benefits. They don't care that you're a dragon, as long as you're an able-bodied one." She glares at me. "And you're going through twenty pounds of meat a day. Do you know how much that costs?"

I shrug. "What can I say? Dragons get hungry."

"Why are you always so selfish, Myron?" she says. "Why can't you graze in the back yard like a horse or something?"

"I don't think dragons like grass," I say.

"And that's it?" she demands. "You won't even try?"

"I'll try, I'll try," I say with a sigh, and go out to the back yard. It doesn't look like Caesar salad, but I close my eyes, lean down, and open my mouth.

Sylvia hides me in the basement just before the fire department comes to save what's left of the garage.

* * *

"You did that on purpose!" she says accusingly after the firemen have left.

"I didn't," I say. "It's just that my flame seems to be getting bigger every day."

"While our bank account is getting smaller," she says. "Either you get a job, or you'll have to ask your brother Sidney for a loan."

It is an easy choice, because when Sidney dies they will need a crowbar to pry his fingers off the first dollar he ever made, and every subsequent one as well, so I go out to look for work.

You would be surprised at how difficult it is for an honest, industrious dragon to find work in our neighborhood. Stuart Kominsky puts me on as a sand-blaster, but when I melt the stone he fires me after only half a day on the job. Herbert Baumann says maybe I could give kids rides on my back when he reopens the carnival, but it is closed until next spring. Phil Rosenheim, who has never struck me as a bigot before, says he won't hire anyone with green skin. Muriel Weinstein tells me she'll be happy to take me on, just in case some out-of-town dragons come by to look at some of her real estate listings, and she'll call me the moment that happens, but somehow I know that she won't.

Finally I latch on with Milt Fein's heating company. Winter's coming on and he's short-handed, and when a furnace goes out he pays me thirty dollars an hour to go to the scene and breathe into the vents and keep the building warm until he can get there and solve the problem. The first week I make $562.35, which is more than I have ever made in my life, and the second week we are so busy I get time-and-a-half on the weekend and take home almost seven hundred dollars, and Sylvia is so happy that she buys a new dress and dyes her hair bright red.

And just when I am thinking that things are too good to last, it turns out that things *are* too good to last.

One day I start breathing into the ventilation shaft in an office building, and nothing happens, except that Milt Fein lays me off.

Two days later I wake up and I have hands again, and the next morning most of my scales are gone.

"I knew it!" screams Sylvia. "You finally find something you're good at, and then you decide not to be a dragon any longer!"

"I didn't exactly *decide*," I say. "It just kind of happened."

"Why are you doing this to me, Myron?" she demands.

"I'm not doing anything," I say. "I seem to be *un*doing."

"This is terrible," she says. "Look at you: you're hardly green at all. Why does God hate me so?"

Four days later I am the old Myron Blumberg again, which, as you can imagine, is quite a relief to me. Two weeks after that, Sylvia packs up her clothes and the portable T.V. and the Cuisinart and leaves without so much as a good-bye note. The divorce papers arrived six weeks later.

I still get cards from her every Yom Kippur and Chanukah. The last time I hear from her she has married a gorgon. Sylvia, who hates snakes and can't stand to be stared at.

Boy, do I not envy *him*.

STRAW INTO GOLD: PART II

by Mark A. Kreighbaum and Dennis L. McKiernan

He was young (for a Dragon), was Smael, and good natured ... and, it must be admitted, a bit lazy, still living in the lair of his father even though Smael had come into his flame several millennia ago. So, one morning, when his ophidian sire sent him off to burn a few huts in the local village and collect their overdue gold tithe, Smael balked. In the first place, you see, he didn't much care for gold because it was too heavy, hard to store, and was always attracting pests in chain mail. (This opinion would have earned him a swat in the wing had his father heard it, and so Smael generally kept it to himself.) A more compelling reason, however, was that the smell of burning thatch made him gag.

That morning, in a somber mood Smael flew away from the great Dragonslair high on the

steep, raddled slopes of the unclimbable obsidian
mountain in a quandary ... er, that is, Smael
was in the quandary, not the mountain. It was a
disagreeable dilemma, for in spite of his allergy
to thatch, he had to come up with a pile of gold
by dusk, and no excuses. Oh, what was a Dragon
to do?

Settling down on a mossy mound in the nearby
enchanted forest, Smael pondered his perplexing
problem, his brow wrinkled in uffish thought
(inasmuch as a Dragon can wrinkle a scaly
brow).

Of a sudden, a disgruntled ugly little Man
came hacking and coughing out from under the
mound. (Smael, you see, had settled down on the
ugly little Man's dwelling, his tail covering the
chimney, and smoke had filled the undermound
house right up.)

"Oi, Dragon!" called the ugly little Man churl-
ishly. "Move your butt. You are sitting on my
house."

Smael, not even taking offense at the rudeness
of the ugly little Man, obliged him, saying, "I
hadn't noticed, so troubled am I. You see, I need
a pile of gold by the eventide."

Upon hearing these words, a crafty look slid
over the features of the ugly little Man. "Why,
Dragon, I can spin gold from straw ... and if
you don't believe me, fly up to the castle and ask
the Princess, who is no doubt playing with her
newborn baby." The ugly little Man ground his
teeth in frustration ...

... but then smiled an oily smile. "And, Dragon, if you find I am telling the truth, and I am indeed, well then, I'll spin you a pile of gold from straw for your sire to wallow in ... but *only* if you'll give me your firstborn."

Smael's glittering eyes widened. "Why, how did you know that I was to bring the gold to my Dragon sire?"

The ugly little Man laughed a snide laugh. "There's not much I don't know about Dragons, Smael."

Smael's eyes opened wider still. "And how did you know my name?"

Again the ugly little Man grinned an oily grin. "I tell you once more, there's little about Dragons I do not know. Now give me your firstborn and I'll spin the gold from straw."

Smael looked at the ugly little Man. "Say, don't I get to guess at your name or something?"

The ugly little Man's teeth ground in rage and he shook his head violently. "Oh no you don't, Dragon. I've already been fooled by the Princess with that trick.

"No sir. Nothing will do but that you give me your first baby ... and by the bye, your Dragon wife *is* expecting, isn't she?"

Smael started back, surprise in his eyes. "How did you know that, little Man. I mean, we Dragons keep such things private."

"Pfaugh," snorted the ugly little Man. "Did you not hear me? Why, I know practically everything there is to know about Dragons."

Well, to make a long story short(er), Smael flew up to the castle, frightening everyone practically to death, including the Princess and her new baby.

"Oooo, that Rumplestiltskin!" exclaimed the Princess when Smael explained all. "He is a wicked, wicked ugly little Man, if Man he is. But I must confess, he can indeed spin gold from straw."

Smael flew back. "Well, Rumplestiltskin, I suppose that I will give you my firstborn if you spin me the gold. It seems as if I must agree, because, as you say—"

"—There's not much I don't know about Dragons," interjected the ugly little Man, rubbing his hands together in unconcealed glee.

And so Rumplestiltskin spun the gold from straw.

Smael's sire was well pleased with the bounty.

Smael's Dragon wife laughed when she was told that they would give their firstborn to Rumplestiltskin, and she hugged and kissed Smael for being so very clever as to get gold for the promise of the firstborn.

And millennia passed . . .

And Rumplestiltskin came often to Smael and asked, "Where is my Dragonchild?" and the Dragon always replied, "Soon. . . . Soon. . . ."

And millennia more passed. . . .

And the ugly little Man died of extreme old age. . . .

And millennia more passed. . . .

And finally, Smael's Dragon wife delivered their firstborn into the world . . . exactly to term.

And as a birthing gift, Smael gave his new Dragon daughter a wheel that spun straw into gold, for after all, she *was* the rightful heir.

You see, Rumplestiltskin did indeed know much about Dragons, but not everything—there were gaps in his knowledge . . . the most notable of which you've just learned.

DAW
FANTASY ANTHOLOGIES

☐ **CATFANTASTIC** UE2355—$3.95
   edited by Andre Norton and Martin H. Greenberg

A unique collection of fantastical cat tales—original fantasies of cats in the future, the past, the present, and other dimensions.

☐ **CATFANTASTIC II** UE2461—$4.50
   edited by Andre Norton & Martin H. Greenberg

More all-new and original tales of those long-haired, furry keepers of mankind, practioners of magical arts beyond human ken. . . .

☐ **THE NIGHT FANTASTIC** UE2484—$4.50
   edited by Poul & Karen Anderson

Unforgettable tales of dreams which may become reality—and realities which may dissolve into dreams. . . .

☐ **HORSE FANTASTIC** UE2504—$4.50
   edited by Martin H. Greenberg & Rosalind M. Greenberg

Let these steeds carry you off to adventure and enchantment as they race, swift as the wind, to the magic lands. . . .

☐ **DRAGON FANTASTIC** UE2511—$4.50
   edited by Rosalind M. Greenberg & Martin H. Greenberg

DAW

Melanie Rawn

THE DRAGON PRINCE NOVELS

☐ **DRAGON PRINCE: Book 1**   UE2450—$5.95

He was the Dragon Lord, Rohan, prince of the desert, ruler of the kingdom granted his family for as long as the Long Sands spewed fire. She was the Sunrunner Witch, Sioned, fated by Fire to be Rohan's bride. Together, they must fight desperately to save the last remaining dragons, and with them, a secret which might be the salvation of their people. . . .

☐ **THE STAR SCROLL: Book 2**   UE2349—$5.95

As Pol, prince, Sunrunner and son of High Prince Rohan, grew to manhood, other young men were being trained for a bloody battle of succession, youths descended from the former High Prince Roelstra, whom Rohan had killed. Yet not all players in these power games fought with swords. For now a foe vanquished ages ago was once again growing in strength—a foe determined to destroy Sunrunners and High Prince alike. And the only hope of defeating this foe lay concealed in the long-lost Star Scroll.

☐ **SUNRUNNER'S FIRE: Book 3**   UE2403—$4.99

It was the Star Scroll: the last repository of forgotten spells, the only surviving records of the ancient foe who had nearly destroyed the Sunrunners. Now the long-vanquished enemy is mobilizing to strike again. And soon it will be hard to tell friend from foe as spell wars to set the land ablaze, and even the dragons soar the skies, inexorably lured by magic's fiery call.

THE DRAGON STAR NOVELS

☐ **STRONGHOLD: Book 1**   UE2482—$5.99
☐ **STRONGHOLD: Book 1** HARDCOVER   UE2440—$21.95
☐ **THE DRAGON TOKEN: Book 2** HARDCOVER   UE2493—$20.00

A new cycle begins as a generation of peace is shattered by a seemingly unstoppable invasion force which even the combined powers of High Price Rohan's armies, Sunrunners' magic, and dragons' deadly fire may not be able to defeat.

DAW

Mickey Zucker Reichert

Tad Williams

TAILCHASER'S SONG   UE2374—$4.95

Meet Fritti Tailchaser, a ginger tomcat of rare courage and curiosity, a born survivor in a world of heroes and villains, of powerful gods and whiskery legends about those strange, furless, erect creatures called M'an. Join Tailchaser on his magical quest to rescue his catfriend Hushpad—a quest that takes him all the way to cat hell and beyond.

Memory, Sorrow and Thorn

THE DRAGONBONE CHAIR: Book 1

☐ **Hardcover Edition**   0-8099-003-3—$19.50
☐ **Paperback Edition**   UE2384—$5.95

A war fueled by the dark powers of sorcery is about to engulf the long-peaceful land of Osten Ard—as the Storm King, undead ruler of the elvishlike Sithi, seeks to regain his lost realm through a pact with one of human royal blood. And to Simon, a former castle scullion, will go the task of spearheading the quest that offers the only hope of salvation . . . a quest that will see him fleeing and facing enemies straight out of a legend-maker's worst nightmares!

STONE OF FAREWELL: Book 2

☐ **Hardcover Edition**   UE2435—$21.95
☐ **Paperback Edition**   UE2480—$5.99

As the dark magic and dread minions of the undead Sithi ruler spread their seemingly undefeatable evil across the land, the battered remnants of a once-proud human army flee in search of a last sanctuary and rallying point, and the last survivors of the League of the Scroll seek to fulfill missions which will take them from the fallen citadels of humans to the secret heartland of the Sithi.

DAW

Mercedes Lackey

These are the novels of Valdemar and of the kingdoms which surroun
it, tales of the Heralds—men and women gifted with extraordinar
mental powers and paired with wondrous Companions—horselike bein
whose aid they draw upon to face the many perils and possibiliti
of magic

THE LAST HERALD-MAGE

☐ **MAGIC'S PAWN: Book 1**   UE2352—$4.99
☐ **MAGIC'S PROMISE: Book 2**   UE2401—$4.99
☐ **MAGIC'S PRICE: Book 3**   UE2426—$4.99

VOWS AND HONOR

☐ **THE OATHBOUND: Book 1**   UE2285—$4.99
☐ **OATHBREAKERS: Book 2**   UE2319—$4.95

KEROWYN'S TALE

☐ **BY THE SWORD**   UE2463—$5.99

THE HERALDS OF VALDEMAR

☐ **ARROWS OF THE QUEEN: Book 1**   UE2378—$4.9
☐ **ARROW'S FLIGHT: Book 2**   UE2377—$4.9
☐ **ARROW'S FALL: Book 3**   UE2400—$4.9

THE MAGE WINDS

☐ **WINDS OF FATE: Book 1 (hardcover)**   UE2489—$18.9
